The Slippery Slope

Amelia Greene

First published in 1997
by HEADLINE BOOK PUBLISHING

A HEADLINE LIAISON paperback

10 9 8 7 6 5 4 3 2 1

ISBN 0 7472 5714 0

Typeset by CBS, Felixstowe, Suffolk

Printed and bound in Great Britain by
Mackays of Chatham plc, Chatham, Kent

HEADLINE BOOK PUBLISHING
A division of Hodder Headline PLC
338 Euston Road
London NW1 3BH

The
Slippery Slope

Chapter 1

I'd always felt that a woman who bought herself sex toys had to be down on her luck. From the point of view of emotional gratification and access to the flesh and blood thing (no one can deny that plastic tastes cheap and nasty for a start) she must be operating at a disadvantage. Yet a recent survey showed men preferred playing with gadgets to having sex. So why was I worrying? I believed in equality. Why not simply enjoy lying on my bed with my legs spread wide, a mechanical toy poised at the ready to thrust into my moist pussy? I had my reasons after all. And they were persuasive reasons. Both of them.

Firstly, Catha, my closest friend and flatmate, had made one of her pronouncements only the night before: 'Sex is not the problem. Love is the problem.' And she had gone on to elaborate, 'It's because we treat men as lust objects that our relationships with them are superficial, Alison. To have a meaningful relationship with a man that is mutually self-actualising one has to fall in love. We must stop using men solely for the purposes of physical gratification.'

Sometimes my reaction to Catha's philosophising is that it is a load of old phooey. On the other hand, because she is a Lecturer in Women's Studies, what she says has an authoritative ring which is hard to resist. Also, I'm very fond of her, and the nobility of her profile, her dark good looks and her tone of voice often give her statements a biblical ring that echoes in my mind for a long time afterwards.

Secondly, the recent loss of my prize lust object, Stefan, had left me feeling bereft and therefore vulnerable to what Catha was saying. In fact, Stefan (admittedly after asking me to marry him) had married the lovely Serena on the rebound only the week before.

Serena, a walking oestrogen bomb fresh out of secondary

1

school, but with kindergarten lips that looked as though they had just been prised off her dummy, had shaken my confidence. My self-regard had been partly restored by Catha though. In fact, just prior to Catha using her tablets-of-stone voice, we had been standing in front of the gilt cheval mirror in her bedroom while she ran her hands over my breasts and the concave curve of my stomach. She had knelt to kiss the uptilt of my buttocks, risen to sweep her fingers up through the cascade of my hair to the column of my neck – all the while softly murmuring comments on the reasons for my manifest superiority to Serena. She didn't stop at my physical attributes either but said that my spiritual and intellectual advantages over Serena were beyond question. This being true I felt much better.

No wonder I bought the whole package – I mean, that we had to change our approach to men. We had to give priority to love and downgrade lust for all time. We had to rethink our whole approach and begin from the beginning. Almost immediately. Like tomorrow.

As if often the case when a decision has been taken to make a fresh start in life, I felt very positive the next day and eager to prove my commitment. I strictly averted my gaze from several attractive young men in the British Museum Library. I stonewalled one in a cafe in Russell Street because he said he was flying back to Zagreb the next day, which gave me absolutely no time to fall in love – only to fall into bed and, as of today, that was taboo. I was doing rather well until I was on my way home in the tube and found myself crushed up against a very clean-cut six-footer in a City suit who inadvertently got his briefcase wedged between my legs. He had placed it on the floor of the train but, as the carriage filled up, he bent to retrieve it. Before he had had a chance to lift it clear of my knees he had been thrust forward by the press of the crowd and found the case and his hand trapped under my skirt. He apologised profusely. I had no alternative but to tell him not to worry. The situation was as testing for him as it was for me. I couldn't very well ask him to relax his grip on the handle of his briefcase, since in doing so he might risk it being stolen.

Therefore I could not complain that, as the train started to rattle and swerve along the track, the back of his head was engaged in a rhythmical cut and thrust against the damp satin crutch of my panties. Even before Leicester Square I'd begun to feel claustrophobic and rather panicky. Which was why I broke my journey and suddenly found myself breathing in the fresh, or the marginally fresher, air of Old Compton Street.

It was necessary to take some sort of therapeutic action immediately. I didn't even baulk at the idea of paying a five pound entrance fee for the privilege of getting into the shop. I handed over the money and went in. Without looking to left or right, I made straight for the shelves at the back that displayed the dildos and vibrators. I grabbed at the largest. The light was murky but I managed to read the promise of multiple orgasm on the reverse of the pack and gazed peremptorily through the cellophane at the front where a shocking-pink plastic penis of impressive dimensions glittered with silver spangles. It was further adorned with a horn like a crooked little finger which, with quick reference to the back of the box again, I learnt gave instant clitoral satisfaction in addition to the deep vaginal penetration of the dildo. I bought it. At the time it seemed cheap at the price and I was in a hurry. I didn't even look at the serried ranks of suits studying the porn mags in silence or glance at the shop assistant or wait for a receipt. I wanted to get home.

This then was why I found myself in such an uncharacteristic position alone on my bed. My dismay soon turned to despair. When I twisted the cap at the base of the dildo that should have set the vibrator in motion, nothing happened. Not a quiver. Total silence. I lay there for a moment with my legs spread, staring at the ceiling in disbelief. My well-meaning attempt to assuage my physical frustration without making use of a man seemed doomed to failure at the outset. Poetic justice perhaps? No, more likely I was the victim of a cheap joke. Angry now, I leapt out of bed and went for the pack I'd thrown in the wastebin, sitting down with a bump as I read 'Batteries not included'. Tears of self-pity almost blinded me as I wrenched the thing open. Sure enough it was empty and, according to the small print, I needed four AA LR6 batteries. I contemplated getting dressed again and going to Mr Patel's corner shop but then I remembered . . . I made a grab at my Walkman on the bedside table, tipped the batteries out of the back compartment and rammed them into the hollow stem of the pink plastic penis. They fitted perfectly. I breathed a sigh of relief. I lay down again, eased the fingers of my left hand along my slit to prepare for the penetration of the dildo, and tried twisting the top again to activate it. No sign of life. Not a sound. Nothing. In a frenzy of frustration I slung the useless thing across the room and, with both hands clutched between my legs, I rolled moaning onto my stomach.

I hadn't heard Catha come in. 'Darling!' she said. 'What's happened? Are you ill? Tell me. Oh, Ali, tell me, please!'

Between muffled sobs into my pillow I tried to explain my purchase, my hope that it would have some cathartic effect and that I had been conned into parting with thirty-nine pounds ninety-nine pence.

'I blame myself,' she said quietly. And then she laughed. 'But this is not something we can complain about to the Office of Fair Trading. I'll see if I can fix it.' And I heard her retrieve the object from the far corner of the room.

'The batteries must be dead.'

'They're not. I was listening to my Walkman this morning. And I only replaced the batteries last week.'

Without turning over to watch, I heard her unscrew the cap, tip the batteries out and rearrange them before she screwed the cap back on.

'You see?' I said.

'Anyway, you don't need this.'

'I do. I do.'

She sat down on the bed beside me and started to stroke my hair. 'Listen to me, Alison.'

'No.'

'Listen to me while I give you a massage.' She pulled the pillow out from under my head, sat astride my bottom and gently started to knead the taut muscles of my neck and shoulders with her cool hands. 'Recovery from any form of addiction involves withdrawal symptoms. You just have to go with it.'

'I can't,' I said, but I was already beginning to relax as her fingers described descending circles on either side of my spine.

'Experiencing withdrawal means that you are well on the road to recovery,' she added.

'I'll never recover,' I murmured. And I wriggled my bottom

4

a bit as she pressed down to run the palms of her hands upwards, spreading my hair through her fingers and fanning it out on either side of my head.

'Being addicted to instant sexual gratification is a clinical condition.'

'But I'm not. It's Stefan. It's because I've lost Stefan.'

'And you're well shot of him, Ali.' Her hands came to a halt and she lifted her weight off me so that I was afraid she was going to stop her massage. She'd never liked Stefan.

'Well, I know I am in a way.' I wanted to be conciliatory so she would continue to work on my back. 'Otherwise I would've married him myself.'

'Quite.' She settled back onto my thighs so that her hands could start to knead my buttocks. 'Thank heavens your natural instinct for survival got the upper hand. No woman could live at close quarters with that massive male ego without being pulverised.'

She always made Stefan sound like a pneumatic drill and this made me feel wistful. 'Perhaps I haven't lost him though.'

'He married Serena.' Catha was briskly dismissive as she parted and squeezed the cheeks of my buttocks together again in a businesslike way.

'I know. But I can't accept it.'

'Oh, come on, Ali, get real! You went to the wedding. It happened. You have to accept it. They did a big number in *Designs for Life*, a whole centre-page spread. You were there.'

'I wasn't there.'

'You described it to me.'

'I described the nauseating pics of her in her wedding dress made out of a few strategically placed pieces of ribbon, yes,' I said miserably.

'But, Ali . . .' She had stopped massaging me and I wanted her to go on. 'You wore the hat. The little black straw one with the black rose and veil that just skims your mouth. You wanted to make a statement, you said, and show the bastard that you were in mourning for a death.'

'I wore it. But not to the wedding. I wore it the night before.'

Suddenly I realised that my dishonesty over this whole incident that was at the root of my present distress. Normally we had no secrets from each other. Catha and I had a relationship that she termed 'mutually pro-active', which I think means we always grasped the nettle and helped each other to be positive. It was this truthfulness between us that kept me grounded and helped me to cope with whatever happened in my other life with men. Yet I had lied to her. It was time to confess. I said, 'If you keep on with the massage, I'll tell you.'

She pushed my legs apart and settled back on her haunches between my knees as her hands began an automatic sweep of my inner thighs.

I sighed. 'I wore the little black hat with the veil the night before the wedding. When I gate-crashed his stag party at the Waldorf.'

'Oh, Ali, of all the crazy things to do!'

And then I told her:

Unbeknown to me, I arrived at the Waldorf reception at approximately the same time that one of Stefan's male guests had arranged for a stripper to make a surprise appearance for his host's entertainment. This was why there was no hesitation at the desk for a porter to be despatched to show me up to the private room where Stefan's stag party was in full swing.

There were at least a dozen men ranged round a damask-covered table weighted with candelabra, champagne buckets, crystal decanters of port and brandy. Everything was overhung with a haze of cigar smoke. Some had their chairs pushed back, some leant forward heavily on their elbows amidst the detritus of a banquet. All had their jackets off and one or two had their silk shirts undone. One had a bunch of grapes hung from his left ear and another was balancing a brandy balloon on his forehead and barking like a sea lion.

Most of the men were laughing. But my entrance caused a sudden hush, followed by a brief burst of applause during which, I noticed, one of the guests leant towards Stefan at the head of the table and whispered something to him.

At this point I knew nothing of the stripper that had been booked to provide a titillating diversion, so I thought that the favourable impression made by my entrance had something to do with the way I looked.

I knew I looked particularly beautiful that night – an air of restrained sadness can lend a woman a sort of intriguing dignity that many men find very seductive. Added to which I was wearing the hat with the rose tilted over my forehead and the small spotted veil that half hid, half enhanced my eyes and could not fail to add a hint of mystery. Under the circumstances, the demure black suit with tiny diamanté buttons that I was wearing must have seemed a little incongruous at first glance. However, like all my favourite clothes, the severity of the tailoring was compensated for by the very high slit to one seam that almost, but not quite, revealed the top of a black silk stocking.

But the sophistication of the assembled company was equal to my appearance and I was gratified to hear one of the men comment, 'A first class act!' I didn't realise that his comment was meant literally because he thought I was a striptease artiste. I was flattered and stared straight at Stefan at the far end of the table to see if he agreed. After all, I had dressed in a way that I knew appealed to him so as to make certain that he could see what he would be missing.

His expression did not change. If anything he affected a mild disinterest. He asked me then if I had brought my music and, perhaps stupidly, I took this to be a subtle allusion to the fact that we had both chosen a number by Billie Holiday entitled *Please don't talk about me when I'm gone* as 'our tune' the last (and supposedly final) time we had met. I smiled, he did not. One of the other men suddenly stood up and crossed to a velvet curtain which he drew back to reveal a grand piano. He drew up the stool, sat down, rolled the cuffs of his evening shirt and struck a chord. This appeared to be a signal for four of the others to lift the table to one side of the room. Some wine spilled and the cut-glass stopper of the decanter rolled off onto the floor but no one seemed to notice, and Stefan did not move a muscle. After rearranging the chairs in a line backing the table, all eyes were turned on me. The man at the piano launched into a rather ragged version of the cancan but after a few bars he stopped.

Stefan spoke very quietly, apparently addressing me, 'What are you waiting for?'

'What?'

'Why don't you dance?' he said softly.

'Why?' I was taken aback until I saw his blue eyes narrow. A sure sign of anger. I was pleased with myself for provoking a reaction at last. 'Why not?' I smiled, taking up the challenge.

But, still innocent of the role I was meant to be playing, I added, 'If you will agree to dance with me.'

After a surprised murmur from the others, the pianist struck up again but Stefan suddenly brought his fist down on the table and the music stopped dead.

'I've an altogether better idea,' Stefan said. 'A conventional strip can be a bit predictable.' This was the first intimation I'd had that I was expected to undress and I think I must've looked shocked because, from that point on, he began to enjoy himself, no holds barred.

'Why not have a sort of musical chairs?' he went on. 'Or better still a cross between that and pass the parcel?' Now a faint ironical smile was on his lips and I was quick to recover my composure. He had thrown down the gauntlet and he knew I could never resist picking it up. 'But only, of course, if the lady is agreeable?'

The assembled company looked from him to me with a degree of pleasurable anticipation.

'Fine by me,' I said and I bent down to adjust the thin slingback of my high strappy sandals to a general murmur of approval. The pianist immediately launched into an impatient ralantando of random chords and at the same time a noisy argument broke out about the possible rules of this new game.

Stefan picked up a knife and tapped it several times against the side of a wineglass. 'Gentlemen,' he said. 'There is no point in setting out on a course of action unless one has a well-defined goal in view. Furthermore, the method of achieving that outcome must be understood by all participants.'

The man with the grapes on his ear removed them and began to eat in a contemplative fashion. His neighbour burped politely behind his hand and poured himself another brandy. Both said, 'Here, here!'

'What I suggest is this,' Stefan continued. 'The music plays and stops, plays and stops. The artiste' – and at this he inclined his head slightly towards me – 'passes from lap to lap. Each time the music stops the lucky gentleman on whose lap she has come to rest is allowed to remove one, and only one, article of her clothing. The even luckier man to be privileged to remove the last article of her clothing wins the ultimate prize.'

'We should've booked a bedroom,' someone said.

'What?'

'For the winner?'

'The winner can go behind the curtain with her.'

'Well said.'

'Always fancied it on a grand piano.'

'Well, I'm not sure,' I remarked.

'Reserve your judgement till you know the winner,' Stefan told me pointedly.

One of the men glanced back across the table at him. 'That's not a foregone conclusion, I hope.'

''Tis his evening though.' The man with the grapes seemed philosophical.

'Okay, it's Stefan's evening but even so—'

'Play,' Stefan told the pianist before there was time for further argument.

I found myself grabbed by the first man in line and seated squarely on his lap. He was loath to let go of me which meant that the man beside him dragged me rather roughly from his grasp by clasping me firmly round the waist with one arm and securing the other under my knees. The idea that I was going to pass from one lap to another rather than be passed was a non-starter from the outset.

By the time the music first came to a stop, my skirt was twisted up round my waist, largely because the fourth man in line had had the bright idea of seating me on his lap so that I faced him. This meant that my legs were spread either side of him, my stocking tops, suspenders and even the tiny lace pouch of my panties clearly visible. (All of which had been carefully chosen to induce an agony of regret in Stefan alone. And, in this instance, it was clear that he was stereotypically male, as it was immediately obvious from the increase in excitability of the assembled company, that I could not have chosen underwear that had a more universal appeal.)

Perhaps because the lower half of my body was already partially exposed, the first time the music stopped it was the removal of my jacket that concentrated attention. But the large trembling fingers of the man concerned were in trouble with the tiny buttons. I helped him, allowing the jacket to slither backwards off my shoulders to reveal my black chiffon camisole with shoestring shoulder straps. This cobweb of material barely

9

concealed the satin basque with front lacing and half cups that thrust my breasts upward and forward towards the man's agitated gaze. For a brief moment I feared his hands were about to tear the delicate material so that they could plunge into the cleavage of my breasts, but the music started up again and, before either he or I had time to protest, I had resumed my bumpy ride from lap to lap.

As my journey progressed, I became increasingly aware of the general state of arousal as my inner thigh, or hand or pussy brushed against the bulges describing the erect male members in each of the laps I visited and I can honestly say that now I marvel at the degree of self-control exercised by all concerned. But then there did seem to be an instinctive recognition of the fact that a self-imposed discipline is part and parcel of any sport. Oh, and that sport itself often depends for its excitement on a degree of self-denial. And that, when all's said and done, a stag night does depend on team spirit.

If I say that the next two times the music stopped the removal of my skirt and camisole top seemed no more than routine, I would not be misleading you. It was what was happening during the musical interludes that got the upper hand. Hands were sliding in everywhere. If one man found he could lift me only by slipping his hand under my buttocks, it was not his fault if his hand got momentarily caught up inside my panties. If his neighbour had to steady me with one hand behind my back it was natural enough for his other hand to find itself cradling my breast as he tipped me forward. And once a breast had been inadvertently dislodged from the cup of my basque it was not hard to see how, when the next man in line was lifting me, my nipple could fail to engage his mouth. I'm not saying anyone was cheating exactly but it was time-consuming and I was impatient to get to Stefan.

When I finally reached him, I was aroused myself and the most natural thing in the world was to guide Stefan's hand to my wet pussy. To my surprise he resisted and redirected his hand to undo the suspenders of my left stocking, which he pushed down to my knee before patting my thigh as though to say, 'There, there.' Then he shoved me off on my way again. I was mortified. Frankly, I felt he was letting the side down but one glance along the line of chairs told me that everyone

10

else was too anxious to get on with the game to have noticed his lack of sportsmanship.

As things progressed and the men divested me of sandals, stockings and panties, my resistance to their handling became weaker as their audacity increased. Fingers slithered into my sex, gently rubbed and parted the lips of my labia and dug into the crack of my arse. In fact, I was feeling so hot and breathless by the time it came to the removal of my basque that I couldn't wait for them to get it off. And the stupid man who had been landed with the privilege tried to unlace the front. Luckily another man knew better and started to unhook the back, but between the two of them somehow I ended up on the floor. For a minute I thought I'd blacked out but then I realised that the whole pack of them had closed in above me, cutting out the light. It was then I heard the *ting-ting* of Stefan's knife tapping his wineglass, which was meant to bring them to order. But an argument broke out.

My basque was now off and I was sitting naked on the floor. But who had won? Was it the man who had unlaced the front of the garment, or the one who had unhooked the back? I would have said I was past caring until I heard Stefan's voice sternly announce that I was not yet properly undressed. Because I had never felt more undressed I was suddenly alert with surprise. The men turned away from me to look at Stefan for an explanation. One said something about changing the rules of the game, another something about tampering with the ball – in any event they seemed to feel cheated.

'But look at her,' Stefan told them. 'She still has her hat on.'

All turned to me in amazement. I put my hand up to make sure he was right. I spread the veil down where it had risen above my eyeline. All of us had been so engrossed in exposing what was hidden that we had overlooked the obvious – the little straw cap on my head. I laughed. The music started up again and the men resumed their seats in an orderly fashion. I felt quite different too because there is nothing like a hat for making a woman feel fully dressed. I moved from lap to lap in a dignified fashion, carefully setting my own pace so that I ended up with Stefan when the music stopped.

The others clapped good-naturedly enough as he bent to brush his lips across my breast.

'I'm not taking her hat off,' he said. 'Since it suits her so well.'

The pianist had vacated his seat and was refilling the brandy balloons on the table when one of the others started to sing, 'For he's a jolly food fellow,' which was interrupted by a roar of approval as Stefan pulled me behind the velvet curtain and closed it. Once alone with me, he smiled. Then he lifted the veil of my hat very slowly and kissed both my eyelids.

'That's it,' he said and stepped back.

'But . . .' I stepped forward only to be restrained by his hand.

'The lifting of the veil is the climax of many a pagan or religious ritual. We won't better that moment.'

'We will. We must.' But I did not speak with any real conviction because nothing makes me feel so defenceless as a man who acts in a gentlemanly fashion. And I think he knew that because he seemed to have no doubt that once he'd collected up my clothes and given them to me to get dressed I would go home without a murmur.

Five minutes later I was walking in slow motion towards a sign that said 'Exit to Main Reception' along the hushed corridor of the hotel. I was dazed and disappointed, just as though I had been woken from a lovely dream and was already forgetting what it was about. In fact, the thing I had forgotten was the ruthless way Stefan could manipulate a situation to ensure that he always retained the upper hand, the buzz he got from taking a woman by surprise. Indeed, the last thing I was prepared for at that moment was to be rushed from behind and thrust headlong through a door marked 'First Floor Concierge'.

'You scheming bitch.' Stefan laughed as I struggled to recover my balance, mental and physical, amongst the racks of freshly laundered sheets. 'Of all the tricks to pull! Oh, how shall I ever do without you, darling?'

The shock of being jumped on in this way made me icy calm. 'Well, you'll have to, won't you? And mind my jacket, please.'

'Get it off.'

'No. I just got dressed. And after what you said only a minute ago I—'

He pressed his mouth hard against mine.

'I—'

But he only released the pressure long enough to slide his tongue in past my lips and along the ridge of my teeth, as though quickly reassuring himself that the geography of my mouth was his territory and his alone. I think I stumbled backwards because several sheets tumbled down, enveloping me in the soft smell of freshly washed linen which, mingled with the familiar scent of Stefan, seemed to act on my brain like an anaesthetic. My eyes closed as his hands slid expertly down inside my jacket, and up under the chiffon camisole, down into the half cups of my basque in a single movement.

'I . . .'

Very gently he tweaked my nipples, lifting my breasts to cradle them in the palms of his hands so that his thumbs were free to rub from side to side as my nipples hardened. More sheets slithered past me and my natural instinct seemed to be to follow them down onto the floor. But as my knees gave way, his hands slid upwards to hold me under the armpits.

'You wanted to say something?' He breathed the question close to my ear.

'I . . . did I? No, nothing.'

And with that he guided me downwards until I was lying amid the jumble of sheets. I made a futile attempt to get my skirt off without realising that, as he had allowed me to fall, he had lifted it up around my waist. I couldn't find the zip. So I felt for his zip instead and found myself holding his cock, already magnificently erect. Then I made an equally ineffective attempt to get my panties off. As I raised myself slightly from the floor to pull them down, he stuffed a folded sheet into the space I had created under my bottom so that my pelvis was raised up towards him.

It takes time to undress. Neither of us had the time to spare. Suddenly he was on top of me with the fingers of his left hand pulling aside the crotch of my panties whilst his right hand joined with mine to guide his penis straight down into me. I cried out until the side of his hand wedged itself into my mouth. I bit hard as he thrust deep. The extended foreplay of the striptease game and now the uptilted angle of my pelvis combining with the size of his erection brought me to climax very quickly. I wanted to stop and get my breath for a moment but he was just hitting his rhythm. His free hand worked its way under my buttocks and, with each thrust, his fingers drove deeper and deeper into my crack. I tried to ease myself away from him a little but he was quick to sense it.

'I want you to come again.'

'No.'

'Yes.'

He took his hand from my mouth and, whilst increasing the pace of his thrusts, caught a handful of my hair and turned my head to one side, darting his tongue into my ear. He knew me too well not to know where the links in my armour were at their weakest. The magnified sound of his tongue in my ear, the uncompromising weight of his body making a prisoner of me, the relentless rhythm of his hand gliding from back to front to part the lips of my labia so that my clit was exposed to the thump of his pelvic bone, urged me on to rejoin him so that we came together with such force that tears escaped.

I don't know how long we lay there. He may even have had one of those five minute catnaps that make him so maddeningly refreshed because suddenly he was standing over me with his flies done up, running his fingers through his hair to tidy himself.

He surveyed the muddle in the hotel linen store with mock surprise and said, 'Well, we certainly made the sheets sing tonight, baby!'

But I wasn't going to fall for any jokes. 'What are we going to do, Stefan?' and my question had a little sob on the end.

He wasn't impressed. 'Do? Nothing. Not any more.'

I suppose I shouldn't have blamed him because, after all, he was getting married in the morning, but I insisted, 'But really.'

He tucked his shirt down inside the waistband of his trousers before turning to the door. 'You're free to contact me as an old friend if you have some practical problem, of course, and I'll do my best to be helpful but otherwise . . .' And he opened the door onto the long corridor. 'Perhaps I'll see you at the wedding tomorrow?'

I turned my head away.

'Perhaps not, then.' And with that he was gone.

As I was on my way down to the ground floor of the hotel a woman in a thin feather boa and fishnet stockings stepped

14

out as the lift doors opened and I fancied that she was the stripper who . . .

Suddenly I realised that I had got so far into my story that I hadn't been aware of Catha stopping her massage. Yet now I had the feeling that she had stopped some while ago.

'Catha?'

The only response was some noisy breathing. I turned over onto my back and realised that she was lying down alongside me. Her jeans were open, her legs parted and the hand thrust down inside her panties was working hard. She arched her back, her eyelids fluttered, her mouth trembled open, emitting a low moan, and then she lay still as though she had fallen into a deep sleep.

'Catha!' I smiled, a little surprised. 'I'd simply no idea that the thought of Stefan could turn you on like this.'

'What?' She seemed to be dragging herself back from the edge of an abyss.

'I said' – and I briefly rolled towards her and sucked her left ear lobe a moment to rouse her further – 'I hadn't realised before that you could get such a terrific wank over my ex-lover.'

Her eyes opened wide then and she stared blankly at the ceiling before she said, 'You've got to be kidding. He's the pits.'

'Why deny it? I saw you.'

She took a deep breath and pushed the damp hair back from her forehead as though clearing her mind. 'I was generalising,' she said. 'Actually I was into a pretty standard textbook type of fantasy. You know the sort of thing, *The Secret Erotica of the Fair Sex* sort of thing, okay?'

I made no comment but, between you and me, she didn't regain her composure fully till the following morning. And I promise you she hated Stefan.

Chapter 2

Thoughtfully stirring wheatbran into her yoghurt at breakfast time, Catha was getting into alternative treatise: *The Kinsey Report: Sexual Behaviour in The Human Female*, she told me, was unequivocal in its conclusion that women's orgasms increased in direct proportion to the length of a relationship. Whilst the *American Survey of Families and Households* concluded from a sample of 13,000 women that long-term monogomous couples made love twice as often as their single counterparts. *The Janus Report* and *Sex in America* apparently added to a positive deluge of evidence to uphold what Catha was saying.

'Surely you're not advocating marriage?'

'I am simply saying' – and she shot me a glance of withering scorn – 'that the trust, understanding and connectedness of a relationship based on true love rather than on lust makes for the best sex of all.'

'We agreed. Or rather we agreed that love came before lust.'

'But, after what you told me last night, I'm not convinced you've grasped the argument. And,' she added darkly, 'it's ramifications.'

'If what you're saying is that falling in love makes for better sex then obviously its desirable. But I thought the point about true love was that sex was secondary. That sex becomes a sort of spin-off.'

'Oh listen, Ali,' she said, 'I haven't got time to get into one of your chicken and egg arguments this morning.' She stood up and flung her yoghurt pot into the wastebin.

'I must be in love with Stefan then. I mean, since it gets better everytime I—'

'Oh, Alison!' Catha seemed to be personally afronted. 'You know that's not true, darling. He treats sex as a commodity

16

and in doing so reduces his women to objects. And he's married to someone else now. End of story. Deep down you're happy to be free. And, if nothing else, you owe it to Serena.'

'Owe her what?'

'Your consideration as another woman. In sisterhood. Be fair.'

'To that Barbie doll?'

'Exactly. Poor girl. She's perfect for him. Don't you see?'

'I suppose.' I nodded miserably.

'Promise me one thing.'

'What?'

'Forget him.'

'Yes. I'm going to try. I'm going to give it all I've got.'

'And one more thing.'

'What?'

'Talking of commodities – bin that dildo.'

'Well, as it doesn't work . . .'

'Bin it because you don't need it. Bin it for the same reason that you've dumped him. Okay?'

'I will.'

'Go for it.'

'I promise.' I loved Catha when her eyes flashed and she was being positive. She never failed to inspire me when she was in that mood. 'But where are you going? I thought you didn't get into college until after lunch today?'

She took a deep breath, looked up at the ceiling, exhaled and turned to the window to gaze out at the treetops in the square below before replying – so I knew it was serious. 'I'm resigning as Head of Women's Studies, Ali.'

'Oh, but for heaven's sake!'

'I'm sick of those dykes trying to trip me up with their biker boots.'

'But I thought there was only a small contingent of them and that you were winning.'

'Now they're calling me a "Fem Woman". I tell you I'm sick of the whole PC thing.'

'That's no insult, is it? I mean to be feminine?' The tortuous politics of Catha's job often bewildered me.

'But that's the way they intend it. They've never forgiven me for referring to the Chairperson of the committee I set up for "The Deconstruction of Male Language" as a Chairman.'

'It was a slip of the tongue. Surely the sort of mistake anyone could make?'

'Because we had spent a whole term arguing whether the post was to be dubbed Chairperson, Chairwoman, Chairman or simply Chair – I frankly didn't know whether I was coming or going. And now I don't care.'

I thought, *When is a chair not a chair? When it's one of Catha's students*, but I could tell that this was not the moment for even the most innocuous joke, so all I said was, 'But I'm out of work now too'

'Already?'

I'd been on a short-term research contract and, as is so often the case with me, I'd got so involved that I'd worked a fourteen hour day and finished the job early.

'If both of us are going to be without an income at the same time, well then the consequences could be serious.'

But Catha was already out in the hall putting on her coat. She called back to me, 'Well, so be it, Ali. I can only speak for myself, of course, but I tend to put principles before money.' She reappeared briefly at the kitchen door. 'Let's be pro-active about this. After all, as we're making a clean sweep in our lives, a change of jobs can only enhance our chance of success.'

After Catha had left, a quick review of the state of our finances seemed to suggest that we could be in trouble with the rent within a couple of months. Because we worked hard, we played hard. We lived for today without much thought of the morrow. Now, though, it'd be wise to start making little economies straight away.

The first thing that struck me was that it would make more financial sense to return the dildo to the shop and demand a refund than to throw it away. The prospect of having to explain its failure to vibrate did not please me but by the time I left the flat I had calculated that the price of one dildo could feed me for a week.

With this in mind I felt quite enthusiastic. In fact, as I crossed the garden square in the sunshine, I decided to capitalise on the situation by walking the mile and a half to Soho instead of spending money on a tube ticket.

What I failed to take into consideration was that this walk would take me past Stefan's office. As I approached the street where his company had its headquarters, I began to question the idea of feeding myself for a whole week on the money I was going to recover. It was possible, of course, on a restricted diet, no takeaways when I was eating in, and definitely no eating out. The worth of my sacrifice diminished further when I thought of Stefan's final words to me – that I could always turn to him for practical help. He was good with his hands. Probably he could mend the dildo. Catha, after all, was not expecting me to eat frugally on the proceeds of a refund or indeed to get any money back at all. And, if the thing worked, she might be less inclined to want it thrown away since she was often critical of the 'disposable' nature of modern culture.

Ever the opportunist, Stefan had switched from property dealing to software packaging six months before the property-market crash and, conversely, was then able to secure a lease on spectacular offices for his new business at a knock-down price. The minimalist nature of the place always took me by surprise.

A single six-foot palm tree stood in splendid isolation beside a double-height window, and some thirty metres away there was a reception desk of steel and glass which seemed to float on a deep sea of blue carpet. Anchored behind the desk, a receptionist – who looked for all the world like part of the architect's original line drawings – fielded unwelcome telephone interruptions to her day between disposing of visitors by quickly directing them this way or that so as to leave her field of vision uncluttered. She reserved special disdain for people who wanted to see her boss without an appointment. I stood my ground. I knew some domestic details about her that made her less intimidating. She was unaware of this, of course, which made her grudging announcement of my presence into the tiny dot of a microphone that hung around her neck confidently dismissive.

She was annoyed when her boss told her to ask me to wait. Stefan had informed me that the receptionist was 'very good with a needle and thread' so I could imagine her dutifully bending to bite the cotton when she had sewn a button back onto his shirt.

He'd also confided that she did 'a mean foot massage'. Apparently Stefan could graft the mentality of a geisha girl onto the most haughty PA. But no doubt she told herself that, like many a woman, she was bound to find herself on her knees by the end of the day.

In contrast to the reception area, Stefan's room was an impressive jumble of 'work in progress' as he propelled and swivelled on a leather executive chair within the confines of a huge U-shaped work station. Three computer screens flickered and he seemed torn between giving his full attention to any one.

He started tapping at a keyboard, a phone rang, he picked it up and talked, cradling it on one shoulder whilst he continued tapping with his left hand, his right ripping a sheet from the fax machine. He briefly glanced up at me. 'Can't give you long.' And then to the phone, 'Wait while I access my diary.'

Perhaps because I have a natural antipathy to technology, the one thing on his desk that caught my attention was a small memo pad. I picked it up. Printed on the top of each sheet were the words 'A Memo From the Desk of God'.

I laughed. 'Too much.'

'Sorry, what?'

When he had put the phone down I pushed the memo pad across to him. 'Explain that. If you dare.'

He laughed then too. 'California,' he said. 'Remember that trip I took to Silicon Valley? Some crazy Californian woman gave me it. Weekend in Malibu. Hot tub on the terrace overlooking the ocean. Fantastic legs. Could I help it if she wanted to deify me?' I winced slightly but at least I'd managed to bring him back to earth. Suddenly he gazed over the top of the screens to look at me. 'What can I do for you, Alison? Presumably its something important?'

I told him what had happened with the dildo. He took the pack from me and studied it, took the thing out and carefully examined it. He unscrewed the top, slid the batteries into his hand and let them drop back in again. 'No excuse for it,' he said. 'Shoddy workmanship.'

'Yes, but can you mend it?'

'D'you know' – he pointed the large pink plastic penis at me thoughtfully – 'I think there may well be a gap in the market here.'

'What?'

'For a better class of sex toy, Alison. Something more aesthetic in design, using better quality materials and with much more reliable mechanics.'

'Stefan, I didn't come here to offer you a new business opportunity.'

'Me? No, I'm up to my eyes as it is,' he said. 'But I might be able to put you in touch with an entrepreneur, worldwide contacts, a man of catholic tastes, always on the lookout for new products.'

'You mean you can't . . .'

'Mend it? I expect so. Looks to me as though the small metal contacts for the batteries just need adjusting.' And with that he unscrewed the end of the dildo again and ran his thumbnail under the rim. 'Done. Okay?'

'But does it work?'

'Well, there's only one way to find out. And you'll have to come round here for me to show you.' He pushed himself back from his desk. 'Because we're running an internal audit and I want to keep my eye on this screen.'

I must've hesitated because he added, 'Hurry up. I've got an important client meeting in fifteen minutes.'

He stood up, holding the dildo, as I joined him on his side of the work station. 'Face the desk, lift your skirt up and pull your panties down.'

'But, Stefan . . .' I protested.

'Darling, I don't want you to go home and then blame me for adding to your obvious state of physical frustration.'

'Well, I suppose it would be sensible,' I said, lifting my skirt. 'I mean, purely in the interest of research.'

'Well, this is already interesting,' he said.

'Oh?'

'You haven't got any knickers on,' and he narrowed the smiling blue eyes that had so often undressed me in the past. 'How very convenient,' he said.

I turned my back on him to shield myself from his mocking stare.

'Bend over,' he breathed in my ear. 'And let's give this thing a test run, darling.' Suddenly the mechanical drone of the vibrator started into noisy life somewhere behind me. This prompted me to bend forwards, sliding my hands in front of me across the desk as I parted my legs.

21

'Careful!' Stefan suddenly leant over me, grabbed my wrists with his left hand and roughly repositioned them behind my back.

'No!' I suddenly felt powerless.

'Sorry, but you put your right hand on a mouse and for a moment I thought you were going to delete an important file.'

'Oh, sorry.'

'Your left hand grazed the touch screen of the other computer, just on the spot where . . .'

I moaned. He had started to push the thing slowly but insistently into me.

'Is it too big?'

'Well, it is very . . .'

'Tell me to stop if . . .'

'It is very . . .'

'Unyielding, is it?'

'Yes.' I swallowed hard. It seemed to be filling my whole pussy in a delicious and most uncompromising way. And although it felt rigid it did feel warmer than I had anticipated.

'One has to be careful with this sort of thing . . . to get the angle right.'

I gave a little whimper of agreement as he thrust experimentally a couple of times.

'Darling, point your bottom up at the ceiling more, I . . . that's better.' Stefan started pumping the vibrator in and out of me as though to the strict musical tempo of a metronome.

I tried to disengage one of my hands because I wanted to protect my slit where it rubbed against the right-angled edge of the big desk, but he held me prisoner with his left hand whilst his right suddenly shot into my field of vision and answered the phone.

He slowed the pace of thrusts only slightly and I did my best to subdue my moans as he held a conversation about delivery dates and credit terms with a US consortium. He scribbled on his memo pad briefly, touched the screen to his right and then drew the laptop he used as a personal organiser towards him.

'Sorry, about this,' he said.

'Of course. But keep going.'

'You can feel the thrusts? But how about the vibrations?'

'Well, I . . .' Out of the corner of my eye, with my face pressed down onto the hard surface of the giant desk, I was watching his index finger manipulating the roller ball on the centre of his laptop. I'd never noticed before how much a roller ball resembled a clitoris, nor how delicately precise was his manipulation of it. It looked so beautiful I felt like crying. The phrase 'Personal Disorganiser' forced itself into my consciousness because it seemed particularly apt. 'I can feel the thrusts alright,' I managed. 'But I'm . . . I'm less sure about the vibrations.'

'Possibly they constitute too subtle a sensation, but if I slow down a little . . .'

'No, please don't!'

'Like so,' he said. 'Concentrate. We are into a controlled experiment here, Ali.'

I couldn't feel any vibration at the tip which was deeply bedded inside me, but perhaps at its root I sensed it tremble briefly where it entered my vagina. 'Yes, yes,' I said hurriedly. 'It's vibrating. It's definitely working.'

'Ah, well, in that case . . .' he teased a little, grinding the thing from left to right and up and down.

'But I can't be a hundred per cent sure, Stefan,' I heard my voice pleading. 'Until it's delivered the promise spelt out in the wording on the package.'

'Multiple orgasms?' he mocked, but he started to manipulate the vibrator again so that it plunged and withdrew deeper and further than before. 'I thought I knew you better, darling. I thought you weren't so naive as to be taken in by the cynical propaganda of self-serving adverts.'

Before I had time to reply – actually I think I was beyond verbalising at that point – the phone rang again. I won't pretend that I followed the conversation that Stefan had with his caller. It seemed very disjointed to me and punctuated with asides in a deeper more urgent tone that contrasted remarkably with the coolness of his business voice.

'Extended credit on any order over ten thousand,' he said. And then to me, 'Give it all you've got, baby, don't hold back.' And then to his caller, 'I've never been known to miss a deadline. I deliver. On the dot. You tell me when you want it and that's when you get it.' Adding in his different and intimate voice, 'Now, come, give it to me, baby!'

Perhaps it was the idea of his devilish duplicity, the dexterity of his control over two wildly contrasting worlds at one and the same time, that gave my excitement such an edge but I climaxed with such force and so suddenly that I failed to suppress a cry.

In a rather more subdued tone, he said, 'No, there's absolutely no problem this end. But I'll ring you back.' Then he put the phone down. Almost immediately, his receptionist rang through. 'No,' he said, 'Thank you but absolutely not.' He reached for a box of tissues in his drawer and shoved a bunch into my hand before continuing. 'Everything is under control my end. It's just that I've programmed the audio alert alarm on my number two computer from the sound of a dog barking to a synthesised human scream. But thanks anyway. Most efficient of you to react so promptly. Well done.'

He reached into my field of vision again, leaning over me so that it wasn't possible for me to straighten up. He scribbled something hurriedly on his memo pad, ripped the sheet off and then I heard the rustle of paper as he folded it. I tried to stand up but my legs felt as though they had lost the ability to support me. It was his hand dragging at my hair that helped me become upright. As I turned to face him he slumped down into his leather chair.

'Are you . . .?'

'Me? Oh, I'm fine, Ali, thanks. Just the normal pressures of a routine workload.'

With that he dropped the dildo and its packaging back into the paper bag and held it out to me, adding, 'But one more satisfied customer is its own reward.'

In spite of myself, I felt concerned. Perhaps the demands of a new young wife were getting the better of him. 'And Serena?'

'Oh, blooming.' But then he shrugged. 'Very possessive though. Seems to think I should account for every moment I don't spend with her.'

'Oh, tough.' And I know I sounded smug.

He looked up sharply. 'There will be a trade-off.'

'What?'

'For having repaired your sex toy. As you have availed yourself of my services, I may well avail myself of yours.' He became animated again as he warmed go the idea. 'You see, it

24

crossed my mind that a threesome – that is to say, you, me and Serena – might act as a corrective. The act of sharing – sharing me with another woman – would be a salutory lesson for her.'

I didn't answer. I walked away from him to the other side of his work station, dumping a fistful of damp tissues in the steel wastebin as I passed. Then I screwed tight the neck of the paper bag containing the dildo until it started to split.

'Besides which,' he continued, 'the elegant way you overcome the petty problem of sexual jealousy would set her a very good example. A young girl needs a role model, don't you think?'

'Hold it there,' I said. 'You make us sound generations apart but I'm only six years older than her.'

'Darling!' He laughed delightedly. 'Maybe it's all the work I've put into you, but you have an emotional depth and richness to which she cannot compare. Besides I can think of no more beautiful heroine for her to have.'

What could I answer? I wanted to curse him but I was flattered. I said, 'Stefan, don't lay this one on me. Be fair.'

All I was asking for was some respect for my feelings, for the way I'd wanted him for myself, but had never been able to admit it because I'd accepted that he could never be faithful to any woman.

He didn't know. He said, 'You be fair. The memory of you affects everything I do. You think I'm lying? Look. If you want proof.' He began tapping on a keyboard and told me, 'This particular screen is permanently on-line to the Net so I can surf whenever. Best to keep it separate in case a virus gets squirted down the tubes and contaminates my personal stuff. I have an official Web Site and an unofficial one.'

'What?' It all sounded like the blackest of black magic to me.

'On the Internet. My unofficial Web Site address is this.' He swivelled the screen of the computer to face me and I read, 'ali. sons. xxx. pussy. com'.

It was quite a shock. It took a little time for the full significance of what I was reading to sink in. I said, 'Oh, Stefan, but . . . does this mean that all over the world . . . ?'

'There are eighty million people on the World Wide Web in seventy-three different countries. All have access to that address. Chances are that every second of the day and night someone somewhere is reading that Alison's pussy comes if you kiss it. Doesn't it give you a buzz to think of that info winging its way down cables and bouncing off satellites? Pull your skirt down, darling.'

'You what?' I was seriously disorientated.

'It's still hitched up at the back.'

I pulled it down without thinking. My mind had gone blank.

He smiled before continuing, 'You see the power you have? To induce such an apocalyptic vision?'

Often a new idea of Stefan's could throw me. Multiplying this one by eighty million made me dizzy. Perhaps this was how an astronomer felt when he had just discovered a new galaxy on the edge of space. I left the room too dazed even to say goodbye.

The receptionist had to point out the way to the lift three times before I recovered my sense of direction, and then I only reached the ground floor after ascending to the twelfth, getting out at the third and running down the stairs.

Luckily I knew my way home well enough not to have to think about it. Somewhere along the way I sat down for a coffee. My sense of reality returned slowly but surely. I began to realise that it was Stefan's ability to shock that held me in his thrall. The likelihood of something unexpected added a sense of danger to our encounters that enhanced the excitement of having sex with him. This sense of danger was as intrusive as his big cock.

That observation led me directly on to another truth. One that was harder to admit. I ordered a second coffee, this time with whipped cream which I spooned into my mouth while I found the courage to face facts: it had not been the dildo that Stefan had thrust inside me. It had been his erect member that had worked to such magical effect. It had been very dishonest of me to pretend otherwise. Particularly since, with his left hand holding my wrists behind my back and his right answering the phone etcetera, he would have had no way of manipulating the plastic penis. The muscles of my vagina contracted sharply with pleasure at the thought. I smiled at the memory of the ease with which he slid into me, the depth of his thrusts and, above all, the discipline he must have had to exercise to pretend that his penis was something other, was not part of himself, as he carried on with his 'business as normal' comments on the phone.

No wonder I felt satisfied. The empty frustration of the night before, which had been like a dull ache in my stomach, had been replaced with a warm and lazy sensation as though my body was in the process of digesting a delicious meal. On the contrary though, as was often the case with me after having sex, I felt ravenously hungry, which was why I ordered a wickedly large slice of Death by Chocolate to go with my second coffee.

It was not until I needed my purse to pay my bill that less palatable thoughts forced their way into my consciousness. To get at my money I had to dig my hand down under the dildo in its paper bag.

Could I have been more disloyal to my dear friend, Catha? Wasn't it less than four hours ago that I had faithfully promised her to a) bin the dildo and b) never see Stefan again?

I had failed on both counts. The latter situation was irretrievable, but I could make some reparation by getting rid of the dildo immediately.

Whether it was working or not, of course, I didn't know. But one thing was certain – I felt too guilty to want to keep the wretched thing. As soon as I got home I would consign it to the dustbin. There was a practical problem though . . .

The week before Stefan had married Serena, I'd made a clean sweep of some things that he had given me during our relationship. To be honest, I'd kept the pearl studs from Asprey, the Yves St Laurent suit and the Cartier watch but I had thrown out a garter, a plaited leather jockey strap and a satin thong that said 'Fuck Me' in diamante on its tiny front pouch, some tasseled nipple clips and a pack of fruit-flavoured condoms – that is to say, the banana, orange and blackcurrant flavours – since I rather like the morello cherry. As well as these things I had torn up an intimate diary that I had shamelessly entitled 'Stefan Sexploits', mixing everything together with a dismembered chicken carcass in order to discourage any inquisitive attempt by the dustmen to explore the bag's contents.

I had not reckoned on the snappy little dog who lived next

door, though. Seemingly this terrier had an ongoing quarrel with black bags, particularly when they stood on the pavement near his gate and rustled in the wind. He shredded our bag and half the contents spilled out. Catha said it was silly of me to worry because none of the neighbours would recognise my handwriting but I went up and down the street collecting shreds of paper as well as condoms. I found phrases of mine – for example, 'I get the hots when you' or 'I get wet whenever I think of' – wrapped around the spikes of iron palings and plastered by rain high up on lamp-posts. In fact, I was so distraught that Catha went and complained to the owner of the dog. Quite a feud ensued.

Okay, so the silly woman walked her dog every day in the square with a plastic bag draped over her right hand and always tidied up the minute the wretched thing had finished squatting, but apparently good manners did not extend beyond the grass in the square. No doubt that had something to do with the notice which threatened a fine of fifty pounds there. Once back on the pavement the animal ran riot with the ankles of passers-by, prams, postmen and black bags – in short anything that dared to move within a few inches of its front gate. She called it 'Doby' – short for 'dobermann,' she said – which just about sums up the hopelessness of her case because, and I kid you not, this canine most resembled a small fireside rug on legs. But 'Doby!' she would shrill regularly from her window, as the rug rolled itself up into attack mode, her tone apparently inciting rather than restraining its vicious intent.

Anyway, my point is that I could think of nothing worse than having a big pink dildo with its permanently distended knob rolling loose outside in the gutter and, as it were, pointing an accusing finger at the door of our flat.

The answer was to deposit it in a public litter bin before I arrived home.

Chapter Three

If you have ever looked for a litter bin that is suitable for the secret deposit of something personal, you will know what I was up against. Either the receptacles were so full that they were already disgorging their contents onto the surrounding pavement, or they had been squashed flat by vandals, or they were being busily sorted through by vagrants and bag ladies.

It wasn't until I was crossing the garden square in front of our flat that I spied a metal bin that was not only respectably intact but had also recently been emptied. With a triumphant flourish I flung the paper bag containing the dildo into it. It landed with considerable force, hitting the side of the bin with a resounding clunk. As I turned to walk away I felt a tremendous sense of relief. Unfortunately, though, this was cancelled out almost immediately by one of anxiety. The force of the dildo's contact with the bin had set the vibrator in motion. Yes, Stefan had mended it. He would. It worked. Just when I didn't want it to, it'd become violently animated. The empty metal container acted as an echo chamber, magnifying its mechanical drone. What's more, the bin began to shake and rattle against its concrete retaining post.

Should I turn back? I was just about to when, out of the corner of my eye, I saw Doby dart from some bushes and run helter-skelter towards the juddering thing. He skidded to a halt on his little stick legs immediately underneath it, barking furiously and leaping up and down as though the grass was a trampoline.

My instinct was to break into a run. After all, our flat door was only a couple of hundred yards away but I forced myself to walk unconcernedly as I realised that, previously unobserved to me, his mistress was in the shadow of a tree and was now being drawn out into the open by the excitement. Had she seen me? Was the hand she raised wearing its plastic bag waving at me or the dog? I walked on, drawing up the collar of my coat until I was safely indoors.

There was nothing for it – I'd have to begin the day again. I drew down the blinds that overlooked the square, put on a Vivaldi CD very loud and ran a deep bath – to which I added some essential oil of rosemary because, it said on the bottle, it had remarkable restorative powers. As the bath was filling I noticed the light blinking on the answerphone.

There was a message from Catha. She suggested we meet up for a Thai meal after she'd finished college. 'To recharge our batteries, darling.'

I winced. And, as though guessing that she might have touched a nerve, she paused before adding, 'No pun intended. I'll ring you on my mobile when I'm leaving here.'

I glanced at the clock. It was remarkably late. I took the phone with me into the bathroom. There was a speaker extension from the sound system in there already and the swell of the music reverberated off the tiles.

Before I sank down into the water, I soaped between my legs vigorously. I was still sticky with Stefan's come and I didn't want the smell of his sex on me when I met her. My fingers slipped and slithered into every crevice of my sex in an effort to cleanse myself of him. It was harder to get him out of my thoughts though. His mind infected mine and he was demonic. The middle finger of my right hand slipped into my vagina and it felt warm inside.

What was worse, I wondered, discovering a waxed image of oneself under a friend's pillow stuck through with pins, or finding oneself being downloaded onto the software of a million techno heads? I had every reason to feel violated. I wriggled my finger and it felt good. Best to think of other things. I looked at the illustration I'd had framed to hang at the end of the bath. I'd come across it during my last research job on *Archaeological Digs of the Twentieth Century*. It was of a tomb painting of an ancient Egyptian god with a translation of his words underneath. 'I had union with my hand, and I embraced my own shadow in a love embrace,' it said.

Didn't that say it all? From now on I was going to be totally self-reliant. I sank into the water and laid back, deep in thought. My index finger joined the middle finger of my right hand to gently probe inside me and it felt at home in there. My left hand swished the water so that it broke into gentle waves over my breasts. I was going to be self-sufficient until . . . well, until I fell in love, and then . . . the muscles of my pelvis were responding to the probing of my fingers as I stroked my nipples dreamily. Suddenly the phone rang.

'Hello?'

'Alison?'

'Hang on.' I had to reach for a towel to stem the water running down my arm. As I did so I realised Catha's voice sounded unnaturally high and tense. I dried my arm and heard what sounded like faint shouts coming from the receiver. 'Something up?'

'Ali? Are you alright?'

'Yes. I was just—'

'Keep away from the windows!'

'I was just—'

'And get down on the floor!'

'What?'

'You mean to say you don't know?'

'What?'

'Darling, I finished early. Thought I'd make my way home and we'd go out from there. But I can't even get into the square.'

'Catha, please calm down.' All I could think of was that she'd had such a showdown with those dykes that were holding her department to ransom that she'd finally flipped.

'The square has been cordoned off. All approach roads are closed. A bomb-disposal unit arrived five minutes ago.'

'Here? You mean our square?' I was incredulous.

'Suspected terrorist bomb planted in the litter bin.'

I gasped and it felt as if I'd been punched in the stomach. I couldn't say anything.

'You know the litter bin in the centre of the square? Someone was seen acting suspiciously. The bin started vibrating. They say the device must've developed a malfunction. If they can't safely disarm it, they'll evacuate the square and carry out a controlled explosion. Ali? You still there?'

A sort of wailing noise rose from deep inside me. My head was spinning and I only just saved myself from losing my footing in the bath as I stepped out and stood there transfixed in a puddle of water. Catha's voice pressed on. 'I can hear you've got music on. Switch it off so you can hear the loud-hailer in case they use one to make an announcement. Or maybe they'll ring the door. Meanwhile keep your cool, darling, and move to the back of the flat. Shut the doors. I'll be with you as soon as I'm allowed. Oh, and keep away from that bookcase. The one we never screwed to the wall. And remember, if you feel a blast use both hands to protect your face.'

I flung the phone down and before I knew it I was running round in circles trying to find my clothes. I couldn't find them. I tried to fling a coat on to cover my nudity but it didn't seem to have any armholes. I had to get out of here. I had to be ready to evacuate the flat at a moment's notice. It was only when I tripped over the phone flex and sat down with a bump on the floor that I came to my senses.

It wasn't a bomb that was in the litter bin. I was so relieved when I remembered that I started to laugh and cry at one and the same time. I stopped abruptly as the door bell rang. I took a deep breath, wrapped myself in a big towel and walked slowly to open it. I hoped it might be Catha.

It wasn't. The woman on the doorstep was forty, no make-up, a neatly tailored dark suit and open-necked shirt. She said, 'Detective Sergeant Wordsworth,' and flashed some sort of wallet at me which I assumed to be her identity. 'Best if I come in.' And with that she pushed past me to walk purposefully down the hall towards the light in my bedroom.

I hurried after her. 'If you don't mind, I was just—'

'What?' She wheeled round to face me with her back to my bed. A small scar cutting across her top lip decorated the cupid's bow like a faint exclamation mark.

'I was just about to . . .'

She suppressed a smile that pulled at the scar, delicately extending it. 'You were just about to . . . ?' She repeated my words with a mocking tilt of one eyebrow. 'Just about to remove all traces of incriminating evidence?'

'No. I mean, why should I . . . I mean.' I swallowed hard. I couldn't understand why I sounded guilty, except that the steady gaze of her dark brown eyes seemed to bore into me. 'I mean, I never planted a bomb.'

'A bomb? Who said anything about a bomb?' She pretended polite surprise.

'Well, no one, except . . .'. I faltered because her eyes began to travel down to somewhere below my shoulders. I followed her gaze and realised that the bath towel had slipped, exposing my left nipple.

'Why not just make a clean breast of it?' she said, sounding gently persuasive. And then she licked the scar where it blurred the line of her top lip.

I pulled the bath towel up quickly and tucked the corner in securely between my breasts.

She frowned. 'Oh, let's not waste time,' she said and she stepped towards me. 'I'm here to carry out a strip-search.'

'Strip? What for?' I stepped back, clutching at the towel again in self-protection.

'For traces of explosive.' She came so close that I felt her breath stir a strand of my hair as I turned my head away.

'But I told you . . .'. I felt my skin tingle into goose bumps on my arms and legs. 'And anyway I've had a bath.'

'In that case,' she said, and she reached out suddenly and tore the towel out of my grasp so that I was standing naked before her. 'I shall have to punish you.'

'No.'

'Bend over.'

'No.' But even as I spoke it was as though I was fighting to restrain myself, not her.

'Listen, my sweet,' she said, allowing her hands to run down my sides till they rested lightly on my naked hips, 'traces of explosive are not always removed by washing. They can become trapped under fingernails for example, or in a person's intimate parts. But if you would rather be strip-searched at the station by a police doctor and have swabs taken for forensics in front of witnesses you are, of course, free to do so.' Then her hands slipped from my hips around and down onto my buttocks and circled them. 'Added to which, if you would rather face the full glare of publicity, and I am referring to the vultures of the press already gathering outside your door, then you have only to say the word.'

What choice had I got? I was so close to her that my hand went up to touch the scar on her lip. She smiled dreamily. I made one last effort to drag us both back to reality. 'It wasn't a bomb,' I said.

She shook her head. 'You were seen.'

'It wasn't a . . . I promise you.' I came to a dead stop because she had started to nudge my lips apart with her tongue.

'It was a . . .'. Suddenly I felt shy. It seemed a remarkable moment to be overcome by a sense of modesty.

It made her impatient. She stepped back and thrust her hand into her jacket pocket, producing a piece of paper. 'Read it,' she demanded.

As I unfolded it I saw the fatal words, 'Memo From the Desk of God' and my heart sank further as I read on. 'Alison, light the blue touch paper and retire! And once the smoke has cleared, my darling, lie back and think of me.'

'That . . . message was tucked down inside the box containing the device.'

'Well, it's just a private note from a . . . well, from someone I know.' On the face of it there could hardly be a more incriminating piece of evidence.

'Like the head of your cell?'

'What cell?' Frankly I felt as though my guilt had imprisoned me already.

'Terrorist cell, what else?' Then she stepped close to me again and, instead of taking the paper back from my hand, she fondled my breast. Her mouth was close to my ear. 'However, if you cooperate with me now . . .'

Without a word I turned and bent over, hiding my face in the duvet on my bed. I hoped she'd spank me. I deserved it. Instead, her cool hands glided up the inside of my thighs, forcing my legs further apart. I shivered.

'Tell me now,' she said, 'if you are trembling with fear at the thought of your wickedness being discovered, or with desire?'

'Your hands are cold,' I said, because I could no longer be sure of anything much.

'Then I'll warm them.' And with that she thrust both hands up into the hot fur of my pubic hair which was still damp from my bath. I fell forward into the bed and, as I did so, I felt her lips brush the cheek of my right buttock. I clutched at the hands between my legs to draw them closer but she snatched them from me. She must've sensed a movement behind her because in the next instant I heard a gruff male voice close by us say, 'What the hell . . . ?'

34

We both straightened up and turned as one to face a young man with soft blond hair standing in the bedroom doorway.

'How did you get in here?' DS Wordsworth hissed.

'I was waiting outside. Found the front door open.' He held up a pad of paper and a biro as though to demonstrate his credentials. 'Reporter on the local paper. Came to follow up the story.' He glanced past her to me. 'And interview the lovely lady who threw away her dildo.'

At that DS Wordsworth glanced shamefacedly at me before spitting, 'Bastard!' at him as she pushed him aside to get out of the flat.

'Only doing my job,' he called after her. 'Local colour, community concerns and all that!'

The front door slammed. He turned back and shrugged apologetically. He stooped to pick up the bath towel from the floor and handed it to me. Until he did so I'd forgotten I had no clothes on. I'd been too busy studying him.

'I should've knocked,' he said.

He was very young and he fingered his notepad nervously as I discarded his offer of the towel to put on the lace negligee that I kept for special occasions. He pretended not to watch me as I turned my back to take it from the wardrobe, but I could see him in the door mirror. He was watching alright. He didn't blink once as I slid the garment over my shoulders and then lifted my hair, slowly allowing it to cascade down my back. I tied the ribbons at the waist rather too carelessly. The flimsy bodice of the thing barely hung together as I turned to face him. He cleared his throat as though to jog himself out of a trance.

'If you don't mind . . .' he said, but his voice threatened to break so he cleared his throat again. 'Answering a few questions.'

I took a step towards him and the biro he was holding slid from his grasp and fell on the floor. I went down on my knees at his feet immediately to pick it up. I held it up to him. His hand trembled as he took it from me. Because I was kneeling on the hem of my negligee, I had to put my hand on his thigh to steady myself before I could get up. My gaze was on a level with his flies so I couldn't help noticing that the material there was tight across an impressive bulge. As I stood, the hand that had grasped his thigh inadvertently touched where he

35

was at his most vulnerable. He caught his breath and his eyes closed momentarily.

'What questions?' I asked. I went and sat on the end of my bed and patted the space beside me.

He looked anxiously towards the door. 'Shall we go in another room?'

'Why? What for?' I knew my teasing was unfair but I found his innocent confusion most appealing. Here I had, after all, the perfect antidote not only to Stefan but to DS Wordsworth, too.

He seemed to make his mind up. He ignored my invitation to sit and paced the floor to give himself a more business-like air. He flipped open his pad and took the cap off his biro with his teeth. Then he read aloud to himself some words he had already written in an experimental sort of way, 'Bomb Squad in Desperate Bid to Defuse Dildo or' – with a brief glance at me went on – 'Local Woman's Sex Toy Rings Alarm Bells.'

I was going to make some clever remark about getting a rise out of the local police force when the danger of my situation came home to me. This was the sort of publicity that any serious-minded woman could do without. I said, 'Hold it there.'

'Okay,' he said. 'Let's begin at the beginning. What's your name?'

'I'm not telling you.'

He looked surprised, even a little hurt. 'Well, I can easily find out. From the woman who identified you. With the little dog. Directed the police to your door.'

'Unreliable witness,' I said. 'She's got a personal grudge.'

'Oh, really.' He looked crestfallen. Then he brightened. 'But that'd just add another twist to the tale.' Obviously from here on in anything I said was going to be grist to the mill.

'Please,' I said because there seemed no point in beating about the bush. 'Don't publish anything about me.'

'But it's a great story. Loads of human interest. I owe it to my readers.'

'I'm not going to tell you anything,' I said.

'Please!' Suddenly he sat down beside me. 'This is my first assignment. My first real hard news story. Until last week all I'd done was six months on the gardening column. So please!'

'Go back to gardening.'

'But I don't know anything about it.' He put his head in his hands. 'The whole article I did on azaleas was a disaster.'

'Why?' I tried to prise his hands away from his face.

'Got the wrong month for planting them and ...' Suddenly he turned and clutched my arm. 'Three years in media studies and then a chance with this job. All I ever wanted was to be a real journo.' Having reminded himself of his ambition, his eyes narrowed. 'And you're not going to stop me. My first lucky break. I've got the bare bones of the story and if you won't help me flesh out the details I'll make them up.'

'You can't do that.'

'Why not?'

'Because it's dishonest.'

'It's what everyone else does.'

'But not you.' I pushed the blond curls back from his forehead.

'You have much more integrity than that.'

'But ... I want to ...'

His inner conflict furrowed his brow and was painful to behold. I stroked his temples with a deft circular motion of my fingers. His eyelids fluttered closed. I chided him gently. 'You're a much more special person. A cut above the others. You must know that.'

'No, I'm not,' he protested, but less stridently. In fact his strength seemed to be deserting him and he leaned against my shoulder, looking down into my cleavage. I took the opportunity to pull his head down even further so that his lips grazed the swell of my breasts where my negligee fell open.

'Oh, God. You smell terrific,' he murmured.

My hand was gently easing down his zip as I said, 'I'm very sorry to disappoint you.' His zip was so stressed that I needed both hands to undo it fully. As I succeeded he slipped backwards from my shoulder to lie prone on the bed.

'What am I going to do?' he asked. 'I mean, I can't go back to the news desk without ... Unless I ... Your fault if I ...' He was having a struggle to make sense of his objections.

'I shall make it up to you,' I murmured as I slid down onto the floor between his legs and eased his cock out of the constriction of his pants. It sprang up and waivered briefly like a pendulum before my eyes but, with one lick of my tongue from root to tip, it steadied and held rigidly still. 'But first you have to promise,' I told him, and I blew a little spurt of breath into the cleft of his knob before running my tongue around its rim.

'I promise,' he groaned.

'But really?'

'Yes, yes, anything.' His hands were reaching down to clutch at my hair so that he could pull my mouth closer.

'Tell me.' I dodged his grasp.

'What?'

'Say it. Now. In your own words.'

'Swear not to write anything . . .' He was fighting for the words. 'About you. Or name you or . . . anything else that might . . . Oh! Oh, no!'

He tried to sit up, caught a glimpse of me and fell back, flinging his arms above his head in a gesture of helpless abandon. I wasn't holding back either. I was giving him the full treatment. In my left hand I cradled his balls, gently squeezing and releasing them with my fingers. With my right I forced a passage under him to dig into his crack and wriggle up towards the tight circle of his anus whilst I sucked greedily on his cock.

The sound of my sucking began to describe a dance tune in strict tempo. My head rocked back and forth as I controlled my breathing to create a tight vacuum, imprisoning him between my tongue and soft palate. Each time I sensed he was about to climax I held off. I relaxed and played with him a moment, squeezing his buttocks together and, gently rocking his balls, allowing my tongue to flicker and taste the juice that I drew in little droplets from him.

After a while he went so still and quiet that I was suddenly worried that he'd lost consciousness. I clutched at the bedclothes and dragged myself up to sit astride him. His eyelids flickered and he reached a hand up blindly to feel for my breast.

Maybe I could fall in love with him. I felt it was a distinct possibility as I guided his long slim penis back along my slit and into my throbbing sex. My head was thrown back, my hands pressed down on the firm muscles of his torso as his member was thrust upwards into my deepest recess. I moaned and my knees slipped so that I was spread wide open. My head fell forward so that my hair fell like a veil between us.

Instead of moving over him, I began to contract and relax the muscles of my vagina. Suddenly he reached up and clasped his hands behind my neck. He drew my face down onto his shoulder so that my muscles almost lost contact with his penis as my bottom rose to point at the ceiling. With my weight off his pelvis, he'd freed himself to thrust upwards into me. I tried to wrest back control but he was like an unbroken horse, wildly bucking under me. There was nothing for it but to press down into the saddle, grip with my knees and give him his head. Slowly but surely he settled into the rhythm of a gallop.

It was an exhilarating ride and as it neared its conclusion both of us gave excited shouts of encouragement. He climaxed just ahead of me but his youth enabled him to continue thrusting into me until I had come too. I fell on top of him with my mouth pressed into his blond hair in a sort of snapshot of a kiss that could be framed and put on a wall where it would hang for years before it faded. My legs slid back to stretch out straight on either side of him as the whole length of my body unfolded to cover him. He made a brief but gallant attempt to draw the duvet up to cover both of us and failed because it had fallen off onto the floor.

'Why on earth would a woman like you buy a dildo?' he murmured.

'Because she hadn't met you?'

He laughed, his chest quivering deliciously under me. So I went on to warn him, 'Print that if you dare.'

He thrust his hand down between my legs so that the rough hairs of his arm grazed my vulva where it was most sensitive. 'I gave you my word,' he said and then he swivelled his wrist so that it grounded into my wetness.

I gasped and wriggled my way up until I could lick a curl of blond hair that encircled his right nipple.

In response he began to rock his arm back and forth between my legs. Within seconds the muscles of my inner thighs had lazily started to grip and release him. Was he capable of starting over again?

I never found out. The next second I froze. Had I heard a key in the latch? Swift footsteps down the hall? I struggled to kneel up but, with one arm between my legs and the other encircling my shoulders, I was spread-eagled face down. As the bedroom door opened I felt a draught fan my naked buttocks which were raised and separated by a masculine arm.

'You two-faced bitch!' Catha's voice cracked like a whip above me. 'Hypocritical cow, after all we agreed! Only yesterday! I should've known better! Well, this is it! This says it all!'

The door slammed shut.

'What the . . .? What's going on?' He sat up and I slid onto the floor.

What could I tell him? His first big scoop and he'd forgotten to take notes? He had other talents, though. I wished him luck.

Chapter 4

Hair shirt time. I deserved all I had coming to me. As soon as I was alone, I put on some old tracksuit bottoms and a baggy sweater and went to look for Catha.

She was sitting in the kitchen with a Thai takeaway that she'd bought us and she was fingering a foil container of butterfly prawns in ginger. My favourite and it smelled delicious.

'Listen to me, Catha, darling,' I said. 'I know it must've looked bad and you're bound to think the worst of me but' – I went to the cutlery drawer as I continued – 'fact is I felt uncertain of my direction. Now I've turned a corner. Today has been my Road to Damascus.'

I couldn't have put it more clearly. I sat down and tapped my chopsticks on the table top to draw her attention to what I was saying because she was staring straight past me as though she couldn't hear. But I was just getting into my stride, 'Don't mind admitting it's been a bit of a bumpy ride but—'

Suddenly she swept the whole meal, including the butterfly prawns, straight off the edge of the table into the swing bin, which she proceeded to kick savagely before leaving the kitchen. There was a pause and then I heard the key turn on her bedroom door. She'd locked herself away from me.

I was mortified. After checking out the prawns (which had landed upside down on some vegetable peelings) I felt that Catha had been completely justified. Starvation would be too good for me. I wanted to suffer. In fact, over the next two days, I ate so little that I began to wonder if I was anorexic.

Catha re-emerged from her room but only to go out. I felt emptier than I had when Stefan announced that he was to marry Serena. My sense of self-worth hit an all time low.

Forty-eight hours later things began to look up – this being the length of time it took for Catha to talk to me. She only did so because she was having one of her regular crises over what to wear. Luckily she depended on me when it came to accessorizing. I was sitting on the sofa feeling thin and reading a magazine article entitled, 'The Rewards of Monogamy', when she walked in.

'Think I should wear this belt or the suede one?' was all she said.

'Well, the suede, except it's not quite . . .'. I was quick on the uptake.

'What?' She looked anxious immediately.

'Not quite the same navy as the jacket,' I replied, adding apologetically, 'if you want me to be honest.'

'Isn't it always the same with navy?' she moaned.

'What about my belt with the diamante buckle?' She followed me as I got up and went through to my bedroom.

'Mightn't it be a bit too glittery?' she asked as she watched me going through my top drawer. 'So much of your stuff is.'

'Depends,' I said, pulling it out, 'on what impression you want to make.'

She took the belt from me, pulling it around her slender waist as she went to the wardrobe mirror. 'Oh, well, that's simple,' she said. 'I want to be taken very seriously. But at the same time I want to look as though I could easily seduce a millionaire into parting with a nice fat wad of money.'

I was very surprised. I'd never heard Catha talk like that before. But, as I watched her walk backwards from the mirror to judge the belt's effect, I sensed it was too soon for me to ask prying questions. Also, I knew that sometimes she enjoyed being enigmatic.

'In that case,' I told her, 'perhaps you should rethink the whole outfit.'

'Really?' She ran her hands back through her hair. That was when I realised she was wearing not only eye shadow but lipstick too. The conclusion was inescapable – she must've left Women's Studies already. You'd never catch Catha wearing make-up to a place where grunge was *de rigeur*.

'Yes.' I was watching her closely now. I wanted to claim a part of her new image as my own because she looked so beautiful.

Suddenly she undid the jacket to reveal a satin bustier that pushed her breasts up and together so that she had the sort of well-defined cleavage that I'd never seen on her before. I wanted to touch the place where the flesh folded gently together, swelling and subsiding as she breathed.

I did nothing.

She glanced up at me in the mirror, explaining, 'I decided to give myself a much sharper profile. I've even rewritten my CV.'

I refused to be drawn and remarked simply, 'The skirt can be taken very seriously. The cut is severe and the length is very . . .'. I went to stand behind her to share her view of herself in the mirror. 'But perhaps you could be more adventurous with the jacket.'

It wasn't long before half the contents of my wardrobe were strewn over my bed and assorted pairs of her shoes were scattered along the length of the hall.

She hadn't dressed so much as undressed and, as she stood there looking a bit undecided, I finally plucked up the courage to try and find out what had happened. 'Must've been tough.'

'What?'

'With all the women that were gunning for you at college. I suppose they gave you nothing but attitude?'

'In the end,' Catha said, 'it wasn't the attitude of the women that bothered me, it was that of the men.'

'The men?' Another surprise. 'But I thought none of them ever hassled you. I mean, you told me that the young male students were, by comparison, well . . . docile.'

'Quite,' she said.

'And rather bewildered by the blurring of the gender barriers. I think that's what you said. Poor lost souls, you said.'

'Tell me about it!' She sat on my bed and ran a hand up the length of her shapely leg, pointing her toes to straighten her tights before she continued. 'D'you realise not one of those young men ever tried to make me?'

'Perhaps because they'd never seen you as you are now.'

She shook her head. Her eyes flashed.

'I mean you can be a bit of a challenge, Catha.'

'They're all wimps.' She sounded really angry. 'Absolutely pathetic!'

'Maybe most are gay?'

43

'It's worse than that, Alison. There's something fundamentally wrong.'

I'd sat in on a couple of Catha's lectures so I was quick on the uptake. 'Oh, you mean the prevailing decadence of post-modernist culture and slow collapse of a male-driven civilization that's undermined the—'

'I'm talking sperm here!' she snapped.

'What?'

'I'm talking chemistry. Basic instincts. Nature rewards power, thrust, aggression. Because those are the little fellas that shoot up and fertilise the egg!'

'But, Catha . . .'. She'd shocked me before but this was something different.

'And you can stuff post-modernist culture for starters. I'll tell you what's wrong, Ali.'

'What?'

She leant very close to me. 'Oestrogens in the drinking water.' It seemed to come out of nowhere. I drew back from her but she went on. 'Depleting testosterone levels.' Adding with considerable emphasis, after a pregnant pause, 'Impotence, okay?'

There were lots of questions I needed to ask but I didn't get the chance because suddenly she noticed the time on my bedside clock and began to panic. I didn't know what she was going to be late for and I didn't care. All that concerned me was her state of mind. After she'd left, though, my pleasure in the fact that we were talking again got the upper hand. I decided a celebration was in order and went out to buy some food for the first time that week.

On my way out I paused to pick up my post which had been lying neglected in the hall. More to celebrate: two responses to my ad in the *Education Supplement* for work. One sounded promising. It was from a clinical statistician at the Department of Psychology in Cambridge. His name intrigued me – Maximillian Chopin Smith. He was working on something entitled, *Modern Mating Rituals: The Personal Column as the Equivalent of the Marriage Broker.* He requested me to ring him.

As soon as I'd got back and the stuffed aubergines with mozarella were gently bubbling in the oven (Catha's favourite), I phoned. I warmed to him immediately. I'd always liked a cultured American accent and he seemed genuinely grateful to hear from me. After a few preliminaries, during which he said that he needed organisational skills, I began to get a picture of him. Boston probably, quite Scott Fitzgerald-ish, tall and willowy with a cashmere sweater thrown carelessly over his shoulders.

'But as a top priority,' he said, 'I need someone with imagination.'

I had plenty.

'And someone not afraid to indulge in lateral thinking.'

I told him he could count on me there too.

'And how are you with statistics?'

'Oh, thirty-six, twenty-four, thirty—'

'You don't say!' He interrupted with a laugh. 'I like it!'

Obviously he had to meet me to discuss remuneration and so on before either of us could commit to the project and he asked if I would be prepared to go up to Cambridge. He told me that the daffodils were in full bloom along the Backs. Spring flowers never last that long. No point in delaying. I agreed to take the train up the next day.

I couldn't wait for Catha to get back to tell her my good luck. But I was pipped to the post. She returned flushed with triumph and clutching a bottle of champagne.

'To celebrate, darling.' She kicked her shoes off. 'Success! I got it! Congratulate me!'

Obviously for the moment my news was going to take second place. 'You got it? You got a wad of money? Already?'

'What?'

'Off a millionaire. Just like that?'

She laughed uproariously until she saw how puzzled I looked. 'Sorry. Forgot I hadn't told you.'

Catha explained that she had gone after a job that was much more worthwhile, much much more far-reaching in its sociological effects than her incestuous little niche in academe with all its petty politics and self-defeating in-fighting.

In short, she had landed a very prestigious job as Chief Fundraiser for a charity whose main concern was environmental protection. Apparently they were currently concentrating on industrial effluent and the de-sexing of fish in rivers that fed into the public water supply. If fish were

45

losing their ability to breed, what would the outcome be for man? Obviously the chemicals being discharged from factories into our waterways constituted a time bomb. And, personally speaking, Catha wanted to ensure the survival of the human race. In the light of what she was now telling me, I realised that the disjointed statements she had made previously were all connected and made perfect sense. Her disillusion with Women's Studies and all the stuff about oestrogens in the drinking water stemmed from the same source.

'What's the divine smell?' she asked when she'd paused for breath.

In answer I lifted the aubergine out of the oven and set it down bubbling on the table between us.

'Oh, bliss!' Catha said. 'Oh, honestly, Ali, I can't wait to get started.'

I warned her it was hot.

'No, I mean I can't wait to get started on all these fat cat industrialists and millionaires. I'm really going to tap into their consciences. They're going to have to clean up their own mess. I'm going to see to it. They're going to have to pay. I promise you. Mega bucks.'

After I'd told her of my modest little piece of news, she opened the champagne.

'Here's to us,' she exclaimed. 'Isn't it terrific? I mean, that both of us are on the threshold of a new beginning? It had to happen. Here we are about to transform our lives. Make a clean sweep of everything except—' She came to a sudden halt, her glass half-raised to her lips. She replaced it on the table without drinking, her eyes downcast.

I'd been waiting for the opportunity to make a full and frank confession and now I came in right on cue. I told her everything that'd happened, leading up to the moment when she'd walked in on my newspaper interview, explaining how my good intentions had been compromised, not just with the young reporter but with DS Wordsworth and with Stefan too.

'Not that I expect you to forgive me. I mean, nothing can justify my behaviour,' I finished sadly, watching Catha twisting a strand of mozarella round her fork.

'That's where you're wrong, darling,' she said.

She went on to explain that my initial motivation for returning the dildo to the shop had been naive. A few pounds

46

would have made no difference to our prospective debt burden. Therefore it made better economic sense to get the thing mended. And in this I had succeeded. After a fashion. With regard to my interrogation by the police I had no case to answer. Any fool knew that the best hope of being treated leniently was to cooperate. As for the press, any woman worth her salt was bound to pull out all the stops to protect herself from the public gaze. Nowadays an unwarranted invasion of privacy like that could be a matter for the courts. But I'd dealt with it adequately myself.

'There are situations, Alison, where a woman is justified in using every weapon at her disposal. Including her powers of seduction.'

'You really think so?'

'Oh, yes.' She refilled my glass as she went on. 'When it comes to self-defence it can be as effective to give way as to attack.'

'Go with the flow?'

'Quite. And as for the business with the bomb,' she concluded, 'well, that's the sort of thing that can happen to anyone.'

I left for Cambridge with a light heart. The fields speeding past the window of the train seemed greener than I could ever remember. Even the ticket collector smiled at me, and I walked from the station to the Department of Psychology with a spring in my step. There are days when I know I'm a winner and this was one.

Admittedly, Maximillian Chopin Smith did not live up to my mental picture. He was rather short and broad-shouldered with a leonine head, in fact not at all willowy. But I felt relaxed with him from the start and, once installed in his muddled room with paper cups of coffee, we had a real brainstorming session that I think both of us found exhilarating. There was one slight blip when he asked me if I was computer literate. But then I told him, as though to demonstrate just how in the swim I was, about having a Web address named after me. He seemed nonplussed until he wrote it down, 'ali. sons. pussy. xxx. com', and then his lips curved into a slow appreciative smile. He said a sense of humour was essential for the job. I liked his honesty. He liked my enquiring mind. He filled in his background. He was, he told me, an imposter and only in Cambridge on sufferance because his father had endowed the Department with more than enough money to save it from imminent closure. Before his father's hand-out the place had been on its knees.

'The guys around here are involved in pretty esoteric stuff. Like how many times does an eye blink in response to a red light as opposed to a green. Know what I mean?'

I nodded enthusiastically.

'Whereas I'm into the nitty gritty.'

'Sex,' I ventured.

'Current mating rituals. But only from an intellectual standpoint.'

'Of course.' I noticed his eyes had wandered to where my skirt had ridden above my knees. I pulled it down.

'I'm a virgin,' he told me.

'You're kidding,' I relaxed completely, forgetting about my skirt. I'd never felt more safe.

'It's the ultimate intimacy of penetration that scares me.'

'Really?' And my tone had a soothing tell-me-more quality.

'Many women have tried, believe me, but . . .'. He shrugged.

'Poor you.'

'Oh, I get by but . . .'

'How?' Already I had a reputation with him for being inquisitive. He shook his head. Suddenly he was on his guard. I respected him for that.

'Let's get back to the job in hand,' he said. 'Okay, so you can help collate statistics, format the material I've already collected, but would you be prepared to be more creative?'

'In what way?' I asked.

'Well, a list of figures makes for pretty dry reading. I want to flesh that out with some real-life stuff.' He went on tentatively, 'Have you ever advertised in a personal column? For a partner?'

'No.' I laughed at the idea.

'Of course not. You're far too attractive.' He looked downcast.

'I've often wondered though,' I said.

'You have?'

'Could be very interesting.'

'If you were to get some replies . . .'

'Of course I would.'

'I've hardly had any,' he told me.

And then he explained that, purely in the interests of research, he had placed an ad recently in an upmarket broadsheet. He read it out to me, 'Serious-minded academic seeks NS female under five foot five, D-cup, to help him pick up the pieces. Photo appreciated.'

'But that's awful!' I told him.

'It is?'

'It's just so negative. And as for mentioning D-cup . . .'. Words failed me.

'I like big titties,' he said and suddenly looked quite petulant. 'And, okay, back home I'dve been lynched by some women's group – if they could have cracked my cover, I mean, gotten around my box number – but here women are more understanding. Aren't they?'

I was beginning to feel a real responsibility for this man. He needed guidance. He was his own worst enemy. And as for what Catha would have said!

I shrugged.

'You wouldn't answer that ad?' he challenged me.

'I'm too tall.' I wasn't going into my cup size right then.

'Imagine yourself short. Imagine yourself ugly. You still wouldn't answer it?'

'Certainly not.' But I didn't want to antagonise him because I wanted the job. Besides which I'd never tried to imagine myself ugly. I wasn't going to start now. 'You'll simply have to rephrase the ad,' I said. 'Won't be a problem.'

'Just my luck.' He shook his head. 'I paid up front for a three-week series because they offered a fourth week free.' And then he continued, half to himself, 'The darndest thing – the way I totally fail to connect with women. I'm just so unrealistic about them. Of course that's why I'm into this work. I mean, half the guys in this department are nutcases which is why they're hell bent on finding out what makes the mind tick. I mean, isn't it always the way? Take my shrink, that man is so agarophobic he won't even come to the door to say goodbye to me.'

'I cannot accept that a man of your intelligence can be that unrealistic.'

'So what would you put?'

'What?'

'In an ad about me?'

Danger zone. I sidestepped it neatly. 'What to put in my ad is what most concerns me.'

'Legs to die for?' he offered tentatively.

'No.'

'Ah, come on! False modesty!'

'No.'

'Trust me. Stand up, lift your skirt and walk to the far end of the room away from me.'

'No.'

'I said away from me. And stay facing the door. Because I wouldn't want you to come close.'

'Even so . . .'. I was very much in control of the situation and he sensed that too. 'I haven't thought what I'll put in my ad but I'll make it up-beat and kind of unthreatening.'

On the journey back to London I knew I'd handled things well. The fee on offer was more than adequate and, unusually for this type of work, I was going to score on the job satisfaction too. He had made it plain that my creative input was going to be important. He had even suggested that he would acknowledge my contribution to the project in his Foreword so that I would share in its kudos. Obviously he had some personal problems but none, quite literally I thought cosily to myself, that would touch me.

By the time the train pulled onto Euston I had settled on the wording of my ad: 'Sporty blonde of independent means looking for cuddles leading to long-term commitment.'

As soon as I got home I told Catha. She said it was bound to lead to trouble. Which it did. But that was nothing to the trouble she was heading for. And, as it turned out, she'd already had a foretaste.

Chapter 5

Catha had been a tad patronising about the efforts of her predecessor in Fundraising. Pleading letters about the survival of the Marsh Marigold depending on deeds of covenant and her Adopt-a-Deciduous-Tree initiative had been swept off the desk and into the office shredder on day one.

Catha was more interested in the high earners of today than individuals past their sell-by dates with their sad hopes of immortality. You had to take on captains of industry on their own ground, she said, grasp them by their corporate throats and get them to cough up in the here and now.

To this end she planned a glitzy, high-profile dinner with tickets at silly prices that would corral the whole lot of them into the same cattle pen at one and the same time. She had a theory too that the more you charged people the more they liked whatever it was you had on offer. An art auction (paintings, sculpture, etc., on environmental themes yet to be donated) was going to give the dinner an especially classy feel. At this bash Catha planned to divest the bastards of quantities of cash, but she had a hidden agenda too. She did not envisage herself waiting cap in hand in some outer office of a plc she had targeted whilst the Chairman shuffled papers on his desk and thought up ways of saying he was too busy to receive her. No way. The idea of being a *Big Issue* vendor *manqué* made her shudder. No, once she had shown herself to be a charming and effective hostess, indulging in an easy social intercourse with the great and the good, she would be treated as an equal. I just crossed my fingers, hoping Catha hadn't bitten off more than she could chew.

The only problem, she said, was in fixing the venue – particularly as she was looking for a freebie. It had to be somewhere within a short hop of the city in chauffeur-driven limo and yet far enough away from base for everyone to feel that they had made a worthwhile effort. She set her sights on a new conference centre close enough to Greenwich for guests to feel that it, and consequently they, had a personal connection with the millennium. Trust Catha to exploit every angle. But arriving at the conference centre for initial negotiations she found herself having to be even more exploitative than usual.

Her meeting with the Director of the centre had been downgraded. He offered his apologies via the Manager who was to show her around in his stead and make sure she understood that her charity was to be offered a reduced charge and not a freebie.

According to Catha the Manager was a real wimp and she put the fear of god into him straight off. She backed up her observations that all the place had in its favour was space and that most of that was empty by reciting the details she'd read off the information board in the entrance foyer: an IT Security Convention on Level A, room 2, a Backgammon Contest on Level D and a Marketing Seminar for Estate Agents in Lecture Hall 3 on Level B. How, she marvelled, could they be in profit with a heating bill for so many acres, not to mention the business rate, the hire of caterers for the restaurants and bars, the general staffing, cleaning . . . Apparently she didn't get a chance to finish before he interjected rather feebly, 'If you've seen enough?'

'I've seen nothing,' she said. 'Yet.'

'But I've just shown you everything except the high-security area.'

'Oh? Well, no surprises there either I expect. Empty is it?'

'It's luxuriously appointed and includes a banqueting suite. And it is only empty at the moment' – he was on the defensive – 'because it's reserved for overseas dignitaries and top-flight international diplomats. The World Bank booked in for a week.'

'When?'

'Last year.' And then, responding to her look of scorn, he added, 'Anyway it'd be well beyond your budget. That's for sure.'

'Tell your Director from me,' Catha said, 'that his policy is self-defeating. He should take a leaf out of the book of theatre managements. They know that it's better to fill houses with complimentary tickets than to have seats left empty. This place should be humming. It's dead. End of story. Forget it. I wouldn't want to be here. Particularly since all my guests will be corporate financiers, heavy-duty industrialists and the presidents of blue-chip companies. Just the sort of people who book big venues themselves, who regularly fill conference centres to the rafters for Trade Fairs and . . .'. Catha shrugged as though she could not be bothered to go on. But inside she was raging. She was even more angry when the Manager walked off with his wimpish walk as though to say that she was a hopeless case and, as far as he was concerned, she was a time-waster.

To calm herself down she went to the bar on Level A and got herself a double scotch. It helped a little. Then she saw that the IT security party had left a half bottle of red wine and that helped a bit more. The two thirds of a bottle of champagne left by the estate agents changed her mood entirely. She grew introspective. She became morose and began to worry that she was over the limit for the drive home. This was probably why she was so slow on the uptake when approached by someone who shook her hand and introduced himself as the Director of the centre. He was tanned with distinguished silver streaks in his dark hair. She did her best to steady herself by fixing her gaze on the hand-stitched lapels of his double breasted suit and thought 'Saville Row' – and that, she admitted to me, was the limit of her judgement.

'Oh, yeah?' she said without much interest.

He wanted to buy her a drink. When she seemed undecided he took the initiative and ordered her a Pimms which was served up looking like Kew Gardens. Once she'd got her mouth around the cucumber slice, sprig of mint, the boring old slice of lemon and floating umbrella, Catha thought she'd never tasted anything more delicious.

As far as she could remember he did not once allude to the fact that his manager had briefed him. Yet he seemed to know what her requirements were and was very keen to satisfy them.

'Cut the crap,' she told him.

He leant forward picked the cucumber out of her Pimms, took a bite, and then said, 'Follow me, and I'll show you something.'

She couldn't remember following him, but suddenly she

53

found herself in what he called his 'holy of holies'. If there's one thing that distinguishes Catha, its her ability to hang onto her principles even when she's feeling a bit squiffy. She said, 'You don't say! Looks to me like a boring old VIP suite with so-so catering facilities.'

However, she told me that in all honesty she had been quite overcome by the opulence of the windowless banqueting room, its ante chambers and sweeping staircases that branched off from a central atrium at several levels, the whole being overhung with tropical plants and glittering chandeliers.

At the time, as she reported it to me, she was much less impressed with the pros and cons of the computerised security system that guarded this inner sanctum than with the decor. But this was to change soon enough.

Sir Harvey was as keen to demonstrate his in-built surveillance and anti-terrorist devices as a young boy with a new train set. Catha, always a sucker for enthusiasm, began to like him.

'You mean to tell me,' she asked, suppressing a hiccough, 'that the archway leading from here to the banqueting . . . thing, where that mile-long table . . . thing?'

'Precisely!'

'What?'

With restrained gallantry he offered her his arm so that she could steady herself before he went on. 'This archway has an in-built laser sensor which operates on the same principle as those things you have to step through at airports.'

'That detect metal . . . those things.'

'Precisely,' he said as he steered her through the archway.

'Well, it didn't go off,' she teased. 'So now we're through security clearance when does the plane take off?'

'It wasn't activated but if I . . .' His hand slipped up the column supporting the arch and a tiny red light began to wink somewhere high above on the ceiling.

'Bingo,' Catha said, looking down quickly so as not to lose her balance.

'So now if I walk back through . . .' He walked back through the archway and turned to face her smiling.

'You mean you haven't got a gun or a knife?' Catha laughed.

'Now you walk back towards me.'

If she'd hesitated, Catha told me, it was only because she

felt challenged to demonstrate that she was sober enough to walk in a straight line. As well as that she was beginning to have to fight off an irresistible urge to be close to him. She took a deep breath, drew herself up to her full height and walked.

All hell broke loose. The chandeliers dimmed, a powerful spotlight clicked on above her and the wail of a siren momentarily swamped the place. Sir Harvey leapt to the column, depressed the hidden switch and silence reigned.

He was so close to her that she could hear his breathing. 'What sort of weapon are you carrying?' he asked.

'I'm not.' But she was in shock. She felt herself rocking back on her heels and tried to catch at him to steady herself.

He stepped back sharply. 'Then you must be wearing something.'

'I'm not.' She felt close to tears.

'A locket or chain or something?' He stepped towards her then quite menacingly.

Catha undid the top two buttons of her blouse to show him. He undid the next two. His finger probed down into the gap between her breasts. His anxiety seemed to subside a little but he still wasn't satisfied.

'You must have something about your person . . .?'

'No, unless . . .' She was fighting to remember whether the suspenders of her basque were made of metal when she realised she didn't have it on. 'All I've got on, I mean apart from what you can see, is a pair of silk french knickers and a bra which . . . I wonder?'

'What?' Suddenly he was easing her jacket off back over her shoulders. It fell to the floor.

'Well, if the hooks and eyes that fasten my bra . . .?'

Her blouse was already undone so it was easy to slip it off. As she allowed that to fall to the floor she turned her back on him so that he could ascertain whether or not the fastening was made of metal. He undid her bra. Too late she remembered. 'But I'm pretty sure it's just a plastic loop that . . .'

Her bra had joined her blouse and jacket on the floor. His hands had slid round to lift and squeeze her breasts. She looked down in some surprise, she said, to observe two manicured thumbnails with perfect white moons teasing the nipples which were already erect.

Everything in her wanted to give way to the sensations stirring deep within. Nothing could have been easier than to lean her weight backwards into his embrace. But something stopped her. She sobered up fast. The motivation for her visit and all her serious intentions came flooding back. She used her elbows to break free from him and found herself running towards the exit. It was a long run. By the time she reached the huge door with its blue velvet padding and brass studs she was breathless.

She wrenched at the handle. Nothing happened. She turned around and leant back against it.

'Where's the key?' she panted.

'What?' He was a long way off. He hadn't moved.

'Unlock it.'

Slowly, he walked towards her, delving into his breast pocket. She had time to appreciate just how self-assured and attractive he was again. He produced a small plastic card.

'Keys are a thing of the past,' he told her calmly.

She stood aside as he swiped the card through a slit in the frame of the door. Nothing happened.

'This is most unusual,' he exclaimed.

'Oh, pull the other one!'

He raised a quizzical eyebrow as though offended. 'Most untoward,' he said.

'So now you're going to pretend that you are the victim of your own technology,' Catha sneered.

He shrugged. He tried swiping again before he pocketed his plastic. 'Maybe the central computer went down.'

'I've heard that somewhere before.'

'Where?'

'My bank, of course.' Catha was scathing. 'The whole thing crashes on a weekly basis. Millions of pounds of customers' assets get sucked into a black hole out there in space at the flick of a metaphorical switch.'

'Which reminds me,' he said, walking away from her again. 'You're here on business. Or that's what I was led to believe. So? Perhaps you'd care to explain?'

There was nothing for it. Catha laid her case before him, and, as she talked about the advantages to be had from supporting a charity, both in the realms of self-advertisement, giving moral leadership and mopping up on tax avoidance, she began to feel that their incarceration together was more to her advantage than his. In fact, he turned his back and walked away from her until, in the far distance, he sat down alone at the vast top table in the banqueting area. He looked lonely. Catha followed him to better gauge his reaction to what she was saying.

He watched her as she walked towards him, waited till she got close and said, 'Have you any idea what beautiful ellipses your breasts describe as you walk?'

She decided to ignore his remark in favour of clinching her argument. 'And that's why you'll never regret it,' she told him.

'I never regret anything,' he said. As he spoke, he eased himself forward in his chair and put both his hands down under cover of the table. 'Especially not business with a beautiful woman.'

It did cross her mind that he was unzipping his flies but she pressed on, 'It's not business exactly.'

'Then what is it?'

Was he playing with himself, she wondered, and if he was did it matter when she was so close to achieving her goal? 'I'm offering you the chance,' she said calmly, 'to allow a well-deserving charity to use this space just the once for free.'

He smiled kindly. 'I tell you what I'll do. I'll give you a fifty per cent reduction on the regular tarrif in exchange for . . . well, if you meet me halfway.'

'How would I do that?'

'Remove the garment obscuring the remaining fifty per cent.'

'What?'

'Your skirt,' he explained. 'Take it off.'

'But . . .' Catha's hand went to the button at her waistband. 'This simply isn't good enough.'

'Okay,' he offered reasonably. 'Take off the french knickers you said you were wearing too and we'll really start talking.'

So near and yet so far. What a coup to get a place like this for her first big event. What a setting for her to start building a reputation as a hostess. She hesitated only briefly before making up her mind. Her skirt had hardly slid down to her ankles before she was stepping out of her silk knickers.

Immediately he stood up and she felt suddenly nervous. His trousers were already off and his member was majestically erect and reflected in the polished surface of the table. She'd been so involved with the women at college that she hadn't seen anything like it for some time. It looked, she told me, like the impressive gavel that a toastmaster might bang on the table to call an assembly of guests to order.

She needed to orientate. She needed to give herself space and get a run up to this thing. A bit of a chase around the table might do the trick. But as she started to sidle away along the far side, he climbed across it.

Knowing that there wasn't any real avenue of escape, and only wanting to create a playful interlude, she made for the stairs that curved upwards into the double height of the atrium. He followed her to the foot of the stairs and there he stopped, apparently content to watch from below as she ran up the open treads past the palm trees and the chandeliers towards the glass dome. It only struck her afterwards that he must've had an intriguing view of her pussy winking between her legs as she sped along.

The stairs led nowhere. Like those on a stage set, they stopped dead at the top. She leant against the brass rail and looked down. The heat from the chandeliers seemed to wrap around her, making it hard to breathe, and she had a sudden sensation of vertigo. This was the reason she turned back and started to descend towards him. By this time he was coming up. He was coming slowly, one hand grasping his erection and stroking back and forth, one stroke to each step that he ascended. They met halfway.

'I just have to be sure you'll keep to your half of the bargain,' she murmured. 'And won't withdraw . . .'

It was as though he could not stop climbing until he was into her, as though the only possible brake on his progress would be her offering herself as a buffer. She sat down with a bump on a stair above him and spread her legs, but he was already onto the next stair so that his penis was on a level with her mouth.

'. . . Withdraw your offer.' She only just managed to finish her sentence because as soon as she opened her mouth to speak he snuck in there. His hands dug down into her hair, pulling her head towards her. For a moment it seemed as if there was no space left in her for thoughts let alone words. But then she remembered what to do.

It's like riding a bike or swimming, somehow you never forget, she told me. She sucked hard whilst leaning back, clasping his thighs to push herself away from him. He let go of her hair. The way he had to flex the muscles of his legs to keep his balance excited her. Then, arching her soft palate to accommodate his length as it slid from mouth to throat, she pushed forward again, feeling the rasp of his pubic hair against her lips. She had him trapped. She half-teased, half-threatened with her teeth at the throbbing root of his penis. She heard him moan. He'd got the message.

'Anything!' he gasped.

'What?' His penis slid out and for a moment Catha forgot the purpose of her visit.

He put a hand under her chin and tilted her head back to look down deep into her eyes. 'I'll do you a deal on the catering too. The cordon bleu for the price of my standard menu.'

Another angle she'd neglected. She began to really like him – as well as to really want him. In answer she closed her eyes and opened her mouth wide to take him inside again. But he reached down and, with his hands under her arms, started to lift her up. As he did so, his mouth on hers, all she wanted was to lie down and open her legs wide. But just as her knees began to give way she remembered she was on a staircase. She turned to kneel on the step above him so that he could enter her from behind. But he seemed to be oblivious to the precariousness of their position and thrust into her before she had got her balance. Suddenly she found her head and shoulders suspended through the open tread of a stair, a few feet above the top of a palm tree. She cried out in alarm but then the whole weight of his body descended and she realised she was held fast. She forgot the danger – or maybe because of the danger, combined with reassurance of his big member thrusting inside and pinning her down even more securely – she began to feel as though she was flying. She went into free fall. A tremendous sense of release from all the petty earthbound concerns of the preceding weeks and months enveloped her.

The palm tree and the table and chairs below rocked and receded until they were tiny dots. There was a roaring in her ears and the air seemed to be getting thin. She gasped out a warning before she climaxed and both of them juddered to a long-drawn-out halt, braking a hair's-breadth from the far end of the runway.

Her eyes were closed and she opened them slowly. Just as there is a lull inside a plane after an emergency landing, neither of them moved for a minute. She slowly became aware of the sweat binding their two bodies and the warm trickle of his semen from her vagina as he pulled away. For a minute she was so cocooned in a warm glow of physical satisfaction that she was not conscious of him descending the stairs behind her.

She'd just begun to think that an enforced spell of celibacy was the best form of foreplay, when she looked down to see him using her french knickers to clean himself up. Experience told her that it was hard to get semen out of satin so she eased herself backwards from between the stairs and stood up. Her legs only just supported her. She descended a little uncertainly, thinking of the way men rarely have the sensitivity to recognise how a cuddle can round things off. But she held her peace. She'd got an awful lot of what she wanted after all. Now was not the moment to complain. Even so she was shocked by the speed with which he became an efficient businessman once more.

By the time she had found her own clothes he was looking very much the picture of smug Saville Row again. Ignoring the offer of her damp, crumpled knickers, she started to dress. She had only just begun to button up her shirt when he got the plastic out of his breast pocket and was striding to the exit. He swiped the card and the door swung open instantly.

'Well, of all the dirty tricks,' Catha said without any surprise. She hurried after him pulling on her jacket.

As he strode out into the open space of Level A, he called back over his shoulder as he raced ahead. 'Something happened in security. Want to find out what.'

They arrived in reception just in time to witness the tail end of some disturbance. Several people were still milling about. It turned out that the central computer had indeed crashed but had been brought back up again by the leader of the IT security seminar. Catha followed as he went through an unmarked door to thank the man in question. The room was lit only by a flickering bank of video screens. In front of these, the computer freak sat hunched with a clutch of biros in his top pocket.

'I can't thank you enough.'

'My good luck,' he said. 'I've proved my recovery procedures in front of an appreciative audience. They've all signed up for the next series of seminars.'

'Most fortuitous.'

The two men shook hands. Catha noticed the IT expert had what looked like a large damp patch on the front of his trousers which became apparent as he stood up. It was only then that she realised several of the screens were relaying pictures of the VIP suite, including one of the stairs. She was shocked. How many of them had been watching?

'My pleasure.' The man licked his lips staring past the Director's shoulder to where Catha was standing. 'It's not often I can offer the boys such hands-on experience.'

Catha decided it was time to go. She excused herself, saying that she would be ringing to sort out details, and hurried to the car park. She was just straightening her hair in the rear-view mirror when she caught sight of the computer expert clutching his bobbing biros as he ran towards the car. Her instant reaction was to engage the ignition and hit the accelerator. She had to turn the car and pass him to make the street. He tried to flag her down with . . . what was it he was waving as she sped past? Her knickers?

Catha hid her face in her hands after she had finished her story. I could see she felt depressed and humiliated. I stroked her hair and tried to get a look in between her fingers.

'Darling, listen,' I said.

She jerked away from me. 'It's no good, Ali.'

'No good? But you did brilliantly!'

'No.' She sat up and flung her head back to look at the ceiling. 'I can see the way things are going to go. It's no good.'

'But you mustn't blame yourself.'

'I do. I behaved abominably. My first project and before it's even got off the ground I've got my legs open and . . .'. Her voice faltered. 'I'm starring in a porno video for an audience of techno heads.'

'Ah, well, that was something else. It was only the denouement to your story that left you with a nasty taste in your mouth. Up to the point where you found out about the video screens you'd had a ball.'

Tears came to her eyes. 'But that's what's so awful, Ali. Lust, pure unadulterated.'

'Your ideals were pure though.'

'I know but . . . I have to face it – nothing is for nothing. So much for charity. I shall have to resign.'

'Catha, there are situations when a woman is justified in using every weapon at her disposal.' I spoke with authority. 'Including her powers of seduction.'

'The end justifies the means? You mustn't say that. That's highly suspect.'

'But that's what you said.'

'Is it?' She looked genuinely surprised.

'Yes. When I felt so disgusted with myself at how weak I'd been. You remember – my Road to Damascus day?'

'Oh, yes!' She smiled. 'And I was sure I was right at the time.'

'You were.' And I didn't stop there. I said, 'Catha, maybe before asking other people to give to your charity you will have to learn to give of yourself.'

She nodded mutely and took my hands in hers. 'You're right. I'm going to give myself unsparingly. I'm going to give it all I've got.' She hugged me then and added, 'Thanks, darling, for being such a friend.'

So Catha's problems with regard to her work were sorted out quite simply. Mine still needed resolving. Particularly the stack of mail that was being sent on from the broadsheet that had run my ad. I'd already received seventy replies to my box number. Because I had been so helpful to her, Catha insisted on giving me a hand and sat down with me one evening to sort through them. Anyway, she was as curious as me to see what the cat'd brought home.

We soon got stuck into a sort of production-line technique, passing, stacking, inspecting and identifying rejects. First to go was cheap paper, smudgy biro, writing that sloped backwards or from a manual typewriter with clogged up e's and o's.

We then turned our attention to those with photos. Of the conventional portraits most had something wrong – lips too thin, eyes too close together, a receding chin or a leery grin. One looked very passable but, after studying the blurry background to the picture, we could see a bird in flight. I said the photo had been taken outdoors but Catha said no, it was a flying duck on his sitting room wall, so he bit the dirt. There was also a photo of a foot resting on a window ledge with the London skyline in the background. Catha thought that this was quite a witty comment but I was worried he might be a foot fetishist.

Then there was a polaroid of a penis with a matchbox alongside it – presumably to give a sense of scale. It looked impressive to me until Catha said it could be the sort of mini matchbox sometimes given away in restaurants. Anyway, a man who indulged in this form of self-advertisement was not for me and, as Catha quite rightly pointed out, this sort of thing was not what I was after in any case.

We were left with ten letters on good notepaper which were either written on quality PCs with laser printers or handwritten with fountain pens and which would have been a graphologist's dream. These claimed to be from company directors, city luminaries or to be coming hotfoot from chambers in Lincoln's Inn or mansion flats within the division bell. Naturally we decided that this little lot should be treated with extreme scepticism.

'Why would such people respond?' Catha asked me.

I didn't know. Anyway, it was getting late and Catha had to hit the road in the morning to start touting for paintings and sculptures to be donated to her art auction at the conference centre.

'Quite frankly, Alison, the whole process has exhausted me,' she said.

'I know,' I agreed as I tried to squash the discarded letters down in the overflowing wastepaper basket.

'And as for the QC who says he can't take anything less than Janet Raeger underwear! How naff can you get?'

'I know.'

'And when I think that only two weeks ago I was invited to edit *The Handbook on Non-Sexist Language in Electronic Media*.'

'Too much. I know.'

But then I remembered it wasn't my responsibility alone, or Catha's. It was down to Max. I'd ring him in Cambridge in the morning and he could decide.

Chapter 6

I didn't have time to relay my news before Max had blurted out, 'Hey, hey, guess what? I got an answer. A real pro. Answers everything. A genuine advertisement freak. She's into free offers and competitions like you wouldn't believe.'

She didn't sound like the sort of research material he was looking for to me, but I didn't want to be a spoilsport, so all I said was, 'Oh, super! Well done, Max!' And he didn't need any more encouragement than that.

'Wait till I tell you,' he enthused. 'She came to my rooms in a micro-mini with this kinda glitter boob tube and no pants.'

'And she was forthcoming, I mean with regard to . . .'

'You bet. I told her, "Stand over there. Keep away from me. Just roll the boob tube down, bend forward and wiggle them about."'

'And she did?'

'Are you kidding? No sooner had she done that than she turns around, lifts her skirt and jiggles her big juicy strawberry-jello bum at me.'

'But Max, didn't you ask her any questions?'

'What d'ya say to something like that? I just got my willie out and that spoke for itself. Actions talk louder than words, okay?'

'You mean you had sex with her?'

'Of course not. I communed with myself. I told you. I keep my privates private.'

'So you didn't make headway with your research? *The Personal Column as the Modern Equivalent of the Marriage Broker*, remember?'

'Oh, sure, sure.' He sounded a trifle deflated. 'But I am very visually orientated. Some guys are tactile and some . . .'

I was sorry I'd asked. I wanted to reawaken his enthusiasm for the project in hand so I told him, 'I had seventy replies to my ad. Until today – when I got twenty more.'

There was a pause. Then he whistled through his teeth. With no hint of a grudge, he said, 'Alison, welcome on board!'

Nothing inspires a women to give of her best in the workplace more than a little personal appreciation. I was soon voicing my reservations and asking for his advice.

'Hey, hey, don't bother your pretty head. It's me that sets the agenda.' He sounded in control again. 'Allow me to decide the parameters here.'

'But since none of these men are worth following up?'

'You follow them all up.'

'What?'

'Alison, your personal preferences do not enter into the scheme of things.'

In the light of what he'd just said this seemed a bit rich, but I just murmured my assent for the time being. *Who pays the piper*, I thought, etcetera, etcetera.

'We're talking psychology here,' he went on, growing ever more earnest. 'We are talking primitive mating ritual subsumed by the intellectual quote urban quote postmodernist culture.'

This was just the kind of talk I couldn't take – even from Catha. I said, 'Okay, so you want me to question all of them. Get them to talk on a confidential level, no holds barred.'

'Fax me detailed notes,' he said.

'Could be risky. I don't want to lay myself open to any sort of trouble.'

'Of course not. You follow the advice printed alongside any of these contact columns. You meet in a public place. You tell a friend where you're going to be.'

'I'll tell Catha.'

'And fax me a photostat of your legs.'

I told Catha.

'Darling, I think I'd better come with you,' she said.

Neutral territory. I chose a Holiday Inn. Happy hour. I didn't want to make a statement. I was wearing a red rose on my lapel only to establish my identity, oh, and to cover the buttonhole mike. I wanted anonymity.

With Catha seated at the next table in the Sundowners Bar (she claimed that she wanted to be sure I was safe, but I really think she was as fascinated as me to see the authors of those letters in the flesh) and with my interviewees pencilled into a timetable I was ready to go. The last thing I wanted was to arouse suspicion. Heaven forbid that any of these men should conclude I was snooping or, even worse, into blackmail. So Catha was providing back-up. she was within earshot, her Power Pad open in front of her, a pile of her charity's bumph alongside, as though she was making notes from that. She needed something to do anyway, she said, because she didn't want to stare. The men concerned were bound to be on their guard. She'd also lent me her mobile so that in the event of some unforseen emergency she could go out to the booth in the foyer and contact me.

It was kind of Catha to be so helpful. However, there was a sting in the tail of this arrangement. She'd been so disappointed with the standard of donations to her art auction that I had reluctantly agreed to act as porter for the event. That is to say I was going to wear my froufrou mini, six-inch heels and basque and, much like a pom-pom girl struts into the ring holding aloft the number of the next round at a boxing match, I was going to display the lots to the prospective bidders. She had brushed aside my misgivings, saying she simply had to add a little pazzaz to the collection of prints of fruit and flowers and the tacky oils that she'd grubbed up to date. So she had, in a manner of speaking, already got her pound of flesh.

The first clutch of my respondees proved disappointing. The minute I brought up the subject of marriage they clammed up, started to look over their shoulders, made excuses to go to the Gents' and never came back. I was on a steep learning curve. At first I thought my policy of ordering the most expensive cocktail on offer at the Sundowners to test the level of their commitment (a Moscow Mule Double Daquari) was what threw them. I scaled this down to mineral water, lemon, no ice. Still poor results. Catha and I had a quick conflab in the Ladies'. What I had to do was forget that I was interviewing them and be much less upfront. I had to forget about my role of researcher and allow them to take the lead. I had to be shy and diffident. As soon as I'd taken this on board things began to look up.

Still no surprises though. Sad cases, out of work, clinging

on to the promise of recovering a twenty per cent stake in the marital home and dreaming dreams. Predictably, the photo of the foot belonged to a man who wanted to get under the table and suck my toes. Cheap notepaper meant jeans and trainers, manual typewriters meant the double breasted blazer with a dusting of cigarette ash or dandruff. But then, I reminded myself, I had started at the bottom of the heap, working my way up to the classy addresses. I was beginning to long for something, anything, out of the ordinary when my transvestite turned up. No dress. Far from it. A Suit from the City, short back and sides and the merest hint of Calvin Klein aftershave. He not only talked freely about marriage (he wanted a woman who'd swap dresses with him, he said) but offered a short-term compromise. He'd run into trouble in Selfridges' lingerie department and professed to be perfectly willing to pose as my husband if I'd try on things in his size. I declined but I liked him.

When he'd gone, I felt much more cheerful because I'd chalked up my first real proposal of marriage. And I only had one more smudgy biro to go before I dipped into the *crème de la crème* of my respondees. But, before I could, I had my first real surprise in the shape of a genial property tycoon who turned out to be dyslexic. He insisted on buying me a fancy cocktail which was why I found myself back on the Moscow Mule. He was a rough diamond, a real rogue whose heavy gold identity bracelet clunked on the table top as he told me about his rise from jobbing building to one of the prime movers in an international concrete cartel. He was big at the UN, he said, particularly when it came to grabbing a slice of overseas aid to build a hydroelectric dam or similar. But he had a particular weakness for bridges. He wanted to build one to the Isle of Wight and one to the Isle of Man.

'Why?' I laughed.

'Why not?' He caught hold of my hand and squeezed it in his big peasant fist till I winced. 'Call me Mick, by the way.' He winked.

'Because no one wants bridges there, Mick.'

'What's that got to do with it?' he said and started to pull me so that I was leaning towards him across the table. 'Look at the Isle of Skye. No one wanted a bridge there. They had a great ferry service. So? Stuff that. Hey presto. Now they got a bridge.' Suddenly he released his grasp so that I fell back in my chair, which set him off laughing.

It was hard not to warm to the sheer energy of the man, but I had to steer the conversation back on track. He told me he was married already, but he'd divorce her and marry me tomorrow if that's what I wanted. I asked him please not to be flip. He calmed down a little and said if I had doubts about him and his credentials I should come and see his place. It was some pile, he said, Georgian, twenty beds, twenty and a half baths with two acres of park, a gate lodge and a staff of five. Oh, and a stream at the end of the garden called the Thames.

'And your wife? What'd she say about my visit?

'I'd pack her off to our villa in Majorca first.'

I don't think I could have looked as impressed as he would have liked because then he added, 'You like pictures?'

'You've got photos of the place?'

'No, no.' He raised my glass to my lips and tipped it towards me so I had to sip as he went on. 'I got a long gallery full of Old Masters.'

'Full of . . .'. I pushed the glass away from my mouth. 'Paintings? Old Masters of what?'

'Fat ladies mainly.' He smiled, pleased to have impressed me at last.

'Rubens?'

'Rude? What's rude about it?'

'I said . . . oh, forget it.'

I had no chance to explain anyway because suddenly I realised that Catha had started coughing behind me. I took her point. I told him, 'Okay, I'll come.'

'Done!' His identity bracelet hit the table as he stood up.

'As long as you promise to answer all my questions,' I warned him. 'I mean, honesty is what I value in a relationship.'

'Give me your phone number, kid. Now you've met me you'll know I don't hold back. What you see, you get.' He turned away to walk off and then turned back. 'One thing though before I show you my house.'

'What?' Instantly I was wary.

'Come to the opera with me.'

'You like opera?'

'Are you kidding? This is business. Otherwise you wouldn't

see me for dust. But having you there'd make it okay. Give me a buzz having you turn heads. You got an outfit?'

I didn't have time to answer before he added, 'I'll buy you one. Down Bond Street with a slit up the back. Oh, and, kid, thanks for not saying about my spelling and my writing neither but I left school at fourteen. And that's the sort of letter you can't give a toffee-nosed secretary.'

As I watched him go I was sure of one thing – that'd be the first and last time I'd rubbish smudgy biro. Turning my head just a little, I saw Catha was on the edge of her seat and waiting with renewed interest for the arrival of the quality letter writers. She gave me a discreet thumbs up as a tall handsome man with a camel coat worn cloak-like over his shoulders approached.

Without preamble, he swung the coat off, flung it over the back of the chair opposite me and sat down. 'What are you drinking?'

'Oh, hi! Pleased to meet you!' I said. 'But I don't think I want another—'

'I insist.' With an imperious wave of his hand, he summoned the barman to our table. 'The lady will have a sweet sherry.'

'Ah. Hang in there. No, I don't like . . .'. But the barman had already gone. 'Anything sweet and especially not . . .'. My voice trailed off. There was something about his eyes that was hypnotic. I turned my head away.

'Face me,' he said.

I did but I looked down and picked a slice of apple out of my trusty Moscow Mule.

'Look at me.'

I dropped the apple back into its glass. My fingers dripped. I looked at him. His eyes were that violet blue of a sky before a thunderstorm. Unreal.

'I'll come straight to the point,' he said.

I was glad of that. Even more glad that Catha was close by. I could sense her getting restless. I said, and it cost me some effort, 'Me too.'

'Okay. You make your point first,' he responded, his eyes still locked on mine.

I cleared my throat. Before I knew it I'd said, 'I'm researching the personal column as the, as a kind of . . . launch pad for marriage. So you see my own interest in you is purely academic.' After all what could be more of a put-down than that.

A ghost of a smile crossed his lips but did not extend to his eyes. 'Good try,' he murmured.

'What d'you mean?'

'I mean marriage could not be further from my mind either. I'm simply looking for a woman I can rub with my fingers and bend like a spoon.'

Freaky. I crossed my legs tight. In spite of myself I wanted to know more. 'Sorry?'

The barman returned with the schooner of syrup.

'Drink it.'

I took the tiniest sip. Yuk. 'I don't like it.'

'But in other respects we have the same tastes.'

'I doubt it.'

'You want to join Miss Rule's Academy.'

'I what?'

'The club. In Mayfair. My problem is they won't accept single men. I can only gain entry as half of a couple and then only to observe.'

'Observe what?'

'The exercise of discipline. What else?' He seemed genuinely surprised.

Only the sound of Catha's fingers starting to drum on the next table gave me the courage to challenge him. 'Oh, do me a favour,' I said.

'You see!' He leant towards me, the pupils of his eyes dilating. 'I knew it. You deserve a spanking.'

'You'll have to find someone else to go to that club with you.'

'Maybe the other club is more to your liking?'

'Other club? What other one?'

'The Raunchy Rodeo Club.'

'Hey, this is London not Bangkok!' I said and made a mental note of the fact that Catha had gone quiet. Maybe she wanted to travel into the dark side of our metropolis too. It was starting to look foreign alright. My hand was exploring the hem of my skirt. It had ridden up to the top of my thighs. I must've been wriggling a lot.

'The Raunchy Rodeo,' he explained, 'has the same conditions of membership as the latter but there the similarity stops. The men participate. They have to because each woman that gets tacked up in saddle and bridle has to have a cowboy to ride her.' He blinked for the first time for ages. 'And to apply the crop to her naked haunches.'

Catha's chair was suddenly thrust back so it bumped against mine. I didn't turn but I said, 'Are you serious? What sort of woman would trot around like a circus pony?'

'Plenty, believe me. Especially the high-flyers stressed out by executive responsibilities and boardroom politics. They can't wait to rip off their power suits and get into dressage. You know dressage, where the animal is trained to respond to the slightest pressure of the knees? Believe me they can't wait to get the bit between their teeth. And I mean a real bit that pulls at their soft mouths.'

Catha's chair overturned with a thump. I tensed myself, ready for her to land one on his chin and I picked up a wooden toothpick to stab him. Instead I felt a cold draught as she stormed out. I knew what was going to happen. I gave her forty seconds to get to the booth in the foyer. I said, 'You've made a mistake. What d'you take me for?'

'But you answered my ad.' He pointed an accusing finger at me.

'I what? I answered your . . . ?'

'My ad. The one that began "He Who Must Be Obeyed".'

What a turnaround. 'I most certainly did not. You answered mine.'

This threw him. He checked his watch. He said, 'What's today?' I told him Wednesday and he said he thought it was Tuesday. Then the penny dropped. He raised his voice. 'Good Lord,' he exclaimed. 'You're the cuddly blonde!'

This upset me because several people overheard. Two women in the corner giggled. A man reading his paper, lowered it, gave it a shake and looked pointedly over the top of the page.

I hissed, 'So what if I am?'

'No problem.' He shrugged. 'Whether I'm advertising or responding I'm after the same thing and you'll do nicely.'

'Try me Wednesday, Tuesday, Monday,' I told him. 'My answer's going to be the same, "Get lost".' This time it was me who was set on staring him out.

Catha's mobile rang. For a split second he looked as though

71

he thought I was pulling a gun at him. I got it out, shot up the ariel and flipped down the mouthpiece.

Catha's voice cracked like a whip against my ear, 'Get rid of him!'

'I just have.'

There was quite a pause, then she inhaled slowly before she spoke more calmly. 'I hope you realise it was only out of respect for the integrity of your research that I stopped myself from laying into him on the spot.'

'Well, thanks.'

'When I think of all the years I spent promoting a revolution in gender politics . . .'. Her voice trailed off. 'I'm going home,' she said.

'No wait, Catha, I've only one more to go this evening, so please!' I was watching the man with the newspaper. He was folding it up and smiling at me.

'Well, okay, but I feel in need of . . . something.'

'Comfort food?'

'Yes, I'll grab a club sandwich in the Bistro Bar.'

'And then come back here? Promise?'

'Count on me.'

I was watching the man with the newspaper get up and approach my table. 'But don't be too long.' He looked fanciable but after my last experience I was on edge.

Suddenly the pitch of Catha's voice rose again. 'He's just passing through the foyer!'

'Who?'

'Swaggering out with that travesty of a camel coat slung over his shoulders. I'm going to get him. He's not leaving here without a piece of my mind. No way.'

'Wait Catha—'

But the phone had gone dead. The man with the newspaper was upon me. 'Mind if I sit here?'

'Seat taken sorry. I am rather expecting someone,' I said.

'You're expecting me,' he smiled. 'Richard Lloyd-Harcourt.' He extended his hand.

As I shook it, I had the definite sensation of watermarked notepaper and an embossed address. Beyond that I could recall nothing. I hadn't had time to consult my timetable or to turn over the cassette in my recorder. I just hoped Catha wouldn't be too long so she could take notes for me.

'Oh, of course,' I said.

'Forgive my presumption but I've already ordered us a pot of strong Colombian coffee.'

My turn to smile. Nothing could have been more appropriate to the way I felt. 'Most welcome,' I said.

'And may I congratulate you?'

'On what?' I was delighted by his reticence. It offered an interesting contrast to the previous interlude. But there was more to recommend Mr Lloyd-Harcourt than that.

'I'm full of admiration for the way you've been handling things,' he said as he sat down and placed his newspaper to one side of the table.

'You've been spying!' I gasped, overstating my shock to obscure my pleasure in the compliment he was paying me.

'Forgive me, but in my line of work one makes a virtue of caution. One does one's homework. One makes a balanced judgement on the basis of all available evidence.'

Suddenly I placed him. 'You're the lawyer!'

He smiled more broadly, half at me, half at the barman who was approaching with our coffee. I couldn't help noticing that it was a Coutts Gold Card he placed on the tray to make payment. In a flash I decided he must be in litigation, city fraud and major bankruptcy.

'Actually,' he told me, 'a good deal of my work at the High Court is in divorce.'

Eureka. Here was a guy making big money out of the very subject of my research. He must have valuable insights. A wealth of material at his fingertips. Not bad looking. Nice manners into the bargain.

'The irony being that my own marriage is on the rocks.' He looked embarrassed about it.

I really liked him. And it isn't that often one meets a presentable man with a Gold Card who is unencumbered. I said, 'You mustn't feel bad about having marital problems yourself. No, really. Often people only become experts through some defining personal experience of their own. I mean, spouting advice is one thing but . . . I'll tell you something, did you know a lot of psychologists are fruitcakes?'

He laughed, tore a neat corner off a sachet of demerara and let it trickle into his coffee. 'You have proof?'

'I have it on the best authority,' I said and laughed too. I was beginning to hope Catha's club sandwich took a long time.

'You have no idea,' he told me, 'what it means to have a sympathetic ear.' He stirred his coffee slowly. 'A feminine one at that. I held out little hope that in replying to such a . . . and I trust you will forgive me . . . a puerile advertisement that I'd meet someone like you.'

I nodded enthusiastically.

'But I was desperate.'

'Puerile? Oh, poor you. Oh, dear, I'd simply meant it to be, well, unthreatening.'

'And to find myself sitting opposite a . . . well, how shall I put it? A Venus de Milo.'

'But with arms, look!'

'A one hundred per cent woman with a sense of humour too,' he said and shook his head as though trying and failing to wake from a dream.

I was moved. We shared a silence. I put cream in my coffee, which is something I never normally do. I took a deep breath before I spoke again. 'Tell me everything. Feel free. If you have a need to unburden yourself . . . use me.'

He nodded. His gratitude was palpable. His eyes filled momentarily and he looked around at the stragglers in the bar in an effort to control the emotion he felt. I liked him? No, that was beginning to look like an understatement. Maybe I was on the verge of falling in love. Maybe that was why I found myself struggling to deny the sudden urge I had to embrace him, to smooth the frown lines on his pale forehead.

'I'm in agony,' he said.

'Don't hold back. Tell me.'

'In agony from the scrotum up.'

'Ah,' I gasped. I'd never felt so wanted before.

'Haven't had it for months. And now I've got such a hard-on I could expl—' Suddenly he froze.

'What is it?' I asked urgently. I was aware of Catha coming back but that hardly explained his fright.

He sank back into his seat, closed in one himself and whispered, 'I thought she'd gone.'

'Gone?' I pulled my chair in to give Catha room without turning to look at her. 'Who?'

'Someone who might recognise me,' he said, and with that he unfolded his newspaper and held it up to shield his face.

'Discretion is the better part of valour for someone in my profession.'

'I understand,' I said without having a clue what he meant.

From behind his paper he whispered urgently, 'Come upstairs with me.'

'You booked a room?' I sensed Catha had sat down behind me.

'We could carry on our conversation there. With more privacy.' And he pushed a key with a big brass label under the bottom edge of his newspaper for me to see.

I read, 'Deposit this key at reception on leaving the hotel'. I turned the label over and read 'Room 203'. I said, 'Okay, I got that – Room two hundred and three.'

The sound of Catha ripping a page out of her notebook startled me. *Better get a grip*, I told myself. 'You don't mean to tell me all this has been about one thing – getting me into bed? And that right from the start . . .'

'No, no, no. Please.'

'Because that really disappoints me.' If I sounded anxious it was mainly because Catha was trying to push something into my lap. My hand closed over the folded piece of paper that slid onto my knee.

'I wouldn't have dared presume . . . wouldn't even have entertained the idea of sharing the night with you . . .' His voice faltered. 'The truth is I dread going home. More often than not I make some excuse about having to stay over in town.'

I wasn't really listening. While he'd been talking I'd had time to unfold Catha's note. 'Urgent. Meet me in ladies. Now.'

I stood up, realising she'd already gone again, and looked down at him over the top of his paper. 'Sorry,' I said. 'Got to powder my nose.'

'Don't blame you,' he replied, looking devastated. 'Serves me right.'

'No, no, I mean really. Must dash to the ladies.'

'Goodbye,' he said.

There's something about an attractive man saying goodbye that often as not makes me want to stay. I said, 'I'll come back.'

He shook his head sadly. 'Don't worry,' he said. 'I'm going up to bed.'

I hurried along the corridor, cursing Catha every step of the way. I flung through the heavy swing door and there she was, cool as a cucumber, helping herself to the free tissues on the marble dressing table counter.

'What's got into you?' I demanded. 'For once I'm having a civilised conversation with a decent man with real potential for furthering my research and all you can think is sex.' I spelt it out. 'S-E-X. Well, I'm sorry for you. You've got a one-track mind, Catha. The second he suggests I go up to his room, alarm bells ring in your head and in you wade with a sledge hammer. All that concerns you is making sure I stay on the straight and narrow like I promised. Okay, so you want to stop me from taking the risk of going up to his room, but I hadn't even agreed, I hadn't even begun to—'

'I think you should,' she said.

'What? You what?' I shouted.

'Sssh! Go up to his room with him.'

The sound of a cistern flushing was followed by the hurried departure of a woman in evening dress.

'You know who that was?' Catha asked.

'That woman . . . ?' Really, I didn't know if I was coming or going.

'No. The man you've been talking to.'

'Yeah, a lawyer, Richard something Harcourt,' I said, calming down.

'The Judge, Sir Lloyd-Harcourt. One of the youngest to take silk, the youngest called to the Bar this century. Brilliant mind. Mutterings of unfair advantage, of course, because of his connections. The family seat in Oxfordshire, a moated Elizabethan castle, one of the few of its kind still in private hands, even though English Heritage offered—'

She'd lost me. I was preoccupied with a picture of him in his wig and robes. A dignified procession through the Inns of Court. Mega gravitas. He looked great. But perhaps what impressed me most was the way I'd liked him, no, loved him before I had known about any of this.

'So what was the number of his room?' Catha concluded.

'Two hundred and three,' I said and that brought me down to earth with a bump. 'But, wait a minute.' There were still things puzzling me. 'Why would someone like that answer an ad?'

Catha used a tissue to blot her lipstick before stuffing the rest of the box down into her briefcase. 'I suspect this is going to be one of the surprising facts uncovered by your research, Ali,' she said. 'That people of real calibre leading pressured public lives neither have the time nor the wish to compromise themselves by approaching women within their immediate circle.'

Fair enough. But as soon as I'd accepted that argument another question surfaced. I looked at Catha in the mirror and asked, 'But how come you know so much about this man, and his background?'

'Only because he was on my list of possible donors for the art auction. His father is on the charity's board after all.'

'And you met him? I mean you met Richard? Otherwise why'd he recognised you?'

'Last week. I went to his chambers.' Catha turned round to face me and clutched my arm. 'And he's got a Picasso on the wall. Oh, only a doodle but it's signed. Imagine, Ali, the kudos of being able to offer something like that. It'd raise the whole tone of the proceedings. Oh, and more – once I could say someone'd donated a Picasso other people'd respond in kind.'

'But he wouldn't give it to you?'

She shook her head. 'He hesitated though. And I think if the right sort of pressure was applied . . . who knows.'

'So you want me to sleep with him.'

'I never said that.'

'Honestly, Catha, when the chips are down you can be more mercenary than anyone.'

'I'm thinking environmental issues here,' she said, 'Oh, and in case you wondered, the particular doodle in question looks very much like two apples on a woman's torso.'

'Oh, I see! It's ecologically sound!'

'Sort of earthy. But if you'd rather not cooperate, I'll quite understand.' Catha looked deflated suddenly. 'But I don't accept that you'd have to sleep with him. In fact, I wouldn't want you to. With your powers of persuasion though . . . well, this sort of person often tries to get their own way by making a gift.'

I looked at myself in the mirror, giving the matter some thought. A small smudge of mascara under my left eye distracted me. I reached for a tissue from the box on the counter. It was empty. Catha dug into her briefcase quickly and presented me with a handful. As she did so, something that looked like a business card fell to the floor. I bent down to pick it up. I read, 'Probationary Membership. The Raunchy Rodeo Club. Novices Hurdles. Tel. 0171—' I didn't have time to read anymore because Catha snatched it from me.

'What's this?' she said.

'You tell me.'

She squinted at the card in disbelief. 'Oh, what a disgrace!'

'Catha?'

She screwed the thing up and flung it into the rubbish bin. 'I told you I'd give him a piece of my mind.'

'Yes, but . . .'. I'd forgotten, but even so . . .

'So he comes straight back at me with something about defamation of character. Shoves a card in my hand saying we better swap solicitors' addresses. So naturally I thought that . . .'

'Forget it,' I interrupted her. If I hadn't known Catha better, I would've entertained some serious doubts. As things stood, my mind was elsewhere.

Chapter 7

The door of Room 203 was slightly ajar. I knocked timidly. No answer. I knocked loudly, no point in hanging back. I put my head round the door. The sound of his voice was raised above the noise of water splashing.

'Room service?' he called.

I didn't answer. He must've ordered a meal from downstairs to have as soon as he'd showered. As I stepped inside I saw his clothes strewn across the bed. The newspaper he'd used to screen himself was screwed into a tight ball.

'Just leave it on the table.' His voice had a confident and commanding ring.

Yet I was already familiar with his more private and vulnerable self. And I think that was why I was drawn to the door of the bathroom. Without thinking of the consequences, I went in. A mental picture of him in his robes was all very well, but I wanted to dig below the surface. I was after the naked truth. I was not disappointed. He was soaping his shoulders. The well-defined muscles of his chest glistened. He stopped dead, water cascading in a steady flow over him as he turned full frontal. He was amazed to see me.

'If only you knew how I longed to . . .' he said.

'I know.' I took my jacket off. It slipped to the floor.

'How I did not dare to hope . . .'

His voice ensnared me. It was like a drug and I was already addicted. He held out his hand towards me. He did not need to make the gesture. I felt myself drawn inexorably towards him. And as his hand reached out so his penis engorged with desire and beckoned me. I forgot about the rest of my clothes, I forgot about everything right down to and including Picasso. As I stepped into the shower, the water engulfing me was part of him, flowing all over me. I tilted my face back to hurry the moment when I'd drown.

His mouth closed over mine. His tongue was my lifeline and it entangled me, pulling me deeper and deeper below the surface of consciousness. Then, as if in an effort to save me, he gripped my hips, pulling them hard against him. But I went on floating down until my mouth anchored itself on his penis.

Somewhere above the crash of the water I heard his voice calling. No sooner had my mouth chained itself securely than his hands were dragging at the waterlogged mass that was my hair and he was pulling me up to the surface again. As he did so, he tore at the wet bandage of my skirt until it was up around my waist.

I spread my legs as he lifted me until I straddled him, arching my back so that my pelvis was thrust towards him. As he entered me, I encircled his shoulders with my arms and I licked his eyebrows and lashes where they dripped. I was dissolved in him and he was so much a part of the cascading water that I was like a surfer riding the big one, the ultimate wave. He thundered into me. My sex was washed and oozing and washed again.

'Richard!' I called to him. What was the name of those sirens who enticed sailors onto the rocks?

Somehow he found the strength to pull clear of the water and to carry me with him onto dry land. Suddenly I was on the bed and he was using the sheets to mop water and come from between my legs. Then his whole weight descended on me. Now I felt him inside me in a different way – hot and dry. Now I could feel the thickness of his penis deep inside me. He lifted my legs and placed them on his shoulders, then he knelt up a little and placed his hands under my buttocks to allow him to drill deeper.

'Alison!' he called, as though acknowledging that his vocabulary had been reduced to a single word – as had mine. And with that he withdrew briefly to turn me and enter from behind. I tilted my arse up to facilitate his entry and he bore down on me with his full weight again, using a knee to separate my thighs.

This way round was a tight fit and as he pushed ever further my pleasure deepened. I moaned into the damp sheets as the inner muscles of my vagina contracted and relaxed, responding instinctively to each thrust.

Just as I had been lulled into a false sense of security by the repetitive rhythm of his movements, suddenly he became an unruly self-willed savage. For a dangerous few seconds I fought the primitive frenzy of his passion before I gave in and went with it. When he climaxed I came for the second time and I think I was crying as he rolled off me. I tried to roll over too, but only half made it before I heard the crash.

At the time I couldn't have told you what happened exactly. All I knew was that suddenly Richard and I had an entire tray of chicken satay, soup of the day, roll and butter, not to mention wine and cutlery tipped over us. In view of the fact that we were feeling pretty wasted at the time we were slow to react. I tried to sit up, fell back and closed my eyes just as the bedroom door slammed shut.

Richard said simply, 'So much for room service,' grabbed a pillow and buried his head under it.

Within seconds I heard regular deep breathing, interrupted only by contented little snuffles and snorts. I decided it would be wise to go home. But then, out of the corner of my eye, I spied my sopping wet skirt and panties on the floor. No way could I get dressed in those. Best stay till morning. I was drifting off when his arms scooped me to him. I wriggled my backside into his sleepy warmth.

'Angel?' he whispered. 'Wake me in the morning. Usually stay at the Savoy. This place is further away . . . take longer to get to court.'

After that I was awake all night, tussling with a growing conviction that I was falling in love. I decided not to tell Catha but to wait till I was sure. I didn't drop off till the pale light of dawn was seeping under the curtains – which was why he was late and in a bit of a panic. I phoned down for a cab while he threw on his clothes. He didn't blame me. He didn't want to go. He backed out of the door, his fingertips caressing my breasts, saying how he never wanted to leave me, how we must never be parted.

'Come to my chambers at one. I'll just have time to take you over the road to the Wig and Pen for lunch.'

I nodded and then ran after him to kiss the fingers that had been so reluctant to detach themselves from my breasts. He looked as though he was about to weaken and retrace his steps to the bedroom. But somehow I found the strength of mind to give him a little shove and send him on his way down the corridor towards the lifts.

I did my best with my skirt and top in the trouser press and used the dryer to coax my hair into some semblance of order. However, I knew I looked a bit wrecked when I got home to find Catha just finishing a phone call. She gave me a cool look.

'I shan't say anything,' she said as she replaced the receiver.

'Good.'

She took a deep breath. 'Thrice you denied me,' she said.

'I . . . ? Pardon?' I never know how to take a biblical quote particularly when it comes from someone like Catha.

'I knocked on that bloody door three times.'

'What door?'

'Room two hundred and three. I called your name. I feared the worst. I pushed it open and what did I see? A maelstrom of naked tit and arse, legs and arms flailing, sheets and clothes scattered in every direction.'

'Oh, come on! You asked me to.'

'I . . . ?' Catha opened her eyes wide. 'I categorically did not. I made a point of saying that I didn't expect you to fuck him.'

True enough. Even more true – I was in love but I wasn't going to tell her. I wasn't going to make excuses either. She didn't deserve it. She was being hypocritical. Playing dirty. If anything, what she deserved was a punch below the belt.

I said, 'Oh, by the way, I got the Picasso.'

'You . . . ?' That winded her alright. Her mouth dropped open before it curved into a long slow smile. 'Oh, darling!' She got to her feet and hugged me. 'Oh, how can I ever thank you! Oh, Ali, I'm so grateful.' She held me at arms' length then and her eyes filled with tears. 'You really are a true friend. Anything, yes, anything further I can do to help you with your new job . . .'

I shook my head. She was so effusive in her thanks I began to feel guilty. I was also uneasy about the Picasso. But I'd get my chance with that at lunchtime. Yet even contemplating taking advantage of Richard in such a way seemed at odds with the notion that I was falling in love. I covered my confusion by continuing to be aggressive.

'Just don't pull that trick again, Catha.'

'As if I'd . . . What d'you mean?' She sounded hurt.

'I mean, next you'll be telling me I don't need to sleep with Mick to get you an Old Master.'

'Oh, waste of time, darling. No, your builder baron's a different kettle of fish entirely. I mean, it's not art he's into, it's investments. And he's far too shrewd a businessman. I tell you what though . . .'. She brightened suddenly. 'For that very reason he'd make an ideal guest at the auction. Bet he'd love a Picasso under his belt. Yes, you see if you can flog him a couple of tickets for the dinner.'

I told Catha I had to spend the rest of the morning writing up my notes. Anyway, I'd inspired her to search out some dealers in contemporary art, she said. She didn't want to waste time chatting either, she was off to a gallery in Cork Street.

'But you won't forget about this evening?'

'This evening?'

'Catha, I've still got a whole cartload of blokes to interview.'

She pulled a face and then remembered that she owed me. 'Oh, okay. I don't think the role of your madam-in-waiting is really me but . . . oh, there's a point.' Catha found the notepad she'd used the night before. 'Grouped under various headings look. Purely as an aide memoire.' And she read aloud, 'Unprincipled Bastard, Bedable Hunk, Sadistic Pig, etcetera. And here in the margin I marked them out of ten for Marriage and Psychological Potential.'

'Thanks,' I called after her as she sped to the front door. 'Oh, and lots of luck, Catha!'

I'd faxed ten pages to Cambridge by the time I left the flat for my lunch date. I surfaced at the Aldwych feeling pretty much in control. During the course of the tube journey I'd reached a decision. When two people love each other, openness and trust are integral to the relationship. I'd make a play for the Picasso but I wouldn't push it. If challenged I'd come clean about my motivation.

In fact, as soon as I was shown into Richard's chambers I spotted the picture. Not difficult because it was the only thing framed and hanging on the far wall. I couldn't really see it properly. From where I stood it looked like a rather indistinct scribble.

'Darling!' Richard breathed as soon as his clerk had shut the door behind me. 'It's been an eternity!' He started to circumnavigate his desk, which was stacked with papers and scrolls tied with red ribbons, but I stared past him to the wall. He came to a stop in front of me, his arms outstretched before he looked back over his shoulder to follow the line of my gaze. 'You like it?' he asked.

I smiled faintly and nodded.

'Then you shall have it,' he said. And, without more ado, he unhooked the Picasso from its place on the wall and hurried to present it to me.

'No, no, really I can't,' I said.

'It's yours.'

I clasped it within my arms, the cold glass pressing hard against my breasts.

'Aren't you going to look at it more closely?' He seemed amused.

I shook my head mutely, too overcome to express what I felt.

'Aren't you going to read the signature on it?'

I shook my head again.

'Darling,' he went on, growing ever more serious. 'How right you are. It's not important. What's in a name? It signifies nothing. Either one likes a piece of art for its own sake or one doesn't. And that's how it should be. So often people's judgement is clouded by considerations of what's fashionable or expensive. But you . . . you have a simplicity of mind, a purity of judgement that's above the mundane and self-seeking.'

I started to sob uncontrollably.

'What's the matter?'

I tried to tell him but I couldn't get the words out. They choked me. Very gently, he took the picture from me and propped it against the side of a big leather wing chair. Then he started to lick the tears that dampened my cheeks.

Almost apologetically, he asked, 'If you'd do something for me?'

'Anything,' I managed, my breath coming in uncertain gasps. In answer his hands started to search for a way into my dress which was a tight sheath with a high neck. I said, 'Zip's down the back.'

He found it. Seconds later I was standing naked in the middle of the room and he'd locked the door. I shivered with emotion.

'Darling, you're cold,' he said quickly. 'Put on my robe.' And with that he took the long black robe he wore in court from a hanger on the back of the door. It was so big on me that it was like a tent. It slipped off one shoulder and fell wide open down the front. 'You look so much better in it than I do. Delectable. Vulnerable.'

I looked down at my breasts peeping out at him, nipples already erect as he bent to suck them, his head moving from left to right as his hands fondled and squeezed. I can't say I felt any more vulnerable than usual. But in the face of his generosity I certainly felt an overwhelming desire to please. I'd do anything for him. Anything he asked. He did ask.

'Would you mind, darling, putting on my wig?'

It was with some surprise that I looked to where he was pointing. The long judge's wig of stiff grey curls was sitting on a block. I didn't really fancy it. Under the circumstances, though, I felt obliged to humour him. Besides I can carry most things off. And this presented the sort of challenge that an overlarge hat does at a wedding. It's only when a woman looks self-conscious about it that the thing looks silly. I went straight over to it, the black gown billowing behind me as I walked, and put it on. And then with a raffish air of mock dignity I went and sat down in the big swivel chair behind his desk.

He was delighted. He sighed a long sigh of contentment as he contemplated the picture I presented – a parody of justice if ever there was one. He undid his trousers and stepped out of them to walk around the desk towards me. He was carrying quite a packet. As he approached, he pushed his blue underpants down at the front so that his erection sprang out. There was just room for him to sit on the desk facing me, his member on a level with my mouth. I did what comes naturally, but no sooner had I leant forward and opened my mouth than he gave the chair I was sitting on a little shove with his right foot so that it swivelled slightly to the right. I turned the chair back and realigned my mouth with his penis. He gave the chair another shove with his left foot so that it swivelled the other way. Okay, so if he wanted to tease . . . I started to rock the chair, then slid a hand down between my legs and slowly eased my index finger down through the brush of my pubic hair and into the top curve of my slit, where it searched out the hard pearl of my clitoris.

He leant forward to get a closer look but I quickly pulled the folds of the black gown across my legs keeping the secret from him. I sighed as he began to pleasure himself, rocking and delicately rubbing. Pretending to close my eyes, I watched him watching me intently. Suddenly he grew impatient. I opened my mouth a little and ran my tongue around my lips. But, instead of responding by turning the chair back so that he could present me with his cock, he looked away and ripped some of the scarlet ribbon off a big bundle of legal documents beside him on his desk.

He made a grab at me, pulling my hand out from between my legs and, using the ribbon, tied my wrist to the carved arm of the chair. A fragile restraint. I could have untied it myself with my other hand. Instead, I raised my left leg and propped it up on the desk beside him, nudging his thigh with my toes. He got the idea. Soon I had a scarlet ribbon decorating each ankle with a floppy bow, one foot resting on either side of him on the desk. This way the ribbon looked much more decorative than it had on the legal scrolls.

Together we admired the effect. Things were looking festive. I pointed my toes until the muscles of my calves were strained taut, their shape sculpting the flesh. He ran his hands up the insides of my legs, leaning forward as he did so to probe the tip of his tongue into my mouth. Without moving my head, I used the moment to withdraw my feet from the desk and spread my legs wide. I wanted him in me. As his tongue quivered against mine it was getting urgent.

With my free hand I tried to pull him down onto me. He resisted as though still in a slightly detached and experimental mood. Stubbornly keeping his position above me on the desk, he withdrew his tongue and leant back. Then he used the flaps of the wig to pull my head towards him. My eyes closed as the silky skin of his penis brushed my lips. But before I got the chance to take him in my mouth he had spun the chair full circle. His penis slapped my cheek as I sped past. My eyes opened wide with surprise. He moaned as if it was all too much to bear but he kept the chair revolving. Each spin was punctuated by the gentle smack of his member close to my mouth where droplets of his semen collected on my top lip like beads of sweat. A real fairground ride. As a child I often went on the Big Whip but inevitably I got dizzy and screamed a lot and halfway through I always wanted to get off.

'Stop!' I cried.

The chair juddered to a halt. He stood up and pushed it back so that there was room for him to stand between me and the desk. I felt so giddy that I tried to cover my eyes with my hands but, of course, one of them was still tied. I'd neither the presence of mind nor the time to free myself before he pulled me off the chair onto the floor. I think he'd forgotten I was still fastened to the thing too because he seemed to want me on all fours. Probably, the voluminous folds of the gown, as he thrust it up to expose my buttocks, obscured my arm, which was now stretched out behind me. The only way I could achieve a steady position was to duck my head into the dark kneehole of the desk.

My head was still swimming anyway so it hardly mattered that the darkness under there was as effective as a blindfold and the scarlet ribbon had me firmly tethered. He stroked my buttocks gently, as though to reassure me, before insinuating a finger into my crack and teasing my anus. I tilted my arse upwards, inviting him into my vagina. Suddenly he thrust in to me with such force that my head was pushed deeper into the dark and the ribbon bit into my wrist. Then suddenly it snapped loose. I'd almost regained some semblance of balance when he withdrew and thrust again. Deep inside me he touched a little soreness left over from the ecstasy of the night before. It was my turn to moan. In response he began riding me from behind more gently, the rhythmical in and out motion of his penis massaging the pain into a tiny pinprick and then into oblivion. I forgot where I was. The alien surroundings of his legal chambers and the strangeness of what I was wearing dissolved into the familiar sensation of his cock. It was mine and I was his and the whole world was spinning again to the tune of the old whirligig.

It was as if Room 203 had simply witnessed the foreplay that would lead to this. And probably because of that we both climaxed easily in unison and with such completeness that neither of us had time to make a sound. All my strength seemed to have been taken away from me, sucked into outer space through my arms and legs. His strength deserted him at the same moment and he fell on top of me. Neither of us was capable of movement. His hand had somehow twisted under him so that his fist was crushed into my back. One of my hands had been trapped under my breast, the other under my forehead, its torn red ribbon dragging across my mouth. I don't know how long we lay there. Or for how long there'd been a rapping on the door.

'Can you hear me, sir?' The anxious voice of the clerk of the court penetrated dimly. 'M'lud?' The court waits to convene!'

Richard held onto the edge of the desk to drag himself to his feet. He took a few uncertain steps away from me as I crawled out backwards into the light. He was looking round the room as though seeing it for the first time. Then he said, 'Where's my gown and wig?'

'M'lud?' The disembodied voice from beyond the door was spiked with anxiety.

'Thank you!' Richard shouted. The effort made him sway slightly. He focused carefully on me as I stood up beside him. He saw his gown and wig and smiled his relief.

'Tissues?' I asked, because some of his spunk was tricking down my leg. He was trying to get his gown off me so he could get dressed in it himself. He shrugged unhelpfully at my question, so I grabbed a fistful of the material near the hem as he struggled into the thing and used that to mop my sex.

'Trousers,' I told him as soon as I'd finished drying my inner thighs, because he looked rather odd in the black gown without any. He glanced down at his bare legs in some surprise, then crossed to where his trousers lay in a heap on the floor and hurriedly pulled them on.

While he was doing so I noticed a silver-backed hand mirror on the table near the wig block. Before giving him back his wig I wanted to see what it looked like on me. Not remotely flattering. Ugh. It didn't suit me one bit. I took it off and threw it at him.

'Take it,' I told him. 'It's all yours.'

'But you'll wear it again?'

'I most certainly will not.'

'If I had my way you'd always wear it.' And with that he donned the wig himself.

I started to laugh. I couldn't help it. It didn't suit him either.

'What's the matter?' he asked and snatched the mirror from me to check his reflection.

'Nothing.'

'Yes, there is.'

'Perhaps just . . . that I'm not used to seeing you in . . .'. I pressed my hand over my mouth because he looked annoyed.

'It's not meant to be a fashion accessory,' he snapped. 'It's meant to be a symbol of my authority.'

'Oh, sorry.'

He glanced down suddenly at the picture propped against the wing chair. The last thing I wanted was for him to take it back. 'Darling, I'm getting used to it already. And . . .'. I tiptoed up to him reverently and stroked the grey frizz where it enveloped his ears. 'Think of me in court,' I whispered through a kiss to his cheek.

'Bound to.' He smiled. 'Unavoidable. With the smell of your sex on this . . .'. He lifted the hem of his robe and sniffed appreciatively before he unlocked the door and strode off down the corridor.

Chapter 8

Two thoughts surfaced on the journey home: one, I was hungry because I'd never made lunch at the Wig and Pen, and two, I was glad I'd held back from telling Catha I was falling in love.

I didn't have time to formulate my doubts about Richard (one can hardly fall out of love with someone just because they look silly in a wig) because, as soon as I'd shoved a pizza in the microwave, I played back the answerphone and there was a message from Max. Obviously he'd wasted no time in responding to the material I'd faxed.

'Ring me asap Alison,' was all he said.

Perhaps he was dissatisfied. I rang Cambridge immediately but needn't have worried.

'You went ballistic. We got lift-off,' he said. 'Let me put it this way – there are opportunities in the works. Things are occurring my end with some rapidity.'

'Oh, yeah?' I sounded a little tentative only because he seemed so pent-up that I thought perhaps he had a hard-on.

'Things here are Byzantine!'

That seemed to confirm it. 'Meaning?' I asked, a touch frostily.

Why did I have such a one-track mind? All Max wanted to impart was that my research had inspired him to think beyond the confines of his original remit. With my human interest stuff he'd raised his sights. Why produce an anaemic little research paper when he could write a full-blooded book? Something that cut through the inward-looking boundaries of academe to hook in the regular punter. It seemed he was already visualising the book on display stands at international airports and even the best-seller list.

'Hang on there, Max,' I said. 'Let's be realistic about this.'

'Oh, sure, sure,' he agreed. 'Hey, but are you aware of how

many copies of the *Hite Report* they shifted, or *Kinsey* come to that?'

I took his point. Catha had copies of both.

He went on, 'And you know something? My father's got a friend in real estate who always advertises his houses with a nude on the doorstep. Male, female, depends where he's pitching, of course. West Coast mainly. You with me?'

I was. I said, 'Now you mention it – I saw an ad for an antique fair the other day with this really dishy guy naked, draped over a Victorian commode?'

'You see!'

'But, Max.'

'The point is, whatever you want to sell nowadays you need sex. And what we're talking about here is selling sex with sex. No contest.'

'Even so,' I said, rather hesitantly.

'Listen,' he told me. 'I got connections. This publisher, okay?'

'Who?'

'I'm coming into town next week. I'll introduce you.'

'Where?'

'I'm open to suggestions. But some place out of the ordinary. Non-scene. Select. Want to make sure he knows where we're coming from – like he's dealing with someone special here.' And he added, 'Pencil in Friday.'

'Friday? But that's . . .'. And without pausing for thought I told him. 'That's the day a very dear friend of mine is having this huge dinner party. A high-profile social event with a sort of fun art auction thrown in.'

'Perfect.'

A sudden vision of myself in mini froufrou doing a cabaret turn holding up the pictures on offer interrupted my flow. It wouldn't be appropriate. 'Invitation only,' I said.

'But if it's a dear friend of yours?'

'And the tickets are expensive.'

'Tickets? How much?'

'One hundred pounds each,' I said.

'Including dinner?'

'Well, yes, but . . .' *oh, what the hell*, I thought. Catha would be pleased after all. 'I'll book it,' I told him.

'Before you ring off . . .'

91

'Yes?'

'What sort of panties are you wearing?'

'Um . . .'

'Come on. You know you're safe with me.'

That was true enough. But I'd never been much of a one for phone sex. I said, 'Actually they're rather plain black . . .'

'Hold it there!' Max cut in. 'Aren't they very flimsy? Aren't they tiny bikinis? Lace with a split crotch? Aren't they?'

'Well, okay,' I said because he seemed to have made his mind up.

'And your bra? Isn't it semi see-through, very thin shoulder straps and peepholes for the nipples? Isn't that what it's like?'

'Yes,' I agreed because I saw no point in arguing.

'You're truly inspirational, Alison,' he sighed. 'But, seriously, I'm beginning to think your input could have a long-term influence on me.'

For my part, I felt inspired by my success at selling tickets for Catha's charity bash. I thought I'd strike while the iron was hot and get on the phone to Mick. Sure enough he was intrigued by the idea of picking up a cheapie Picasso and said he'd got a friend who was a bit of a collector too. He'd put a cheque for a couple of hundred pounds in the post on one condition – that I sat with them and brought along another woman for his friend. No problem there, I said rashly, though I did warn him I'd be otherwise engaged during the auction. He seemed disgruntled about that until I'd explained.

'What's a froufrou?'

'You know, like a high-stepping pom-pom girl wears when she's leading the parade and baton twirling. Only more so.'

'This is going to be worth every penny, kid,' he said. 'I'll bike the money.'

I ran to the door to tell Catha when she got back but forgot my news temporarily in the rush to unload a whole cab full of stuff she'd trawled up. About twenty paintings, a sculpture and even something she called an 'installation' in a wooden box. She'd done well. I was surprised she seemed subdued. She said it was only stuff left unclaimed by artists after shows.

'Even so Catha!' I said, surveying it all spread round the living room.

'No, don't do that!' And she snatched what I'd thought

was a piece of wrapping paper with some paint splashes on it. She told me it could be a Jackson Pollock Unsigned.

Looked doubtful to me. But I told her, 'I just wanted to see in this box.' And I lifted out a heavy object and put it on the coffee table. 'What is it?'

She gave me a look so I stood back to get a better perspective. It appeared to be a freestyle plaster cast of a penis.

'It's entitled "Leaning Tower of Pisa Re-erected",' she said gloomily. 'You press a little button on the side and it straightens up.'

I pressed the button and jumped back in alarm.

'Quite.' Catha grimaced. 'And you try squatting over that when it happens.'

'Oh, Catha!' I went and sat beside her. 'Tell me about it.'

'Suffice to say,' she said, 'that I found myself thinking fondly of your pink plastic dildo.'

She'd tell me about it in her own time. Meanwhile I wanted her to cheer up. 'Guess what. I've just sold four tickets for you.'

'Oh, well done.' She smiled, but a little wanly. 'And what about your brush with the law?'

'My . . . ? Oh, yes, I got the Picasso.'

'You mean it's here? But that's fantastic!' She hugged me.

'So you see we're making real headway, Catha.'

'But at what cost?' She stood up suddenly to pace the room.

'Well, speaking for myself I'd have sex with Richard anytime and even with his wig on I suppose—'

'But don't you see?' she interrupted. 'It's all so ironic. I mean, how come we have both ended up with jobs dependent on the casting couch?'

'Catha, that's not something we could've foreseen.'

'Exactly. I mean, let's just think job description a minute. Nightclub hostess? Cruise ship croupier? Oh, okay, par for the course. You with me? But fundraiser? Research assistant?'

'I know,' I said because I could feel a long session of soul searching coming on. 'Which reminds me, Catha, you are coming with me to the hotel again, aren't you? Because we should be leaving.'

'I've had such a day.' She sat down.

'Me too. And I've spent most of it working for you.'

'That's true,' she agreed and seemed to pull herself together suddenly. 'Besides you might flog a few more tickets for me.'

'This evening? Well, I dunno . . .'

'You're on a roll. I can feel it, Ali. Let's go!'

Back at the Sundowners Bar things went with quite a swing. I'd learnt from the night before there were dangers in not focusing on my research. I'd got much better at sifting the wheat from the chaff. I'd compiled a questionnaire worthy of a market research team. If by question number three – 'How often do you read the personal column?' – they were still saying something like, 'A fluke I picked up the paper last week and read it only because I missed my train', I knew they were going to play their cards too close to their chests for my purposes. They only got one more chance with question four: 'Do you think personal ads work?' If they responded to that by saying a friend of a friend had had some luck, or so they'd heard, but they'd no first-hand experience, then I labelled them liars and time-wasters, dumping them swiftly in favour of the next person.

Three men stood out. Firstly a company director in import and export who admitted straight away he'd met his last wife through an explicit contact magazine in LA. She'd advertised herself with a quarter page colour spread of her pussy, long, well-manicured fingers delicately spread to stretch open the glossy lips of her labia. In fact, he admitted to not looking at her face properly until after the marriage in Vegas and by then it was too late. He said he'd buy a ticket to Catha's function if I could put him in touch with someone who developed film of a sensitive nature. The guy in Kilburn he'd used had been raided and his darkroom trashed. He had four rolls of hot stuff that he couldn't take to a regular chemist. I said I might well be able to help and made a mental note to ask Stefan.

Then there was the Scottish laird – so painfully shy, he said, that his only hope of making a conquest was by preserving his anonymity via a third party. Using a newspaper was a handy way round the problem. Promising material. He looked like confirming the central premise of Max's research.

'And now you've met me?' I coaxed him on.

'I'm overcome. Indeed you see this is what happens to me.' A blush was spreading across the fair skin drawn taut across his high cheekbones.

94

'What's your name?'

'Bruce.'

'Trust me, Bruce,' I breathed, closing my hand over his.

'Well, I'd like to but . . .'. He swallowed hard. He wanted to withdraw his trembling hand and hide it under the table but he just managed to restrain himself.

I wanted to help. I wanted to protect him. He brought out the nurturing instinct in me. Until he suddenly blurted out, 'D'you like babies?'

'Do I what?' I couldn't have been taken more unawares.

'Because I need a son and heir.'

'D'you mind repeating that?' I was genuinely shocked.

'Well, sorry but . . .'

'No, don't worry,' I said thoughtfully. I shouldn't have been shocked because this was an important angle. But, before I could follow it through, Catha started coughing behind me. I said, 'Yours is a problem that needs some thought. But perhaps by next week I could . . . Could we meet again then?'

'Well, if you tell me a time and place.' His mouth quivered as he looked down to where my hand had withdrawn from his. 'I'll be there. That I promise.'

'Friday. Eight p.m.' I said. And I went on to tell him the location of the conference centre and that the function was unfortunately ticket only. 'You don't mind?'

He shook his head. I sensed Catha nod hers approvingly. Frankly, I was beginning to find her presence quite intrusive. As soon as poor Bruce had taken out a purse and counted five twenty-pound notes for his ticket, he left. I turned to Catha and told her she could go home too if she wanted. She said she was quite happy and that she'd passed the pain threshold as far as her exhaustion was concerned. Now she may as well see things through to the bitter end.

She looked even happier and more firmly anchored to her seat as my next respondee approached. Hand-stitched lapels. A white rose wilting in his buttonhole. Blue silk shirt intensifying the green of his eyes. He slumped down opposite me without taking his hands out of his pockets. He stretched his long legs to one side of the table, crossing them at the ankle. Gucci boots. But then this degree of detached arrogance meant only one thing – money.

Without even looking at me he said, 'I suppose you're starving hungry?'

'No.'

He raised a quizzical eyebrow. 'So where d'you want to eat?'

'Nowhere.'

He took a long hard look at me then. 'You sure?' He seemed genuinely puzzled. As he got no answer he went on, 'So far every women I've met like this is looking for a free meal.'

'Oh, so you make a habit of this sort of thing?'

'On and off over the years. I don't like staying in and if I haven't got a party or a dinner . . .'. Suddenly he gave a raffish grin, leant sideways and looked under the table at my legs. 'Well, this is a turn up for the books,' he said. 'Can't see anything wrong with you at all.'

'Just wait!' I warned him.

He laughed and ordered a bottle of Krug because he said we ought to celebrate.

'Well, I can understand that you have cause to celebrate,' I told him as the waiter set up the ice bucket beside our table. 'But have I?'

'You've met me.'

'And what's so great about that?'

He shrugged. 'Not much, except I'm rich and . . . I want to put it in you. I want to fuck you rigid.'

'Oh, is that all?'

'No.' He raised his glass to me and lowered his voice so that it purred out of him. 'I want to get to know you first.'

Fatal. He knew his stuff alright. There's a line that is almost impossible for any woman to resist. Within ten minutes I'd given him a careful précis of my life and was about to start filling in the detail when the sound of Catha yawning at the next table pulled me up short. I asked him about his life. It appeared not to interest him much, but I insisted. With a few careless brushstrokes he painted the picture: Eton, county family but with extensive interests in French vineyards, chateau in the Loire, wanted him to go and bone up on techniques in the Napa Valley but he wasn't interested in the stuff. Except as a drink. Only one passion.

'Women,' I interrupted obligingly.

'Well, okay,' He seemed unimpressed with the idea. 'But if

you want me to be honest – Formula One.'

He'd lost me. I'd never been to a Grand Prix.

'But you surely . . . I mean, you must've been to Silverstone?'

'No.'

'You must come. I've got my own car.'

'You mean you're a racing driver?'

He shook his head. 'No, I mean I put money into a car. I finance the team.'

'Well, I don't think it's my scene exactly but—'

Suddenly Catha was standing over me. 'Alison! It isn't! It is!' Imagine my surprise as she kissed me on both cheeks. She quite winded me.

'Long time no see!' she said, turning her chair around smartly and sitting down beside me.

Frankly I was furious. She was meant to be taking notes of my interview, not muscling in on the act like this.

'Well, aren't you going to introduce me?' She laughed her tinkling laugh.

I was dumbstruck. What'd got into her? Okay, I thought, so I was taking my time getting round to asking if he'd buy a ticket for her dinner but after his opening gambit what could she expect?

He introduced himself. 'Harry de Burgh Walton,' he said and extended his hand to Catha, adding with an amused nod in my direction, 'Looks as though your friend has seen a ghost from the past.'

'The past?' Catha turned to smile at me too. 'Well, yes, but we keep in touch. In fact we spoke on the phone only last week about a charity function I'm organising because—'

'Harry is only interested in one thing, Catha,' I cut in. 'Racing.'

'Gee-gees?' She opened her eyes ultra wide.

'No.' I snapped at her viciously because I knew perfectly well she'd heard it was Formula One. 'Cars, stupid!'

'Oh, not Formula One?' she asked Harry, calmly turning away from me.

Frankly I felt like throwing up as she started to bang on about Monaco and things I knew perfectly well she'd only ever seen on TV. Harry found it all fascinating though. And before I knew it Catha had accepted an invitation to Silverstone in a month's time, along with stand seats and a pass to the pits.

'And can my friend come too?' Catha asked him, indicating me.

'I don't want to, thanks.'

'Course you do, darling.'

'Please come,' Harry said with a conspiratorial wink to me. I changed my mind and agreed immediately. After all why should Catha have him to herself? I'd put a spanner in the works the minute she brought up the question of Harry buying tickets for her dinner too. But she never did. Never mentioned it once.

As soon as he'd gone I questioned her about her motives.

'Nothing sinister, darling.' She smiled. 'No hidden agenda, or at least nothing that'd be obvious to you.'

'Then what on earth . . . I mean, he's not exactly your type.'

'There you go!' She laughed and then got serious. 'Alison, you know the way they use these cars to advertise? Anything from cigarette brands to woolly jumpers, brand names plastered all over them. And you know I'm designing a new logo with the name of the charity entwined around the trunk of an oak? Suddenly I got a flash of my design whizzing past, zooming over and over across a million TV screens. Imagine the impact of something like that. Zapping Joe Public's subconscious!'

'But, Catha . . .'

'Okay, so I'm racing ahead. Ha, ha, no pun intended,' she said quietly.

'I've got to hand it to you though. You never miss a trick. Which reminds me . . .'. And I went on to ask her if she would make up a foursome with me, Mick and his friend at the dinner.

'I'll be far too busy. And anyway it's a matter of principle with me – no blind dates, never have had, never will, sorry.'

That was why I rang Stefan next day. Ostensibly it was to ask, 'Where d'you get your dirty pictures developed?'

'Who is he?'

'Who?'

'I demand to know.'

'Be serious.'

'I am. I want to know how he posed you. In detail. And if

you don't tell me now I shall order a set of duplicate copies for myself.'

I could see this conversation getting nowhere fast so I changed tack. 'Stefan, the other thing is – would you lend me Serena? Just for one evening next week. Well, Catha thinks it'd be a good idea too.'

'Listen, sweetheart,' he said. 'If you and your crazy friend want a three ball – it's me you'll need, not Serena.'

I explained about the charity dinner and the fact that we were a woman short at my table.

'That never presented you with a problem before,' he mocked.

'How come you've got a one-track mind?'

'That's the effect you have on men, Ali.' He sounded serious for the first time.

I ignored his remark. Although he'd never admit it, perhaps he didn't trust Serena. 'I'll chaperone her,' I promised.

'That's what's worrying me.'

I refused to give up on the idea. 'I thought you wanted her to be less focused on you anyway.'

'Well . . .' He suddenly made up his mind. 'Okay, it'd give me an evening to myself and there is something I'd like to see to.'

'What's her name?'

'Pass,' he said. 'You don't answer my leading questions, I don't answer yours.'

Why did he always leave me feeling that I was missing out on something? I comforted myself with the thought that my arrangements for next Friday were more or less complete already. I just hoped that Catha, who was having to run to keep ahead of herself, managed to meet her deadline.

It was an unqualified success. Mega bucks flowed into the coffers. Catha's eminence as a fundraiser was established. Her reputation as a hostess par excellence was to be unchallenged for some time. A rather lurid pic of her in *Hello*'s diary bore testament to her arrival on the social scene.

That's not to say there weren't a few hiccoughs during the actual event. And, as Catha pointed out afterwards, there was a Pope who died of hiccoughs once – which only goes to show that the most saintly can suffer from them. At least ours weren't life threatening. They did have a knock-on effect though.

Firstly there was the problem of Serena and Bruce – not something anyone could have foreseen. Serena, in her Barbie-doll party outfit and Bruce in his dress kilt and furry sporran made the most unlikely pair. In fact, I think it was their rather extreme modes of dress that drew them together.

When they arrived and surveyed the restrained decorum of the assembled company – two hundred classic DJs and scores of marvellously plain Nichol Farhi numbers in crumpled linen – they both instantly felt self-conscious. Bruce knew he would. He started apologising as soon as he stepped inside the VIP suite. He hadn't brought a DJ down to London and had only the kilt with him because he'd had to attend a whisky distiller's bunfight at the Guildhall. (Apparently his mother was a major shareholder in a particularly fine malt and he'd been detailed to represent her.) He grabbed a glass of champagne off the proffered tray and tried to make himself inconspicuous by standing behind one of the potted palms to one side of the central atrium.

I don't know what Serena's excuse was because she didn't make one. I wondered what Stefan had told her. Perhaps she thought she was coming to a film premiere or at least somewhere she'd have to hold her own among the stars. Her backless satin dress in midnight blue with diamante halter swooped down to within a smidgen of the cleft of her arse. She did her best to neutralise her lack of judgement by keeping her back to the wall. She walked crab-like around the outskirts of the circular atrium until she found her way blocked by Bruce hiding behind his potted palm.

Trapped in this way, she admired his knees. With nowhere to turn, he admired her handbag, which was in the shape of a heart shot through with a diamante arrow and matched her dress. She said the thingie in his sock looked just like a dagger. He took his dirk out and unsheathed it for her. She'd barely had time to admire the six-inch blade before a security guard swooped and disarmed him. They both protested. Now they were firm allies.

She showed him the way her locket (also heart-shaped) unlocked. It was warm to his touch from where it had nestled in between her breasts. They agreed that they would sit down to dinner together. Following her to the nearest table, the easy blush of Bruce's fair skin deepened and rouged his cheeks as he watched the cool whiteness of her back and the sway of her high buttocks barely contained within her gleaming dress.

His shyness was deserting him. It disappeared altogether at the realisation that there was a seating plan. She was to eat her dinner three tables away. This emboldened Bruce considerably. He made eyes at Serena all through the meal and she responded. When she wasn't staring at him directly, she took a heart-shaped mirror out of her bag and pretended to check her lipstick when, truth was, she was holding up the mirror at such an angle that she could capture his reflection.

I was annoyed because I'd only got her there to keep Mick's friend sweet after all. But that's something I'll come back to later.

By the time dinner was over, Bruce and Serena were hot for each other. Using the hubbub of the art auction as cover they made their escape and met up on the landing of Level A. They kissed with the passion of long-lost lovers. Their enforced separation, although it had only lasted for two hours, made them feel that they'd known each other ages. His hands delved down her back and were soon clasping the soft naked flesh of her buttocks. She couldn't be blamed for not wearing any pants because they would've spoiled the line of her dress. Her hands moved instinctively to stroke the fur of his sporran. He wasn't wearing pants either and no one would expect a Highlander to make any excuse for that.

'Where shall we go?' she whispered the words straight into his mouth.

He breathed in her breath. 'Docklands. Not far. My cousin's flat. Where I'm staying.'

'But?' She'd lifted his sporran and, as she did so, his kilt sprang up underneath and filled her hand.

'He's out!'

'I know.'

'I mean, my cousin!'

'Let's split,' Serena demanded with growing urgency. She'd felt the back seam of her dress beginning to give as his hands clasped inside its skirt, lifting her off the ground and pulling her upwards into him.

'Wait! no!' Suddenly he relaxed his grip on her. The back seam of the dress tore a fraction. 'I must get my dirk back from security first.'

With that he'd grabbed her wrist and they'd run down the stairs together. After asking at the desk in reception they'd gone in through a door marked 'No Entry'. There was nobody inside and the only light came from a bank of flickering video screens, many of which relayed pictures of the gathering they'd just left. They both felt as though they were in a dream.

Suddenly they were on the floor. He was pulling up her dress and she was lifting his kilt with one hand whilst her other tore his shirt open so that she could feel her breasts, flesh on flesh, being crushed under his weight.

He felt her breasts spread and pillow him. She thrust her hips upwards and he felt their hardness nudge into him. As though unable to withstand the rich mix of sensations, he slid off her but only to pull her on top. They rolled around the floor and as they did so each became more entangled until it seemed they had spun a web of tentacles that held them fast together. So busy were they for a while, tongues probing, hands stroking, gasps of *ah, ah, ah,* spiralling upwards and their eyelids blinking in the flicker of the greenish light, that Bruce forgot to enter her, and she forgot to invite him in.

Serena remembered first. She pushed him away a moment to offer up her welcoming pussy, but tilting her pelvis as she raised her knees to let her legs fall apart. Catching his breath, he looked down at the flesh framing her sex which blossomed into a strange exotic flower, unfurling its dewy petals in the hushed warmth of a humid hothouse. Its dark centre glowed with nectar already as sweet as honey.

He wanted to touch, rub. He wanted to lick, slurp, bite. He wanted a confusion of everything at once. But then her hands grasped his penis and he understood that there was something she wanted too. She wanted to be filled. She didn't have to guide him. He pushed down with his arms to raise himself off her and aim his member into the deep well of her opening. As he did so she relaxed her grasp, her hands gliding up to the base of his penis to tease his balls, her fingers curling into his scrotum, beckoning him to come, come, come. He slid into her easily and deeply and they lay together and sighed. Then he raised himself again and slid all but the very tip of his penis back out. He looked down and she pushed herself up on her elbows to get a look too. Now he was glistening. They smiled at each other briefly before he slid back into her, fitting as smoothly and neatly as a dirk into its sheath. Her head fell back, his head fell forward, her tongue flicked into his ear. He tried to turn his head away but her fingers clutched at his hair. In answer he grasped her hands, entwined his fingers between hers and raised them above her head, pressing down on them with this weight and using his knees to push her legs further and further apart.

As he raised his buttocks to re-enter she was fully stretched, wide open to him, her head rocking from right to left as she moaned her desire. Only the savagery of his need to get back into her silenced them both momentarily. Then the voluptuous machine of her body and the tense piston that was his took over and drove them on relentlessly, faster and faster.

The frenzy of his heart pumping made a roaring in his ears and she, dragged again and again into a collision with his body along the length of hers, felt the flesh on her face pulled back as though by G-force or a rushing wind, a precursor to the speed and ferocity of her climax. They lay a long time folded together like dead animals amongst the wreckage of her dress. And here's how I got to hear about it:

First thing I knew that anything had gone amiss was when I spotted Serena wandering in a daze between the tables looking for her handbag. I only saw her because of my vantage point on the dais erected for the display of the paintings and artefacts. In fact, I was doing a twirl and holding up something rather abstract which Catha had confidently announced was 'Untitled Number Ten' when I caught sight of her. Luckily, Mick was standing closest to the dais, this being the best possible vantage point for an uninterrupted view up my skirt. As soon as the bidding finished I knelt down and whispered to him, 'Tell Serena to meet me in the Ladies'. Only one more lot to go and I'll be with her straight away.'

He spotted her immediately. After all she had been sitting between him and his friend for the duration of the dinner.

'Leave her to me,' he said. 'She's drunk. I'll take care of her.' And very gallantly, I thought, he pushed his way back through the press of people and grabbed her arm.

I didn't notice what happened after that because Catha announced, 'And now the final lot. An installation entitled, "The Leaning Tower of Pisa Re-erected" by . . .'. She consulted the sheet of paper in her hand but, before she'd had a chance to read the name of the artist, I had held it up and someone had shouted, 'Looks like me!'

Quite a laugh went up. In fact, by this point in the proceedings, everyone had enjoyed the evening so much that there was an irresistible air of relaxed bonhomie.

Catha shot me a look as though to say she'd kept everything under control so far and now it was up to me. She indicated that she had to go to the Ladies' and made such a speedy exit that I had no time to say that she was bound to bump into Serena there – or so I thought.

'What does it do?' someone shouted.

More laughter. Then I remembered the little button on the side that made the model of the penis straighten up. I pressed it. General applause.

'Have you got a reserve on it?' called another voice.

'It must do more than that!'

'Let's see her demonstrate.'

I was looking round rather anxiously for Mick, and finding no sign of him when a voice close to me said, 'One hundred pounds!' I looked down to see Catha's benefactor for the evening's venue, the Director of the conference centre, looking up at me.

'I'm bid one hundred,' I called out. 'Do I see two?'

A hand was raised.

'Fine – two. And three. Three and four. Four in the corner. Thank you, sir. Five? Five and Six and . . .'. How extraordinary, I thought to myself, the way people are led by the nose, like sheep, like lemmings. 'And a six. Any advance on a . . . ? And seven by the palm tree? Yes. Shall I settle at seven. Seven, one last chance, ladies and gentlemen, before I—'

'Eight,' said the Director standing below me.

A gasp went up, a sigh, several people turned away as though the price was getting silly. It certainly was. The Director got it. I felt quite sorry for him. He seemed oblivious.

'If you wouldn't mind bringing it to my office?' he asked.

'No, no, of course not. But I must go to the Ladies' first,' I said.

Chapter 9

Sometimes it feels like these formal functions last a lifetime. It'd been a long night already and I find I often get this need for a calm moment to myself before relaunch.

The fact that there was no sign of either Serena or Catha in the Ladies' was not uppermost in my mind. One thought surfaced and refused to go away – I wasn't going to deliver a modern sculptor's interpretation of a penis to Catha's Director dressed as I was.

She'd told me quite enough to put me on my guard. I divested myself of my basque and froufrou and slithered into the plain grey silk sheath with single bow on one shoulder that'd cost Mick an arm and a leg in Beauchamp Place – a street which, as I'd told him at the time, had overtaken Bond Street aeons ago.

Lucky old Catha, I thought, as I fastened the concealed zip at the back of my neck. She may have had a last-minute panic over the floral displays and catering arrangements. She may have had a hard time of it, but at least she hadn't had to keep changing clothes. She had looked as cool as a cucumber from start to finish. Her black full-length gown, whose sole decoration was a corsage of oak leaves hung with little acorns (strictly in accordance with the charity's new logo which she had designed), gave her an almost nun-like air. Okay, the dress was strapless and showed off her shoulders to some effect but only in the way that a marble statue dares the casual onlooker to touch briefly before recoiling from the coldness of the stone.

When Catha gets stressed out she doesn't get hyper but becomes aloof and puts out these other-worldly vibes which make her seem quite saintly. People pray to saints. Saints get respect. And I'd just seen it happen. Mick's friend, Don, had been on his knees, for heaven's sake! Metaphorically speaking, he had become her acolyte during dinner. Without exchanging a single word with her, he had seen the light. Or so he said. Mick said so too.

We'd barely got stuck into the Lamb Cutlets with Honey and Rosemary before he was telling me, 'Hugh Hefner got nothing on Don, believe me. Don had bunny girls popping out of top hats and silk hankies, never mind centrefolds.'

'What happened?'

'You can have too much of a good thing. He was going to become a recluse before I met him. I told him, and I'll be straight with you, Ali, by this time I had a vested interest, all he had to do was settle down, get married, end of story.'

'What vested interest?'

'Look at him now,' Mick said. 'You'd think he'd never set eyes on a woman before.'

Don's fork was poised, motionless, halfway between his plate and his mouth as he listened to Catha making an announcement and proposing a toast.

'Catha's no bunny girl,' I told Mick.

'Quite. From what you've told me she's right up his street. The street he wants to move into anyway. Bit of a blue stocking, is she, kid?'

'Catha is a revolutionary feminist.'

'Good luck to him!'

Serena said, 'Freaky!'

This being the sum total of her conversation for the entire meal so far, all of us paid her immediate attention. However, she made no attempt to back up this comment with reasoned argument. Instead, she ran her tongue around the open pout of her lips with her gaze firmly fixed on the middle distance – or rather on where Bruce sat – then she directed a smile away from us, beaming it towards him, revealing a perfectly matched row of milk-white teeth. I could have slapped her. No wonder Don's interest in her had been impossible to sustain. And to think the only reason I'd invited her was to amuse him. Wait till I told Stefan. Meanwhile, I asked Mick again, 'D'you mean by having a vested interest that you are looking for an intelligent bonk too?'

He laughed. 'A bonk's a bonk, kid. The only brain a woman's got is between her legs.'

I must've winced visibly as I said, 'I shall return the dress. Tomorrow.'

He shrugged. 'Sorry, just slipped out. You know how it is.'

Truth was I did. The awful fact of the matter being that a few years in the thrall of a man like Stefan prepares a woman for the grossest calumny. That does not mean that I forgave Mick (or Stefan) but I changed the subject back to my original enquiry.

Mick explained. 'Yes, well, Don and I are hand in hand over a coupla projects. Currently a holiday complex and a casino.'

'I thought he had lots of those already.'

'Oh, sure, he's king. Worldwide. Leisure International. At the moment he's buying big-time in Albania. But fast.'

'Albania?' I couldn't help being surprised.

'Only bit of virgin coastline left in the Med.'

'Just as well Catha can't hear this conversation,' I told him.

'Casino's going to be in Kendal.'

'You don't mean in the Lake District?' One of the things about Mick was I could never be quite sure whether he was serious or not. And I think he played on that.

'Greenfield site. Usual trouble with the planning. Appeal. Appeal. Always get it in the end.'

I began to look at Don in a different light. My first impression of him having been as a person of no consequence with a carefully slicked quiff and a fake tan, I suddenly saw him as being powerfully evil. His handsome, fading-pop-star exterior and *Come Dancing* smile were a clever smoke screen. Broken down into their component parts his features told another story. The set of his mouth, the gleam in his eye, the flash of a diamond in the signet ring on his finger bespoke his ruthlessness.

In contrast, Mick seemed genuine and comparatively harmless. 'No bridges?' I asked.

'What? Where?'

'Across the Lakes?'

He laughed good-naturedly. Then added, 'What about between Italy and Albania?'

'You're not serious?'

He shrugged. 'Listen, kid, the wife's away week after next. How about it? The house isn't far. Near Henley.'

'I'll see,' I said. 'I thought I had to come to the opera with you first.'

'Oh, don't remind me,' he replied.

* * *

It was at this point in my recollections that the door of the ladies' room swung open and Serena staggered in. She took one look at me and made as though to beat a retreat, but I grabbed hold of her and pulled her towards the mirror.

'What happened?' I demanded.

'Oh, nothing much,' she said, but then caught sight of her reflection and realised that this statement wasn't convincing. She looked wrecked. Mascara made dark circles under her eyes and her lipstick was smudged as though her lips hadn't had time to recover from their most recent injection of silicone. Her dress was not only crumpled and torn but was decorated down the front with what looked like the silvery trails of a snail across a midnight garden. I hated her. She had made a travesty of acting as an escort for Mick's friend. Worse, far worse, she had married Stefan.

'Tell me everything,' I hissed.

'No. You'll only tell Stefan.'

'I won't.'

'You tell him everything.'

'Who says?'

'He does.'

'Oh, great. Oh, super. Well, I tell you something, Serena – he doesn't know the half of it.'

'He doesn't know much about me either,' she said. She glanced from herself to me and her baby-blue eyes filled with tears.

From that moment on I hated her less. In fact I began to like her and smiled at her in the mirror. 'Don't tell me then,' I said.

'But I'd like to,' and with that she washed her hands and held them under the hot-air dryer as she began her story. Obviously detail was important to her. She spared me none in her desire to get things off her chest. I began to admire her. In particular I began to understand that she shared a certain naivety with Bruce that made her his perfect partner.

'But you haven't been married long,' I told her. 'And I thought you'd still want to be faithful.'

She hung her head. 'I know, but the trouble with Stef is he makes a girl feel so sexy . . . it kind of spills over.'

I nodded sagely and knew just what she meant.

'Some days even the sight of a traffic bollard can set me off.'

Poor Serena. I gave her a little hug. 'Look,' I told her, 'Bruce was a one-off.'

'But after Bruce there was Mick,' she said, pulling away from me to give some attention to her hair.

'Mick?' I was stunned. My admiration for her was growing by the minute. 'You mean to say . . .?'

She was just about to launch into that story when there was a loud groan. We both turned to see where it had come from. For the first time I realised that the door to one of the cubicles was locked.

'Someone in there?' I called. Another moan. I knelt down and peeped under the door. To my horror I saw a little bunch of acorns and some oak leaves on the floor. 'Catha!' I cried.

A rustling and scrabbling came from within the cubicle. Serena and I clutched at each other and stepped back as Catha appeared swaying at the door of the cubicle. She staggered out and pitched forward as Serena and I rushed to support her. All three of us ended up leaning heavily on the marble counter by the washbasins, staring straight into the mirror.

I'd thought Serena had looked badly mauled but she'd looked sleek and positively groomed compared to the state Catha was in. Yet it'd been less than twenty minutes ago that she'd presented an enviable image – not a hair out of place, the folds of her gown flowing out from her neat waist in perfect symmetry, exuding an air of inner harmony and calm authority. Now her hair stood on end, the voluminous skirt of her dress was crumpled up into a damp ball, the bodice had slipped down at one side so that one of her breasts tumbled out, and – worst of all – she had a black eye.

'Oh, Catha!' I said.

More to the point, Serena asked, 'Who was it?'

'Well, I don't know his name,' Catha dragged at her hair distractedly. 'But you must. He sat between you two all through dinner.'

'Mick's friend? You don't mean Don?' But I knew enough of his background and his fascination with Catha to be pretty convinced already.

'The creep!' Serena said. 'I never liked him from the off. Just wait till I tell Mick!'

'Thank you, Serena,' I said. 'But I'll handle this.'

'No, no, no,' Catha protested and then added with a rueful smile into the mirror, 'You see I think it was . . . a bit of a misunderstanding.'

Serena and I cast anxious glances at each other over the top of Catha's bowed head.

'You see, I dashed in here a bit urgently because I'd had no chance all evening,' she explained. 'Didn't look to left or right. Certainly didn't notice that a man was standing with his back to me in one of the cubicles with the door open. Till I came out. Then obviously I challenged him. He looked startled. Deep in thought. Said he'd assumed it was the Gents'.'

'Oh, per-lease!' Serena said

'Before leaping to conclusions – let's hear Catha out,' I said.

'Okay, the general atmosphere of the party was pretty uninhibited by this stage. Everyone was well tanked up and so on but I wasn't going to take any nonsense. Incumbent upon me to keep things under control and so on. And he hadn't done his zip up.'

I could just see Catha facing up to this crisis, standing her ground, smoothing down the unruffled folds of her dress, and coolly asserting her authority.

'This, sir,' she had told him, without deigning to lower her eyes to his exposed member, 'is a room reserved exclusively for the use of the ladies.'

Quick as a flash he'd responded, 'And this, madam, is reserved exclusively for the ladies too.'

Before she'd had time to gather her thoughts for an appropriate riposte he was upon her, penis in hand as though to ram home his point and – although she turned her head away – she clearly saw it stiffen and its knob distend until it touched the front of her dress. This turn of events overtook her with such speed that she forgot her self-assertiveness training for a moment. Instead of kneeing him in the groin or stamping down on his foot whilst poking her fingers in his eyes, she said, 'Oh!' And knowing she was backed up to the marble shelf by the washbasins, she gave a little jump so that she was sitting on it – the move, she said, at least giving her a height advantage.

Unfortunately though this did not have the desired

psychological effect. Far from it – because now his erection was exactly in line with her pudendum. In short she'd landed herself right in it. Her other misjudgement was that the shiny material of her skirt on the marble shelf gave her no purchase but made her position as precarious as a toboggan on ice. And here he was coming at her like a sexual juggernaut.

Catha said that what flashed through her mind was that the whole of western culture was based on this sort of high level testosterone surge. And that's why oestrogens in the drinking water were such a threat.

An observation which was lost on Serena, of course, who simply cried out, 'Go on! Tell what happened next! Did he stick it in you?'

He'd grabbed her legs, Catha reported, and she'd shot forward into him with the spectacular velocity of a ski jumper. In an effort to save herself, she slid sideways and grabbed onto the corner of the hand dryer. Before she could get away she fell off the shelf with him still grappling her, hitting the side of her head on the hot air button as she did so.

This went a long way to explaining why her hair was standing on end because she then found herself on the floor in what she described as a rerun of Desert Storm, a hot wind blowing straight across the field of battle. Her skirt had billowed up around her waist and within an instant his face was plunged into her corsage for all the world like a pig snuffling for truffles. At the same time, his hands were busy with her panties. They were very tight around her slender hips and he was having trouble. She took advantage of his concentration and made a supreme effort to stand up. To her surprise he allowed her to do so and she slid her back up the tiled wall, again using the hand dryer to steady herself. The hot air, which had only just stopped, came on again. Another serious misjudgement: he did not let go of her knickers as she straightened up. This meant that by the time she was upright her panties were round her ankles and her attempt to step away from him was hampered by her legs being tied together. Immediately she bent down, lifting one foot, to remove her underwear. But this meant that she was completely off-balance for a moment. And it was precisely then that he made a grab at her. When she hit the deck for the second time it was minus her panties. And, as her skirt had billowed out once more,

111

he'd dived in there right underneath it.

Maybe it was the intense heat from the dryer which made Catha feel as though she was melting. Maybe it was the stress of the preceding week, the build-up to the function, the hours spent on the phone, juggling menus and seating plans, etcetera, that made Catha feel that she had had enough of struggling. In any event, she slumped back against the wall as her legs slid out straight on either side of the man that only later she was to come to know as Don.

Her eyes closed as he began to tongue her, expertly parting the rippling folds of her flesh to expose her clitoris, his hands kneading the softness of her inner thighs to encourage them apart even further. She had no strength left anywhere in her. She heard her voice rise in a moan, sucked up by the hot wind to echo against the tiles. His fingers slid around under her buttocks and insinuated themselves into the opening of her vagina while his tongue still worked at her clit. She relaxed for the first time in days. She had no option but to just go with it. Then she was overcome by a long shuddering climax, and still he hadn't entered her.

'I'm so hot!' she'd cried. 'I'm burning up!'

He stood up immediately, lifting her with him and turning her towards the basins where he'd run the cold tap. He cupped his hands under the icy stream as she had leant forward to support herself against the marble shelf. He splashed water along the length of her long bowed neck and across her bare shoulders. Then, lifting her skirt again, he scooped more water to let it trickle down over her bottom and legs. He turned her slightly so that she was in profile to the mirror and said, 'Look. Watch.'

In the mirror she saw him as though for the first time. An impassive profile, tanned skin, his hair slicked back as though riding into the wind. She saw his strength and thought how everything about him seemed firm and erect as he began to enter her from behind. In contrast to the cold water that trickled down her legs, his penis felt hot and large as it plunged in and out of view.

He didn't hurry. He was feasting his eyes too. His gaze locked into hers and, with the same unflinching obsession as his cock, it seemed to penetrate her, delving rhythmically deeper and deeper, exposing her innermost secrets to the light, digging for treasure in the dark until, without any warning, he climaxed.

He stood motionless with his eyes fixed on hers in the mirror. His penis remained firm. She understood he wanted her to come again. He withdrew, turned her slowly to face him and lifted her. He sat her back on the marble shelf where the process had begun.

She had the curious feeling that this was going to be one of those circular stories that had no end. But there was a difference this time – she did not slither about because it was her bare bottom that was in contact with the marble. And she was hot and sticky with her own come as well as his which meant she was stuck fast.

He raised her legs and placed one across each of his shoulders so she was tipped back with her head against the mirror and her throbbing sex glowed red against the white marble. Again he entered her with deliberation, staring directly into her eyes this time rather than at their reflection, and gently, very gently, her rocked in and out of her wet vagina. She'd wanted him to thrust harder but when she'd opened her mouth to tell him, he had stopped her with a kiss. It was a short kiss and he drew back from it to look at her. She drew breath to say 'harder' again but the same thing happened. She gave in gracefully.

Slowly, slowly, he was dragging a climax out of her. The tension in her body mounted as though each of her limbs was being drawn taut by strings that bound her to him. She closed her eyes and her hands groped up to his face like a blind person's as her breathing quickened. He turned his face this way and that, sucking and biting at her fingers, whilst his own hands were squeezing the lips of her labia together around the root of his cock, making its passage tighter and tighter.

'Ah, no!' she pleaded.

'Then come,' he begged. 'Please.'

'No.'

'Yes.'

She came. He pulled her forward to lean against him because she was in danger of banging her head again. She sobbed, not because she wanted to cry, but because she had to let her breath out quickly or she would've choked.

* * *

Her story over, Catha grimaced apologetically at me in the mirror and then tucked her straying breast down into her bodice.

'Yowee!' said Serena.

'But that still doesn't explain the black eye,' I said.

'She hit it on the thingie.' Serena pointed at the hand dryer.

'No.' Catha shook her head. 'That happened afterwards.'

'He punched you?' I was horrified.

'He didn't mean to.'

'He . . . ? How can you punch someone without meaning to?'

Catha explained how. He was just about to make his excuses (his 'excuses' if you please!) when he'd suddenly realised that he hadn't seen her breasts. Somehow they'd been left out of events. He grasped the top of her bodice at the front to pull it down. But by this time Catha was beginning to recover and get some sense of what she had just been through. In short she was coming back to normal. She'd wised up. The bodice, being strapless, was very tight and well boned and he was surprised at the resistance the thing put up. He renewed his efforts. But this time Catha was forewarned. He gave it a terrific yank up. He lost his grip on the shiny material and his fist shot straight up into her face. She reeled back, clasping her eye.

'You bastard!' she'd screamed. 'You brute!'

Genuinely horrified at what'd happened, he stepped towards her to offer some assistance. Instinctively, she recoiled and threw her hands up in front of her face to protect herself.

'Get the hell out of here!' she'd spat at him between her fingers.

The shock of her reaction and the fact that he had almost knocked her out brought him to his senses. He'd stood for a moment, transfixed by appalled indecision, before apparently coming to the conclusion that there was nothing for it but to do as he was told.

'He left you.' Serena sounded a bit let down.

'I went into the cubicle and . . . well, delayed reaction I suppose, passed out.'

'Just wait till I tell Mick,' Serena said.

'No, you won't,' I said.

'Just wait till I tell Stefan then.'

114

'Tell that shit anything about me and I'll murder you,' Catha said.

Serena opened her baby-blue eyes very wide and looked as though she might cry again.

'Now, listen, you guys,' I said. 'This is the time to stand together as sisters. A degree of solidarity is called for on this one, okay?'

Catha smiled approvingly but Serena said, 'I'm going to get a cab home.' She'd only made an ineffectual stab at tidying herself up. What would Stefan think if she arrived back looking like that?

'I don't care what he thinks,' Serena blurted out as she made for the door.

I went to stop her but Catha caught my hand. 'Let her go.'

Serena tossed her head and went.

'The evening's nearly over anyway. Just a mopping up operation left. See the stragglers off and then we can go too.' And Catha set about smoothing her hair. 'Going to take me ages to unwind tonight though. Just been so incredibly . . . stressed.'

'Shame we can't go somewhere,' I said, realizing that I'd been the only one not to have an adventure. Nothing. Zilch all evening.

'You go on if you want,' she said. 'Now let me think . . . have I thanked everyone? Don, did you say his name was?'

'Catha!'

'I think I made the rounds, exchanged a few words with each and every guest but . . .'

It was amazing how quickly Catha got herself back into hostess mode. Suddenly I remembered.

'Oh, no! Oh, lord!' I said. 'Did you speak to Max and his publisher friend? Of all people! I mean, Max is employing me after all and I never even caught sight of them.'

'You did,' she chided. 'It was him who outbid Mick for the Picasso.'

'Was it? Well, I saw Mick alright but I couldn't see any detail beyond the first couple of rows because of the spotlight.'

'You looked fantastic,' she said. 'You still do.'

'Yes.' I looked at myself in the mirror. Not a hair out of place. Bandbox fresh. 'I promised to take the . . . that installation to your Director's office. Imagine paying eight hundred for it! D'you know where his room is?'

Catha caught my hand again as I turned to the door. 'Not so fast,' she said. 'I told you what he's like. I'd better come with you.'

'I can look after myself, thanks,' I said, adding provokingly, 'Or not, as the case may be.'

'Darling, you don't want to put yourself in a compromising position, now do you?'

'Don't I?'

'Of course you don't.'

'Oh, I suppose not,' I said crossly. All in all I was feeling decidedly sulky as we rounded the door and bumped straight into Max. He stepped back from me.

'Hey! How's the cuddly blonde?' he asked good-naturedly.

'Oh, Max!' I exclaimed. 'So sorry I haven't . . . Let me introduce my friend.'

'The ice maiden?' He stepped back even further. 'What a pair!'

Catha looked quickly down at her breasts, fearing they might've popped out again but I knew Max better. He was simply getting us both in frame.

'And the publisher?' I asked him.

'Just gone for his coat. But I must introduce you to Jasper before . . . Hey, here's a thought. Why don't you two come along to Jasper's club. An all-night watering hole, he calls it, in Mayfair.'

Catha gave a sigh preparatory to refusing but at the same instant I said, 'Oh, we'd be delighted, wouldn't we?'

Her whole demeanour suggested that all she wanted was to get back home and flop into bed so I added, 'Catha would be especially interested. Jasper publishes ecological-type books, doesn't he?'

True to form, Catha perked up immediately whereas Max looked as if he hadn't heard my question, saying simply, 'Change back into your other outfit, okay? Jasper's a leg man, leg and bum, you with me?'

I didn't change. I was glad I hadn't. Those drinking clubs are all the same. The timer clicks off the heating around two a.m. – the assumption being that by then clientele have either stoked a fire inside themselves with enough alcohol to combust spontaneously or else they're past that point and wouldn't notice flames licking around their ankles, let alone the draughts whistling in from the icy waste of Shepherds Market. Besides I hate the feeling of a dusty plush banquette tickling my thighs. A sensation that always prompts a picture to spring to mind of the place in daylight, ugh.

The conversation, once we had breached the excitement of gaining entry and ordered the obligatory champagne, was desultory.

'Great legs, C.B.' Jasper said to me.

'C.B.?' I queried.

'Cuddly blonde. Max told me.'

Max flicked some ash off the pink damask tablecloth onto the floor.

'Max told me,' Catha said, 'that you publish books on ecology. Anything on the rain forests?'

Jasper was nonplussed. He went on addressing me, 'Soon as I saw your legs I said to Max we should put them on the cover.'

'What cover?'

'Stockings, suspenders, six-inch heels and slingbacks.'

'Jasper's got his eye on the commercial potential of our material,' Max confided.

'And a gold anklet,' Jasper added.

'What about high patent boots and a whip curled around the calf?' Max asked him.

'Been done already,' Jasper advised.

'But what, if one may ask,' Catha interjected tartly, 'is going to go between the covers?'

Jasper shrugged. He seemed to have a short attention span. Smiling at me, Max said, 'Our book!'

'Ours?'

'Already talked to Jasper about you getting a cut of the royalties,' and with that he leant towards me across the table. 'Provided you cooperate.'

Jasper got interested enough again to remark, 'The biggest slice of the budget for any book goes on the cover, right?'

I ignored this in favour of asking Max, 'Cooperate? I trust you mean with the research?'

But before Max had time to elucidate, Catha, grinding some

ash into the carpet with her foot, made another stab at getting a response from Jasper. 'What titles have you published,' she asked him, 'on green issues?'

'Green? Green Books?' Jasper looked puzzled. 'Don't you mean blue?'

'I beg your pardon?'

'Blue books. Me? Goes without saying.'

'Bet Jasper uses recycled paper though,' I said.

But it was too late to retrieve the situation. Catha retreated into her shell after that. In fact, she didn't speak for the rest of the night, except to comment vaguely, 'Don must be short for Donald, don't you think?'

I made a mental note to check with Mick that Don was not to be amongst the party for the opera – since I wanted to save Catha from that. And that reminded me that I had to ring Stefan as well – to check on his reaction to Serena's arrival home. I really didn't want her to be in trouble there.

As for myself, well, I'd come through unscathed. With Catha, Max and Jasper accompanying me to the Director's office on our way out of the conference centre, there was no chance at all of any hanky-panky.

Any twinge of resentment I felt at the time was forgotten by the next day. In fact I woke full of the joys of spring, with a clear conscience and feeling incredibly upbeat. I leapt out of bed to make brunch before I woke Catha. Too busy and distracted to eat the night before, she'd be in need of sustenance. As soon as the porridge was bubbling (oats being a natural anti-coagulant and so good for the heart) I rang Stefan.

'So!'

'So what?' he asked.

'So what did Serena have to say for herself?'

'That it was a very boring evening and that she'd left early.'

'I see,' I said.

'In fact I wish I'd known she was going to get back before me. Luckily she went to bed and fell asleep, so she didn't know I hadn't got in till just before dawn. And she looked like an angel, curled up under the duvet, the picture of innocence, so what did I do? I screwed her. Which surprised me because I'd been out all night screwing someone else. What did you ring for?'

Well, sod you too, I thought and put the phone down. But even as I did so I could see the positive side: I had something on Serena now and one day it might prove useful. I picked the phone up again.

'Hi, Mick, how you doing?'

'Like the back end of a bus this morning, kid. Even Picasso looks better'n I do and that's saying something.'

'Good. Just wondering . . . you know this opera thing?'

He groaned, 'You're a sadist!'

'And you wanted to know if Catha'd be free to come along? Just a bit worried you might be setting her up for Don again?'

'Again? Don't know what you mean. Anyway there'll be quite a party of us. Worse luck. No need for her to feel . . . anyway he said something about . . . oh, my head!'

'And what about you and Serena?' I pressed him.

'Think you can OD on Alka-Seltzer?' He burped. 'Sorry, kid.' He burped again so loudly that I had to hold the receiver way from my ear.

'Talk nearer the time,' I shouted but by then the line had gone dead.

I woke Catha. At first she seemed unable to move. She'd got herself in an armlock with her hands between her legs. She disengaged herself painfully, unfolding from the foetal position to straighten out on her back and murmur, 'Why'm I so sore?' She blinked up at the ceiling gathering her thoughts before she said, 'Oh, let me die.'

'Catha?'

'I want to die. Please, please!' And she rolled her head from side to side on the pillow in quite an alarming way.

'Listen, darling,' I told her quickly. 'Last night was a triumph. You made more money in six hours than the charity normally makes in six months. Plenty of people thought you were being over-ambitious but you confounded each and every one. Your reputation as a fundraiser will soon be second to none. You can't give up now.'

'Yes, but you see I feel so . . . used.' She struggled to sit up.

'Okay, so one is bound to have to make sacrifices. And, well, we had some little hiccoughs along the way but . . . when you think that only a few short weeks ago . . . well, we've come a long, long way.'

'Yes,' she said. 'You seem to have made a mark with your job too.'

'I've already progressed from being a humble researcher to co-author of a book,' I agreed. 'And it's all down to you.'

'To me?'

'It was you who decided we should change our lives.'

'Yes,' she said. 'But . . . I meant something else.'

'That we should put love before lust?'

'Don't!' And she clutched her head between her hands despairingly.

'But now we're in the perfect position, don't you see? Of all the extraordinary things to happen, both our jobs have led us slam bang into the heart of, the very cradle of, the eligible bachelor, Catha.'

Catha looked worried as she said, 'Well, I suppose that's one way of putting it. I mean, we have landed some rather ritzy invitations recently. And from some pretty powerful men.'

It seemed to me the observation that women go where the money is and then fall in love was nothing short of prophetic. But all I answered was, 'How can we fail to find a lasting love from amongst that lot?'

'But the last thing I wanted or expected when I took on this job was to get mixed up in a privileged social scene.'

'Exactly. Me neither.'

'Can't really blame ourselves, I suppose.'

'I wasn't to know that so many of my would-be suitors'd be high calibre.'

'Nor that some of them would turn out to be fodder for me.'

'Oh, and vice versa.'

Catha sighed deeply before she said, 'Quite reassuring. I mean, that we can sort of double up on things.'

'Overlap.'

'Be mutually supportive.'

'And combine efforts in our quest for True Love. Gives a while new meaning to job satisfaction, Catha.'

'Yes.' She smiled at last and swung her legs out from under the bedclothes. 'Better get going. Both of us've got a hell of a lot to get through.'

Chapter 10

We kicked off with the opera.

Mick said that Glyndebourne, being in Sussex, was only just down the road so he'd drive us in his limo. Four hours after setting off we were just clearing Croydon and he was looking forward to arriving so late that we'd be lucky to get there by the dinner interval.

Frankly, I was disappointed but determined to be jolly because Catha was sitting in the back in quite a temper. She'd had to reschedule a meeting with the charity's accountants to be ready for the early start from London. It was only because I'd reminded her of my contribution to her fundraising dinner and art auction that she'd agreed she owed me one and dutifully pitched up in full evening dress.

To be honest I hadn't dared pursue enquiries about whether or not Don was to be at the opera-fest. I'd allowed myself to be reassured by the fact that Mick had made no mention of him. I'd stressed to Catha that our host for the evening was to be the squillionaire industrialist, Sir Jonathan Coombes, and left it at that. It was just enough to whet her appetite and make her feel that she might be able to do some business of her own.

After having made some observations about the number of poisons contained in airborne pollutants from petrol and their lethal concentration in traffic jams, Catha had fallen into an uneasy sleep with her head locked between the back shelf and side window of Mick's red Merc.

I decided to risk it and whispered, 'Is Don going to be there?'

Mick checked Catha was out of it in his rear-view mirror before he whispered back, 'Ever given head to the driver before?'

'You answer my question first,' I demanded, watching him raise himself off the driving seat to unzip his trousers.

'Up to Johnnie.'

'Who?'

'Sir Jonathan. See, kid, he supplies Don with the timber.' He paused to ease his penis out of his underpants. It was as soft and limp as a rabbit's ear. 'For the log cabins and A-frame holiday homes Don provides on his leisure parks. How d'you get into this dress?'

I pushed Mick's hand away. I increased the volume of my voice by several decibels and turned towards Catha in an effort to rouse her, 'First tell us more about Sir Jonathan.'

'Just give us a feel of your tits to get me started,' he said, glancing down at his supine member.

Instantly the car behind us honked because Mick had missed his cue to cover the three-metre gap opened up by the car in front moving off. Catha snuffled and her eyelids flickered. Mick accelerated, braked and rechecked his mirror.

It was hot. The air conditioning was off because it drew in fumes. The thin grey silk of my dress was sticking to the leather upholstery. The silver threads of the evening wrap I'd bought to compliment the dress glinted in the sunlight like a spider's web around me. I pushed the fine gauze of the material off. I would've liked to take my dress off too. It was getting creased up. But there were faces all around me, looking and pretending not to look. In fact the car and the style of dress of its passengers invited attention. Mick undid his velvet bow tie and eased the collar of his finely tucked shirt.

I said, 'Well, perhaps when we get going. You can have a touch up.'

Mick concurred. Inclining his head towards me, he winked appreciatively. Placing a sweaty hand on my knee, he said, 'Johnnie? Let me see – lives near Lewes, take him five minutes to get there today. Castellated manor, two vast tithe barns, olympic pool in one and a comprehensive games room in the other. Get the picture?'

'Yes,' I said.

'But he's a bit of a dark horse.'

'Really?'

'Bit of a nutter.'

'How?'

'Well, he's got to be, hasn't he? Opera and all that. Lifetime patron of this place we're going to for a start.'

'Well, I'm looking forward to meeting him.'

'You're with me.'

'I never said . . .'

'You're with me. All evening,' Mick warned and, putting his foot down for the first time in ages, he flicked the air conditioning and then swapped hands on the wheel to feel for his penis.

I quickly turned and poked Catha's knee. 'Hey, Catha, isn't that interesting?'

'Umm. Wha?'

'About Sir Jonathan Coombes, darling.'

She dragged herself into a more upright position, 'We nearly there?' she asked. 'How long have I been asleep?' And with that she thrust her head between the front seats to get a view of the clock on the dash. Instead of seeing the time she saw Mick's penis. She laid back in her seat again with a little groan.

I said brightly, 'Flies undone, Mick, hope you don't mind my saying.'

'Can't close my eyes for two minutes,' Catha muttered.

'Nothing happened,' I told her and I smiled a quick little apologetic smile at Mick.

'Worse luck,' he said and tucked himself away before giving his full attention to the road ahead.

And I must say there's something very appealing about a man who can be gracious in defeat. In fact it makes a woman quite keen to give him a taste of victory.

Sir Jonathan Coombes kissed Catha's hand. She barely noticed. She was distracted by the dazzling scene.

Watching Catha's expression, Sir Jonathan said, 'A perfect Glyndebourne evening! Hard to know how to divide one's attention between the frocks and the flowers.'

It was as though the guests for a midnight ball had mistaken the time of day and, caught out by the sunlight, had sat down on the grass to wait in groups and gossip until it was decently dark. Unlit candles and empty icebuckets on little tables amongst the flower beds stood abandoned, women with their skirts spread out around them gazed up in mild surprise at sheep wandering across the distant backdrop of the Downs, while the men consulted their watches in anticipation of a sunset.

'I need a drink,' Mick said and it sounded urgent. 'Where's the bar, Johnnie?'

'Here.' Sir Jonathan drew a silver hip flask from his pocket. He watched Mick glug brandy while he said, 'My man is setting up our picnic by the lake. A couple of our party has already gone in.'

'That should keep me going,' Mick said, wiping the neck of the flask on his sleeve. 'How long is it?'

'The first act?' Johnnie enquired. 'Oh, two hours give or take.'

Mick thought better of screwing on the cap and took another glug. 'Oh, well,' he said. 'Go for it!'

Johnnie smiled. He seemed to be comfortable with Mick and asked, 'Built any good bridges recently?'

'Ah, now you're talking.'

'Later perhaps.' Sir Jonathan cautioned him. 'Meanwhile, if the ladies would like to follow me into the theatre?'

By the time we'd made it to the dress circle, Catha had got her bearings. She was whispering to me about how opera was the ultimate form of elitism. Furthermore it was a microcosm of hierarchical male structures – witness the fact that I couldn't think of a single opera by a woman, could I?

'Ah, ah,' I said, shaking my head and taking in the sweep of the auditorium.

Served her right that she failed to spot Don until she'd sidled halfway along the front row of the dress circle. By that point her way back was blocked by Sir Jonathan. She turned back abruptly, meaning to make a retreat but he responded by tipping down her seat for her. At the same time I pulled her arm and she sat with a bump next to me.

'Why didn't you tell me?' she demanded.

'Because I didn't know.'

'Well, I'm not staying.'

'Look, you've got me and Mick and . . .'. I leant forward to look along the row. 'And another woman between you and him.'

'I'll have to go.'

'Be practical. In the depths of the countryside you cannot walk out and flag down a black cab. The station's miles. You can't hike. Look at the way you're dressed.'

Now Catha was leaning forward. 'Is he . . . with that . . . girl?'

124

We both looked. We saw him pass her a box of chocolates. She took one and popped it into her mouth before, seeing us looking, she passed the box down the line.

'He's with her so you're quite safe. Have a choccie. Bags me the violet cream.'

'It'd choke me,' she said and pushed the box away so roughly that I only just saved the contents from spilling into my lap.

I passed it back hurriedly along the line mouthing 'thanks!' The girl smiled and waved. She was stunningly lovely. Even younger than Serena, I guessed, but without her cuteness and blonde curls. In fact her hair was crew cut to the point of being almost shaved. The severity of her hairstyle exposed her perfect pixie ears to public view and made her large dark eyes seem as big as those of a startled faun. Her breasts were either barely pubescent or flattened by the stark white material of her dress, whilst white shoestring straps rose like exclamation marks on her shoulders accentuating the golden tan of her skin.

'Oh, god, I hate him,' Catha breathed.

'The place is filling up,' Mick said. 'Talk about bums on seats! Confirms my theory: the more you charge for anything the more you sell.'

'Why didn't you tell me Don was coming?' I asked him a little unfairly.

'Got roped in. I dunno.' Mick shrugged. 'Looking for special terms on a new shipment of timber off Johnnie I expect.'

'But you must know about Catha and Don.'

'Know what?'

'Well, that he and she . . . on the night of the charity thing.'

'Go on!' He leant back in his seat to look at Catha with renewed interest. 'He never mentioned it.'

'He must've done.'

'Why?'

'Well, if it meant anything to him.'

'Knowing Don, the more it meant to him the less likely he'd be to talk about it.'

'Care to look at the programme?' Johnnie asked Catha.

'Oh, thanks.' I reached across Catha to take it from him because she didn't seem to hear. I opened it and riffled through the glossy pages without giving it my attention. I was having another peek at Don's angelic androgyne.

'What d'you mean – I'm safe?' Catha suddenly demanded loudly. 'You mean he won't want anything to do with me, with a real woman, when he's got that? I mean, look at me!' she exclaimed heatedly. 'I've got breasts. Oh, yes, a waist and hips and curves. I've got hair, lots of it and—'

'Sssh!' I said.

Johnnie started to clap enthusiastically. 'First season for this conductor,' he remarked. 'Hope he's going to do the new opera I'm commissioning.'

Mick said, 'Tiring drive. Wake me up when it's over, kid.'

When the first act was over we repaired to the lake. Yummy food: iced pea and mint soup, a lobster mousse followed by a fairly run-of-the-mill chicken and lemon thing, but even so. Catha's appetite wasn't up to much but I helped her out. In fact, the gastronomic delights combined with the evening scent of flowers and the dying light blurring the pastoral scene with a misty gauze made me wish I could write poetry. First-class nymphs and shepherds stuff.

The conversation was a bit leaden though. Sir Johnnie asked Mick what he'd thought of it so far.

Mick shrugged. 'Can't understand the lingo.'

'But you can read the translation. The running subtitles over the stage.'

Mick looked at me with one eyebrow raised.

'Mick hasn't got his specs with him,' I told Sir Johnnie.

'You promised to show me the organ room,' Don's angel told him.

Catha snorted incredulously. And I must say I was a bit startled until the girl turned and explained to me, 'Uncle Don promised me. It's where the original performances were held, even before the old theatre was built.'

'Uncle!' Catha laughed her tinkling laugh.

But Don refused to be drawn. In fact he had not addressed a single word to Catha and so far had managed to keep his eyes averted even when passing her the french toast.

Catha, perhaps in an effort to provoke Don, began to make eyes at Sir Jonathan. He proved receptive. He placed a hand on her gleaming knee and said he wanted to know all about her.

'Currently I'm implementing a high-level donor and committed-giving programme.' She sighed and paused to flutter her eyelids before adding, 'And a pilot legacy scheme.'

'Are you now!' He seemed genuinely intrigued.

She sighed again. 'Must be lovely to have the wherewithal to give, don't you think?'

He came straight to the point. 'My slush fund's a bit low at the moment. Stumping up the money for a new opera doesn't come cheap.'

Catha looked away and ran her hands through her glossy hair, as though already thinking of something else.

Sir Jonathan watched, fascinated by the soft white curves of her upper arms. 'But perhaps we should meet and talk next week?'

Meanwhile Mick, having had a good slug of the vintage Sancerre that Johnnie's man had produced to go with the chicken, not to mention the Chablis that went with the lobster, had wedged his left hand under my bottom. With his other hand he was feeding me morsels of chicken. He was in recovery from culture shock, he said. Then he whispered to me, 'What you say I tell Johnnie we're going to doss down at his overnight?'

I hadn't time to reply when Johnnie asked his man, 'Summer pudding, Conningham?'

Conningham, who had been sitting on a canvas stool a little apart, stood up immediately and dug down into the hamper. Like a conjuror, he draped a white napkin over the container he held up only to whip it off as he approached the table.

'And what d'you make of the performance so far?' Sir Jonathan asked him.

Conningham paused halfway through serving the pudding with his spoon dripping blackcurrant juice onto the grass. 'The Queen of the Night has a little too much vibrato for my taste, sir. But the tenor . . .'

'I could eat him for breakfast!' Don's niece interrupted rather rudely.

'The tenor, whilst being vocally secure, should pay a little more attention to the score. Andante means andante after all, sir, and impassionato con brio . . .'. Conningham made an eloquent gesture with his spoon.

Catha looked to Sir Jonathan for an explanation. He said, 'Always buy a ticket for staff. Big screen in the Piazza at Covent Garden? Great stuff. Democratic. Something for everyone. Quite wrong to treat opera as a thing apart.'

From that point on Catha paid him respect as well as attention. So much so that when Don's niece asked her to join them on their trip to the organ room, she answered silkily, 'Oh, we'd simply love to – wouldn't we, Johnnie?'

Unfortunately Sir Jonathan said he'd have a word with Mick first. So whilst Catha, and Don, hand in hand with his angelic niece, walked on ahead, I trailed behind with Mick and Johnnie talking suspension bridges.

By the time we got to the Dress Circle (no sign of Catha and co, of course) I was really looking forward to the second half. That's when I noticed I'd left my evening wrap by the lake.

'That silvery thing?' Mick asked. 'Now you mention it, I think I saw it sort of drift away.'

'Oh, Mick! Why didn't you say?'

'Thought it was a bit of wrapping, or tissue, or . . .'

But I was already heading out of earshot down the stone steps, out across the lawns and back towards the lake.

There was nothing on the grass where we'd been sitting. In fact, all signs of picnics had been cleared away. The light was fading as I reached the water's edge but there it was, drifting like a puff of mist. The silver threads in the material made it look as though it was spangled with dew. Only I would have known what it was. I'd paid a lot for it. A raft of water lilies right in the centre of the lake had saved it from sinking under the darkly glinting surface. How was I going to reach it? I found a broken branch under the trees but it was too short by far. I looked around. There was no sign of anyone to help. In the distance I heard the faint sound of applause and then the orchestra starting up.

Nothing for it. I rolled up my skirt and tucked the hem right up into the top of my bodice, kicked my sandals off and waded in. The bottom of the lake was slimy with mud, the slithery stalks and roots of lilies and weeds curled around my ankles, then my knees, then my thighs, and yet I was still some way off. Was it a little pug dog I could see on the far side? I hesitated, started to turn back and slipped. I struggled a moment and then with a cry sank under the water.

I'm not clear about what happened next. All I know is that as I resurfaced strong arms were suddenly around me and, above the deafening noise of splashing, a voice behind shouted, 'Don't struggle! I've got you! Just float on your back and I'll swim you to the shore!'

He dragged me up a steep bank, leaves and twigs tangling into my hair and the silk of my dress ripping, until I came to rest in a thicket. I tried to turn over to get a glimpse of my rescuer.

'No,' he cried, 'I must put you in the recovery position!' And with that he knelt astride me. 'Don't worry,' he said. 'I've got a bronze medal in it.'

I coughed feebly. I was pretty winded. What could I do except go with it? His hands pressed down on my ribcage. I wanted to tell him there was no water in my lungs but I had no breath to speak. I had even less once he got going. In fact, as he started a rhythmical rocking above and behind me, I think I lost consciousness for a minute.

When I came to I was looking up into the branches of trees dancing in a warm breeze beneath a canopy of stars. I blinked hard in an effort to reconnect with reality. I failed. The silhouette of a blond angel illuminated by the first pale rays of the moon obtruded into my field of vision, blotting out the stars. Diamonds of water dripped down his long hair and were lost in the white wings of his shoulders. I shivered and struggled to sit up.

He said, 'I thought I was dreaming.'

'I think I still am,' I replied.

'No, you don't understand.' He shook his head and a shower of the diamonds fell on me. 'You see I came to sit by the lake looking for inspiration. I mean, I've got a commission to write an opera.'

'Oh, I know about it,' I said remembering Sir Jonathan's comment.

'You do?' He looked at me wonderingly.

'And you're the composer?' I had to ask because he looked so young.

He nodded his head. 'It's based on the story of Hamlet,' he said. 'And I'd got rather stuck on . . . Ophelia's aria when . . .'

'Too much!' I said and I shivered again. But I was beginning to appreciate the background music. Mozart but with the volume turned right down.

'When suddenly I was watching Ophelia . . . I was . . . inspired! But now I've forgotten . . .'. He turned away from me in some distress.

'It'll come back,' I said and my teeth chattered.

'What am I thinking of?' he asked and turned to look at me in some consternation. 'You'd be better off out of that dress.'

'Well, I'm not so sure.'

'I left a sweater on the bank.' He felt along the ground. 'Here! It's dry, look. You could put it on.'

Together we struggled to remove the tight wet tangle that was my dress. My bra was waterlogged so I took that off too. We both looked down. A diamond of water hung from the hard bud of each nipple. Scooping his wet hair up with one hand in a bunch at the nape of his neck, he bent forward to lick the water gathering at the tips of my breasts. His tongue was blessedly warm. I sighed thankfully. Then both his hands began to chafe me, travelling up and down the back and front of me to get my circulation going until, sitting there naked in the velvet dark, I began to warm up. I began to glow. Meltdown. I got the hots.

'You're clothes are wet too,' I said. 'Let's get them off.' And believe me wet jeans are an even worse problem than a silk dress. We managed though.

'Ophelia!' he said, grinding the wetness of his naked body into mine. 'I can hear your music!'

'Play it to me,' I urged as my fingers searched out his instrument. He raised his buttocks and his hand met mine as it closed over his penis, poised above the soft damp cushion of my pubis.

He paused, then said, 'I really ought to write it down.'

'What?' I murmured, a wet strap of his hair across my mouth.

'The notes. Of the music. Before I forget.'

So much for being a Muse, I thought, but all I said was, 'In a minute. For now just keep humming it in your head.' And I rippled the foreskin of his member back with a gentle glide of my fingers.

He made a kind of humming musical sound deep in his throat as he plunged straight into me. If he was remembering he soon forgot. So did I. The night sky and the stars came at me in little spurts, showering outwards from the column of his neck as his muscles strained taut above me.

Then his soft lips sought mine and everything was blacked out. His kisses blindfolded me. There was no point in looking. Everything was taste and tactile sensation. Sounds too, of course. And like a blind person compensates for a lack of vision by becoming super sensitive to the slightest noise, the soft crackling of twigs and leaves under me, the sighing of the branches overhead and the glissando of his well-lubricated penis plunging back and forth, in and out of me, the suck of our lips in a crescendo of kisses was like a swelling symphony.

He withdrew and rested for several beats, then he moved up my body, turned around and lowered his member into my mouth. It was warm with my own juices. He stretched forward and lay the length of his lean torso between my hips. His head went down between my legs. He sucked, I sucked. Contrapuntal. And then he pressed down on his hands, raised his head and turned again.

Now his mouth on my mouth was smeared with my own juice as he re-entered me and it was like we were swimming again. Sinking down, drowning, only to push up from the bottom, up and up until I broke the surface. I orgasmed seconds before him, pulling him after me until we lay panting on the same bank again. Now it was him in the recovery position with one hand thrown out along the ground. He lay still for so long that I stroked his cheek to rouse him. He made strange grunting noises.

'What's the matter?' I asked in alarm.

'I was singing,' he said. 'Must write it down.'

I sat up as he stood. He seemed to have forgotten about his pants. Oblivious, he turned to go.

'Wait!'

'What?'

'What's your name?'

'Adam,' he told me. 'And when I've got it down on paper you'll be the first to hear it.' He turned to go again.

'Adam?'

Suddenly he made a rush to reassure me. 'Oh, my darling,' he said. 'You've released something in me. You've opened a door for me tonight.'

131

That was all very well but I didn't want him to leave me. I'd heard a kind of rustling in the undergrowth and I was scared. 'I believe you but . . .'

'I was a virgin till tonight,' he blurted out.

'No, sorry, that I don't believe.' I laughed.

'I'm quite instinctive. All my talents are untutored. All it takes is for someone like you—'

'Ssh!' I put my finger to his lips. 'There's someone watching us. There's someone . . . Oh!' I pointed to where some brambles nodded in the shadows. Both of us saw a pair of eyes glint in the moonlight. I clutched Adam's hand, pulled myself up and whispered. 'A peeping Tom!'

'Pag?' Adam called. 'Pagliacci? That you?'

A little grey pug dog shuffled out of the bushes. He looked at Adam. He turned his head away from me.

'You should be indoors,' Adam told him, snatching up his jeans. 'Follow me.'

I watched Adam's pale length as he loped off with the little pug trotting stiff-legged in his wake until they were swallowed up by the darkness.

'Adam!' I called. 'I've no clothes on. And I don't know where I am.'

'Stay where you are,' he called back. 'I'll send someone with a torch and a blanket.'

In the event it was Sir Johnnie's man, Conningham, who got to me first. He'd bought a towel and the damask tablecloth that we'd used for our picnic.

'Dear, oh, dear, miss,' he said. And, as though I was a wet puppy or something that'd been for a splash in a puddle, he started to rub me down briskly. A little too briskly. I pushed him away. 'If you'd allow me, miss, to dry between your legs?'

'I'm quite dry there, thanks.'

'Really?'

I didn't like his tone. If it hadn't been so dark I suspected I would've seen a lascivious grin. Anyway he did an excellent job with the tablecloth, wrapping it around me like a sari. And so I made a quite decent appearance in the car park where everyone was now waiting to go. Except for the leaves in my wet hair, my muddy feet, etcetera, I felt that after what I'd been through I looked pretty much together.

'My God!' Catha said. There was something odd about the way she looked too, but at least she was still wearing the same dress she'd arrived in.

Mick said rather sadly, 'Seems like I missed out again, kid, did I?'

Don's niece said, 'Hey that musician guy who told us where you were was dishy.'

'Get in the car,' Don told her. And then turned to Catha to say, 'I want to talk to you.'

To my surprise Catha went immediately to Sir John who put a protective arm around her. Obviously I'd missed out too. As we got into Mick's car to follow Conningham, who was driving Sir Jonathan's Rolls, I asked Catha to explain.

'Johnnie rescued me,' she said.

'That's funny,' I said. 'I got rescued too.'

'Why d'you always have to copy me?' she asked.

'I don't.'

'Yes you do.'

Sleeping arrangements at Sir Jonathan's mega pad were complex to say the least. In the end Catha and I got put in a twin-bedded room in the turret and had the door locked on us.

'I don't want to be locked in,' I complained.

'Well, I do,' Catha said. 'And the key thrown away for good.'

'Why?'

Then she told me that she feared she could no longer trust herself. Apparently, on the way into the organ room, Don's niece thought she'd spotted a member of some pop group or other and had rushed off in pursuit of his autograph. Don had looked pretty annoyed. But the minute she'd been left alone with him, Catha had felt a rush of desire. It was, she said, a sort of throwback reactive memory of their first encounter.

He had the self-same sort of rush, grabbed her hand and, before they knew it, they'd blasted through a corridor cordoned off with red rope, thrust aside a 'Private' sign and dashed breathlessly up some wooden stairs. They'd catapulted straight through a door which read 'No admittance to the public', shut it behind them and had started mauling each other as though possessed by demons. She was at his trouser belt whilst he'd pulled her skirt up and had pushed her against a wall before she looked down and saw they were in a sort of gallery overlooking the organ room with people milling around below.

He only had eyes for her. He didn't care where they were. He'd pulled her away from the wall because she had begun to protest and had bent over the gallery balustrade with her skirt up around her ears. It was from this vantage point, and with Don's hands ripping at her panties, that she looked straight down into the eyes of Sir Jonathan who was, at that moment, looking up at her.

'Catha?' he'd wondered.

'Help,' she'd said rather feebly but just loud enough for him to get the message.

Before she knew it and before Don had had a chance to get his cock out, Sir Jonathan had burst through the gallery door. There was a bit of a scuffle. One of the ushers from the opera house had joined in and dotted both of them over the head with a pair of opera glasses he'd been taking to Lost Property.

I asked Catha what she saw in Don.

'I don't know,' she cried as though the question really pained her. 'It's just a sort of base primeval urge, a sort of . . . almost as though his penis acts as a magnet on my pussy.'

'Madness. Like me and Stefan.'

'Hardly,' Catha said. 'I mean, you know that Stefan's a pig whereas Don—'

'Is a swine . . .'

'Oh, anyway,' Catha shrugged. 'What's so awful is that now I really like Johnnie. And that's . . . well, on a different level entirely. Sort of . . . romantic.'

Romantic was not a word that had played a big part in Catha's vocabulary up till then. On the other hand, Johnnie had always had undoubted potential as a high-level donor. I said nothing. Instead I thought about Adam. The definition of the muscles of his lean torso, his long hair in the moonlight and, above all, his music. 'I think I'm into something romantic too.'

'You see?' she said. 'You always copy me.'

'You copy me.'

'I don't.'

'You do.'

134

Chapter 11

The next highlight was Henley.

Catha made a killing acting as hostess for Sir Jonathan in his marquee. Corporate hospitality. You know the kind of thing: champagne flowing faster than the Thames, strawberries consumed in big enough quantities to make Wimbledon look like a famine zone. But I'll come back to that.

I'd been diverted upstream.

Mick, having conscientiously despatched his wife to their villa in Majorca, was determined to make me feel at ease. He'd given me his tour of the house. Very *Ideal Home*, each room unfolding like page upon page of a glossy magazine.

Now we were standing at the edge of an acre of lawn that ran in velvet stripes down to the edge of a picturesque river. No weeds – they'd been torched. The bank was overhung with weeping willows whose tresses could've been styled by Nicky Clarke.

'The Thames?' I enquired. 'Not much more than a stream.'

'When I go for something, kid, I go for where it's at. I go for the source.'

'Hey, why don't we get in your car and nip down the road to Henley?'

'And here's where its at,' he said as his hand slipped down and lifted my skirt.

'Only take half an hour, Mick. Or even less.'

'Much less in my speedboat,' he said as his hand eased inside the soft material of my bikini.

'Well, there we are!'

He smiled but then looked serious. 'You'd rather be there than here?'

'No, but . . .'

'I've already told you. Bell Catha. I'll send Davies down in the boat to fetch her and her chum up here for the evening. If that's what you want. Stick with me, kid, and what you want you get.'

Davies was Mick's man. His version of Sir Jonathan's man, Conningham. Davies wasn't the old family retainer type though but a slick upstart supplied by a Knightbridge agency specialising in a quick-fix butlers and valets for new money. He wore a shot-silk waistcoat and a smirk. He and I had taken an instant dislike to each other. 'I'll ring Catha.' I agreed with Mick.

Why not make Davies do some work? After all, I told myself, Mick'd had the rough end of the stick so far. Each time he'd come close to having me to himself something had happened. He deserved better. 'I'll ring her mobile from the house,' I said.

'You can give her a bell from the Folly,' he said gruffly.

'Folly?'

'Over there.' And he pointed into the trees at a big hut in the style of a Hansel and Gretel chalet, looking as though it was carved out of gingerbread.

Oh, and folly it was. But I didn't begrudge him. On the contrary I wanted to pleasure him as much as he wanted to pleasure me. First things first though. I called Catha.

'Darling, hurry!' she shouted.

'Sorry. Not coming.'

'What?' Gales of laughter were making it difficult for her to hear. She talked on regardless. 'I've cut a swathe, Ali. Reaped quite a harvest. So many promises. All sorts of lifetime covenants, not to mention legacies. Even Johnnie is a bit . . . What? Scuse I, Ali, but he's trying to tell me something.'

'Catha? Mick says he'll send his speedboat to bring you back here after.'

'What? Oh, great. Johnnie's going now but I . . . in fact I've promised several of my new recruits, high-level donors, okay?' She interrupted herself to give Johnnie a chirpy farewell. 'He's not coming anywhere, he says, but some of the others . . .'

'Mick says he'll send Davies with the boat.'

'Oh, brilliant! Who? Oh, well, never mind. Ship ahoy!'

'Catha, are you alright?'

'Yes. Fine.' At least she sounded as though she was trying to sober up. 'Little too much of a . . . Hey, wait till I tell you.

Bruce, remember Brucie? He of the furry sporran? Well, he's got the tent next door. Whisky promo, high malt content, very high. Anyway, as I was saying, the truth is, Ali, I've rather raised expectations this end by offering a mystery prize.'

'How d'you mean?'

'Well, to the highest bidder, I mean giver. And a surprise boat trip could be just the thing! Jolly boating weather! Magical mystery cruise, you with me?'

During this conversation Mick had been giving instructions so I said, 'Hang in there, Catha, Mick says to wait for Davies on the wooden pontoon above the—'

'We'll be there!' she shouted. ''Bout ten of us.'

'No, no, I don't think a . . . that a speedboat holds . . .'

But the satellite had blinked or something and she was gone. No point in worrying. Down to Davies, he'd get it sorted. Let him sweat. Anyway Mick was already pulling me towards the conservatory-style swing seat at the far end of the Folly.

'Going to be quite a party,' I said as I dropped the phone to concentrate on the belt that held up his trousers.

'Tell me about it!' Mick sighed in contented expectation, laying back on the cushions with his hands behind his head.

There's often a problem when the moment of consummation has been delayed as it had with me and Mick. There'd been several occasions already when force of circumstance or my own ambivalence had frustrated his intentions. In fact, by this stage in our relationship we were being quite brother and sisterly. So, whilst taking his soft-as-a-rabbit's-ear cock in my mouth, I was feeling more friendly than passionate. I wanted to reward his patience though. And I think he felt the same – that a cosy session of fellatio was his due and that I would understand that. I did. He wriggled his bum down into the cushions as I gently rocked the swing-seat back and forth so that his penis glided easily in and out of my mouth with a minimum of effort on my part.

'How's it for you?' I asked after a couple of minutes because he didn't seem to be getting much of a hard-on.

'Beats going to the opera,' he offered. Perhaps because of this remark, perhaps because the rhythm the swing-seat was having a soporific effect, my mind began to wander back to Glyndebourne and to Adam . . .

* * *

Regrets? Well, a few. You see I'd fallen out of love with Adam
before I'd had a chance to fall in. And all because he'd insisted
that I go and listen to the aria I'd inspired. It had been quite
a shock. The soprano he'd press-ganged into singing it for me
was very un-Ophelia. But it wasn't that so much as the music
he'd composed. A-tonal. Mean I'd call it, with lots of jerks
and squeaks – no trace of a tune, whereas I like to tap my foot
and hum along. I'm afraid I couldn't help but take it as a
personal affront. From what the soprano said afterwards I
gathered she felt much the same. She said it was the equivalent
of chinese torture for the vocal chords. And that the top Ds –
this being musical parlance for the ear-splitting screams that
brought the whole abortion to its climax – had drawn blood.
I'd found myself apologising to her. To Adam too. Later I'd
even failed to defend his cause when Catha told me that she
was set on syphoning off some of the funds that Sir Jonathan
had earmarked for the new opera. Not very sensitive of her.
And I was sorry because the idea of falling in love with a
talented artist is always romantic. Sorry for Adam too, but
then artist's do have to suffer. And an opera often has its own
tragic finale . . .

'Stop,' Mick said.
'What?' I'd got so involved reminiscing that I hadn't noticed
what was happening in the here and now. The penis that slid
out of my mouth as I spoke had quadrupled in size.
'Or I'll come in your mouth,' he explained. 'And I want to
wait.'
I started dragging cushions off the swing seat and flinging
them onto the floor. I was taken aback by the size of his
member. I wanted it in me.
'You're not ready, kid,' he laughed.
'I am. Try me.' I lay down quickly, spread my legs and
pulled him off the seat, still laughing, on top of me. It was
only then that I realised I still had my clothes on. I had to get
them off quickly but that was difficult with him on top of me.
I gave him a push but he didn't budge.
He said, 'You gonna let me undress you.'
'No,' I said urgently. 'I'll be quicker.'
'I'll be very slow,' he whispered in my ear.

'Well, exactly!' I tried another shove but to no avail.

'Cos you'll have to be very wet for me to get this lot in you.'

'I'm wet now.'

'Not wet enough.'

His hand was into my panties, pulling them down. I tried to get my hand in too but he caught hold of it and stuffed it in his mouth, his tongue darting in and out between my fingers.

'Oh, please!' I said and I wriggled a little under him to get the message through.

'You gonna let me?'

'Okay then,' And with that I gave in and decided to go with it. Every muscle in me relaxed simultaneously. He rolled off me, lifted my shirt and kissed my palpitating diaphragm before starting to roll the material up to pull it over my head. I tried to help him.

'Don't help me.'

'Alright.' I swallowed hard because he placed one hand above my head and was kissing my armpit before he drew that arm slowly out of its sleeve. As he did so he chased my hand, nipping at my fingers with his teeth. Then the other arm. Then . . . 'Oh, please hurry,' I said.

He didn't answer. He was easing the material of my bra down to expose my left breast. He cupped it with his hand, lifting it slightly as he lowered his head to tease the nipple with little puffs of breath before he tongued it. Then, when my nipple was fully erect, he gently closed his teeth around it and pulled and released and pulled again. I looked down. I'd never seen a nipple stand so proud and pink and pointed. Then the other breast. Then both together, squeezing them to make a cleavage in which to bury his face, grinding the roughness of a hint of stubble on his chin into the softly yielding cushion of my flesh.

I moaned. Still he hadn't got my bra off. He eased its straps, one at a time, off each shoulder, before he slid his hands under my back and slowly pinched the fastening together until it came unhooked.

'Ah!' I cried, arching my back and pushing my body up into him. It was as though this simple action of his, normally a mere prerequisite of foreplay, had brought me perilously close to climax.

Then came my skirt. Thank heaven, I thought, any minute now! He unbuttoned the side fastening. Something snapped inside me. 'Ah, give it to me!' I cried out. 'Let me have it now. Get it in me. Fill me.'

'Just testing before I . . .'. His hand slid down quickly into my knickers and he stabbed two fingers straight into my vagina and wiggled them from side to side. The sound that reached my ears was of a luscious overripe fruit being masticated.

'You're wet,' he said.

'If you don't . . . soon,' I responded with my breath coming in little gasps. 'You'll have lost your . . . chance. You'll have lost your . . .'

'My erection? No chance, it's getting bigger all the time.' And with that he laid it on my bared thigh and pressed himself against me. His member seemed to extend from my groin almost to my knee. I was swooning, almost unconscious with desire for him when . . .

'Are you in there, sir?' Davies' carefully cultured voice preceded a sharp *rat-a-tat* on the door.

'What is it?' Mick called. And then as a quick afterthought he added, 'Don't come in.'

'Is the phone in there not working?'

'Switched off for incoming . . . What is it? What the hell do you want?'

'I took a call in the house,' Davies said, complaining of the imposition. 'Some woman on a pontoon, sir, downstream . . .'

'Oh, no! We forgot Catha!' I groaned.

Mick pushed himself up into a sitting position beside me on the floor. 'Take the speedboat, Davies. She's at Henley.'

'If you'd be so kind, sir,' Davies opined on the other side of the door, 'to give me some clue as to whom I shall be collecting?'

'She's . . .'. Mick looked at me for help.

'Wearing a big cartwheel hat,' I shouted. 'The brim set about with artificial roses and a matching raw silk coat and—'

'Just mug up a placard, Davies, with her name, "Catha", on it. Nice big letters. Use your initiative. Thick felt tips in the onyx pen holder on my library desk. Hold that up as you near the bend in the river. She'll flag you down.'

By the time this was sorted Mick's erection had already

atrophied to half its former size. But I was so concerned about Catha that I didn't notice until he said, 'Oh, sod it. Look at that.'

I looked. 'Let's face it, Mick,' I told him sadly. 'It isn't meant to happen.'

'That sort of talk always gets me going. Now I'm going to have to prove you wrong.'

'But, Mick . . .'

'We'll start over. From the beginning. Back to the drawing board, kid!'

And that's exactly what happened and why, I think, I lost track of time, place and everything. The double dose of prolonged foreplay was exquisite agony. This man, with his stubborn dreams of building bridges across seas, held me perilously suspended above the swirling torrent of my desire for so long I was barely conscious. Each time I was about to fall, he pulled me back from the edge. He revived me, brought all my senses alive again as he plunged down into me, drove me along the surface of the torrent as I clung on and shouted my excitement, thrilled by the danger, white-water rafting, racing us both along at high speed to a spectacular climax.

Afterwards, arms interlocked, legs entwined, we both slept and dreamed. Then he must've carried me up to the house because I was lying on the white silk sofa in the drawing room wrapped in a gigantic white towelling robe when Davies made his entrance.

At first I could make no sense of things. Or perhaps I should say that Davies seemed like a natural extension of what had happened in the Folly. He stood in a pool of light by the double doors to the drawing room like an echo of the interlude I'd just experienced. He was dripping wet, strands of water weed decorated his shoulders and the shot-silk of his waistcoat was stained jet black.

'I swam most of the way back, sir,' he explained. And then, because this didn't seem to be making much of an impression, he added, 'Against the current.'

Mick wasn't inclined to be impressed. In fact, he was so relaxed and pleased with life that he lit a small cigar and puffed a few puffs flicking a little wad of ash onto the floor before bothering to enquire, 'Swam from where, Davies?'

'The island in the river, sir, where the shipwreck occurred.'

141

Mick sat down on the sofa and began to fondle my ankles before he asked, 'You mean the boat's a write-off?'

'Yes, sir.'

'You're bloody useless,' Mick told him. 'Going to ring the agency tomorrow for a replacement. You realise I'm paying them ten per cent on top of your wages?'

'It wasn't my fault, sir. We were overloaded and the woman insisted on taking the wheel. She hit the left bank in the dark, swerved straight across to mid-stream and crashed on the mudbank.'

I tried to push myself up on one elbow to say something but Mick pulled at my ankles and I found myself laid out flat on my back again.

'Sod the woman,' Mick said. 'As if she hasn't caused enough trouble.'

'What trouble?' I managed, trying to get a wavering hold on reality.

Mick looked down fondly at me. 'She's driven a wedge between Don and Sir Jonathan for starters, kid. Don's had the rug pulled from under him as far as his timber supplies are concerned. And now this.'

'You don't mean Catha?' I asked and suddenly took in the disastrous change in Davies' appearance. The full force of the crisis, the implications of what was being said, struck home at last. 'Oh, no!' I cried. 'Oh, please tell me she hasn't drowned?'

'Did she drown?' Mick asked Davies with a marked lack of curiosity.

Davies shrugged. 'Last I saw she was being dragged clear of the water by a couple of men up the mud bank. You know the island, sir, bit of a nature reserve and bird sanctuary?'

'Not the one Don's got his eye on for a nudist camp?'

'Oh, poor Catha,' I cried. 'We must do something! Quick!'

Mick registered my alarm and reacted. 'All hands on deck, Davies.'

'Point is, sir, what deck?'

Once Catha had had a tetanus jab (her insight into the pollution of our waterways had made her particularly susceptible) and was sitting in the guest wing wrapped in a mohair blanket and sipping hot chocolate, she said, 'Pardon

142

me for saying so, Alison, but next time I'm marooned on a desert island I shan't rely on you to alert Air Sea Rescue.'

'The police launch was a long way off and Mick had to borrow a neighbour's pedalo.'

'And when I'm on Desert Island Discs I'll tell them they can stuff the complete works of Shakespeare for a start.'

'What luxury will you take?' I asked, entering into the spirit of things.

Catha gave me a look. 'A year's supply of condoms,' she said.

'Oh, Catha! No! What happened?'

She took a deep breath, thought better of it and yawned instead, before remarking, 'Well, let's just say it wasn't exactly Swiss Family Robinson.'

She laid down and closed her eyes. She looked washed out and, anyway, I was more than satisfied – just to have her back safe and sound. I gave her a kiss and switched the light off. She'd tell me in the morning.

She was cracking the shell of her second soft-boiled egg with the silver breakfast tray balanced on her knees in bed when she finally explained what had happened.

'The thin veneer of civilization cracks under pressure. The base instincts of the neo-cortex soon raise their ugly head.'

'Yes,' I agreed. 'And I think you'd been drinking too, hadn't you?'

'We all had.'

'I wonder if Bruce and the two other men Mick brought off the island are awake yet.'

'Once the inhibitory mechanisms are undermined out there in the wild' Catha explained, dipping a corner of toast into her egg, 'the law of the jungle takes over.'

'But, Catha,' I protested. 'You can't have been a castaway for more than a couple of hours.'

'So?'

'So what happened?'

Catha told me.

Bruce had turned out to be the leader of the pack. (Obviously his experience with Serena had unleashed an untamed Brando streak in him.) Quick to assert his authority, he had delegated the other two men to strip Catha of her mud-caked clothes and bathe her in some clear water scooped up in her cartwheel hat from the river on the other side of the island. This was a lengthy process. Each time they arrived back from traversing the island with a hatfull of water, they splashed it on her and then using a handful of dockleaves, wiped some more of the slimy brown mud off her body. Catha's face and breasts were just clear of the stuff when Bruce took advantage of the brief absence of the other two men.

During one of the previous trips to refill the hat, he'd already taken his kilt off to cover her. Night was falling and with it the temperature. The two men fetching the water were taking longer and longer. The hat had sprung a leak. Meanwhile Bruce, divested of his kilt, began to feel cold too. The obvious thing to do was to snuggle under it alongside Catha. Bruce gave in to what can only be described as a natural animal instinct. Catha didn't mind because she knew a sudden drop in body temperature due to shock can have serious consequences, so she snuggled up too. One thing led to another. He laid on top of her to make her even warmer. This position, much like an involuntary knee-jerk reaction, triggered his penis into life. He pulled her hips down and he thrust upwards at her. His penis missed aim in the dark and slid between her upper thighs. Catha disengaged herself in an attempt to climb on top of him but he thought she was trying to escape and quite a tussle in the mud ensued, or, as Catha put it, a rerun of man's emergence from the primeval ooze.

Finally she squatted over him, thighs spread, her hand guiding his member backwards along her slit towards her opening, when the two other men reappeared. With a whoop of delight (much like the hoot of a gorilla or other primate, Catha told me) one rushed her from behind and the other came charging at her from the front. Bruce simply reacted by locking his arms around her neck and thrusting upwards into her vagina harder than ever. With her bottom up in the air, clouds scudding across an eerie moon above, she had no way to protect herself from being entered for a second time. She was powerless to prevent the cleft of her buttocks being prised open and her anus being ravished. With the pressure of two penises thrusting into her, one from below and one from behind, her head jerked up and back, her mouth fell open with surprise and she gasped, unwittingly giving a third penis the perfect opportunity to introduce itself between her lips.

'Three men at once!' I exclaimed. 'Oh, Catha, and the most I've ever had is two.'

'When?' she snapped.

'You remember that package holiday in Tunisia?'

'Oh, that!' She tossed her head dismissively and scooped some honey onto the remainder of her toast.

'But Catha how d'you square this with your principles? All your resolutions?'

'I don't,' she said. 'This was something other. I plead extenuating circumstances here.'

'Oh, very convenient,' I said, making it plain that I was being sarcastic.

'Apart from which I never lost sight of my professional commitments.'

'Oh, pull the other one,' I said. 'Next you'll be telling me that this event was simply a question of natural selection. A mere blip in the evolutionary process.'

Our argument did not develop further because it was at about this point that Sir Jonathan arrived. He'd come hotfoot as the result of a summons from Mick who was keen to clear the house of uninvited guests so that he could return to giving his undivided attention to me.

Sir Jonathan, firmly cast in the role of Catha's protector ever since he had saved her from Don's clutches, was in a state of considerable agitation. Being a dyed-in-the-wool traditionalist, the only hope he could see for Catha was within the bastion of marriage.

'This unfortunate incident has served to prove that I love you,' he told Catha. 'Marry me. Honour will be restored. Marry me and you won't be violated again. Will you marry me? Just say the word.'

This proposal shocked Catha far more deeply than anything that'd gone before. Up to and including being a castaway. She was rocked to her foundations. She came down to earth with a real jolt.

'What am I going to do, Ali?' she cried. 'I mean, this is just the sort of thing we were aiming for, but . . .'

'Well, um, do you love him?' I asked. I was playing for time because it was a shock to me too.

'How do I know? I haven't even slept with the man!'

'Um, but, wasn't that meant to come last?'

'Last?'

'Like afterwards. Love before lust and so on?' I didn't want to lose Catha to him but I didn't want her to have regrets later and then blame me.

'Oh, darling,' she said, pushing the breakfast tray to the end of the bed. 'I'm into a real chicken and egg situation here. Help me!'

'Sleep with him before you give your answer,' I directed. 'Sexual compatibility is necessary for emotional closeness and commitment. Sextasy, call it whatever, sustains monogamy. Trust, respect, the whole shebang, needs the Big O to make the thing stick.'

'Oh, Ali,' Catha said. 'You're right. What'd I do without you?'

'Well, like you said,' I told her because I was determined to be generous, 'you never lost sight of your professional commitments and you never will. Put your job first because that has got to be your safety net.'

'You're my safety net,' she said. 'My friendship with you. From that I draw my strength.'

'And you'll soon get him involved in the environment. You'll soon have access to a whole tranche of money for your causes. Though I must say, Catha,' I added a little apologetically, 'from first-hand experience, and I speak for both of us, grounds for supposing that testosterone levels are dropping as a result of oestrogens in the drinking water – or anything else for that matter, do seem a bit . . . well, overstated, darling.'

Catha ignored this observation to tell me, 'Before we'd left Henley, Bruce'd already promised that once his mother had died and he'd come into his inheritance, he would make sure his will contained a legacy. One of the others had pledged a deed of covenant for a thousand a year after tax and the other . . . Oh, yes, I forgot to tell you!' she exclaimed. 'The one who I sucked off full frontal? Well, he made a small fortune with a dating agency and singles magazine.'

'Really? Oh, that is interesting.'

'So you see I didn't forget your professional requirements either. Told me he'd got a stack of info. Loads of statistics collated from answers to his searching questionnaires.'

'Well, thanks,' I smiled. 'I'll ring Max. Make sure the material comes within my remit. Meanwhile I might just nip down the corridor to where the men are sleeping and get a handle on it.'

Minor misjudgement. The man concerned had obviously been overexposed to the sort of intimate photos with which women advertised their wares in his magazine. He was very up-front.

Mick rescued me in the nick of time. Quite a bout of fisticuffs ensued. There was no doubt at all that Catha and I were being offered safe conduct along life's tortuous path by two very caring men. Whether we wanted long-term protection or not was another question. And one we decided to defer until after Silverstone.

Chapter 12

Before Silverstone I rang Max. I told him that I'd got access to an impressive wad of info from a dating agency and a singles mag but that it might not fit under his heading of *Modern Mating Rituals: the Personal Column as the Equivalent of the Marriage Broker*.

What did he think?

He said, 'Outta sight. Just keep it coming, baby. Give it to me! Give me all you got!'

'Yes, but you see, Max, strictly speaking—'

'Thanks to you this whole thing's taken off.'

'We don't want to lose our focus, do we?'

'Focus?' he said. 'We're probing outer space here. We're going super nova.'

'Yes, but shouldn't you check with Jasper? I mean, he's publishing the book.'

'Which reminds me,' Max said, sounding ever more serious. 'He fixed a photo shoot for tomorrow. Balham somewhere. Pencil it in. Can you meet me at Euston?'

'No, I'm going to Silverstone.'

'Cancel, baby. Never heard of it.'

'Race track. Formula One. And it's a long-standing engagement, Max.'

'Okay, okay, my fault. No sweat. We'll reschedule.'

'You could get someone else to pose for the book cover, surely? Couldn't you?'

'You kidding? Anyway, we'll be shooting for inside the book as well as out.'

'You mean . . . ?'

'Whole new conception. Coffee-table presentation. Lavish illustrations. Top-of-the-market connoisseur stuff. Whole new angle too with the authors strutting their stuff right in there among the text.'

'Well, I'm not sure about that,' I told him. 'You should've consulted me before you—'

'We'll make it the day after this Silver place. Don't worry, Alison,' Max said, slowing down at last.

'I am worrying because . . .'

'Since when did I take advantage of you?'

'Well, never but . . .'

'Trust me, please. Hey, this is Max speaking, right?'

'Yes, but . . .'

'And it's your mind I love you for, remember that.'

If any remark was ever designed to disarm a woman it was that. It stopped me dead in my tracks. Reservations? I'd forgotten them. Besides, Max was like a dog with two tails over the successful progress of his project and I didn't really want to spoil it for him. Not now anyhow. Why not let him have a couple more days?

Mind you, a lot can happen in forty-eight hours.

'I don't see why we couldn't have met him there,' Catha said as we belted down the motorway to Harry de Burgh Walton's house.

'He said something about the traffic.'

'Quite. So now we have to set out again in his car. This the exit?'

'Then two miles and second left after the village,' I said as we swung off into the countryside, fields veiled with an early-morning mist.

'It's ages since we met him at the Holiday Inn. Will you recognise him, Ali?'

'Heavens, yes,' I said. 'He was quite a looker, come-to-bed eyes and Gucci boots.'

'I see.' Catha sighed her world-weary sigh. 'Say no more. We all know what that means.'

'You must be joking!' I bridled 'I'm still recovering from Mick.'

'Well, I'm out of the running,' Catha said. 'Perhaps for all time. Did I tell you I'd put Sir Jonathan in my phone book under 'L' for love?'

'Yuk,' I said.

'You're just jealous. Real love only develops in a partnership where love is reciprocated equally. It's the moment when both

149

partners, without losing any independence or identity, become a part of each other.'

'You haven't even slept with him yet.'

'All in good time,' she told me. 'I think he and I will talk about it at some length first. Whether or not we should have sex and if so – why? His preferences. My preferences. A frank and adult exchange of fantasies, responsibilities, mutual expectations and so forth.'

She'd lost me. I was gazing out of the window across damp fields to a honey-coloured stone farmhouse nestling in a coppice of silver birch. As we turned up the winding drive through a broken five-bar gate, two golden labradors ran out to meet the car and race it back up to the courtyard where we parked.

No one came to greet us. The dogs, their tails wagging, urged us round the back of the house. Through the leaded lights of the stone-framed windows I spied split leather sofas, old tiffany lamps with their shades awry, huge silver bowls spilling fruit and dried flowers onto the dusty patina of mahogany side tables, and the muted glimmer of a dying log fire. Quite a relief after Mick's designer nouveaux, kinder on the eyes, like an old sepia print after technicolour. The owner of this house had style inbred.

Harry was seated at a scrubbed pine refectory table in the flagstoned kitchen. He was on the phone and motioned us to sit. As soon as we did he used his free hand to serve us a Buck's Fizz. More Fizz than Buck as it happened because most of the orange juice got slopped onto the table.

'Okay,' he was saying. 'They've got the best chassis and they're starting higher up the grid. But we've got the best suspension and gear ratios. You with me?' Harry winked at Catha and me in turn before continuing. 'We take them on the turn in the tenth or twelfth lap. Accidentally, of course. Brake on the corner. We squeeze them off the track. Anyway, less said the better, see you soon.'

Harry de Burgh Walton replaced the receiver and gave his hand to the dogs to lick. They seemed most appreciative.

'Hi,' I said, 'Nice place, Harry.'

Catha dug me in the ribs and told him, 'One sniff of champagne and she's anybody's.'

It was a comment that seemed most unfair to me. Harry thought she was speaking out of turn too because all he said was, 'You two all set? Got your wellies?'

'What?' Now Catha was definitely wrong-footed. She glanced anxiously under the table at her new antelope skin boots with latticed cutwork to the sides.

'Oh, come on, Harry!' I said because I was wearing my stacked cuban heels which weren't exactly waterproof either.

'Not to worry,' he joked and changed the subject. 'Either of you fly?'

'Oh, yes,' Catha responded, dropping herself right in it. 'I've almost got enough Air Miles for Barcelona.'

Harry laughed uproariously at that. 'Nice one,' he said, and then added in a more serious tone. 'Copter or fixed wing?'

'BA actually,' she said.

I laughed then too. 'You mean to say you've got your own plane, Harry?'

He nodded. 'Use the copter today though,' he said. 'No runway at Silverstone. Just a boring old helipad.'

I don't think Catha would have forgiven me for days, but she was so frightened in the helicopter that her short-term memory got wiped. She kept her eyes shut most of the time and confined herself to complaining about the noise. Little did she realise what lay in store. Anyway, I thoroughly enjoyed the ride and kept up a running commentary for Catha's benefit.

'The motorway is at a standstill for miles. Bumper to bumper as far as the eye can see.'

She whispered to me could I find a sick bag but I couldn't. 'Just pinch your nose or something,' I told her, because I knew being sympathetic always made her worse.

Harry said, 'People set out long before dawn. Can take twelve hours to get into the circuit and much longer to get out.'

'Oh, look,' I cried as we circled. 'Look at all the tents.'

'Some people sleep here the whole three days of the Grand Prix.'

'It's a sort of shanty town, Catha. And do look – traffic's worse than Bangkok.'

'Stop/start marathons aren't for me,' Harry said as we bumped and lurched onto the helipad. 'Some jolly unfortunate cases of road rage last year. Not to mention a whole raft of sprained achilles tendons from pumping a clutch for six hours at a stretch.' The blades juddered to a halt. 'Okay, girls? Ready to hop out?'

We'd landed miles from anywhere in the middle of a field and there was no sign of a path. But Harry seemed to know which direction to take and set off at a cracking pace through the fine drizzle. We did our best to keep up but my heels kept sticking and the mud squelched in through the cut-out sides of Catha's antelope-skin boots. Point taken about wellies, I thought. Catha shouldn't have worn her fake ocelot either. We'd only been going quarter of a mile before it looked like dead-in-the-gutter Tom cat. My leather jacket did better but I was worried about the studs going rusty. All Catha said was, 'Beats me why anyone'd want to come here in the first place.'

'For the excitement,' I told her. 'For the adrenaline rush.'

'No comment,' she said through gritted teeth as Harry turned back to urge us on. 'One thing though,' she conceded. 'It's a blessed relief to get away from the noise of those whirring blades.'

The noise in the pits was much worse. 'And now we know what "it's the pits" means,' said Catha.

First, though, Harry had taken us into the paddock – once he'd managed to swipe his security card, which the machine rejected nineteen times. Then we had to have our wrists cuffed with a security code (Catha said that previously she'd thought it was only criminals who got electronically tagged) and we'd been introduced to the Ferrari Press Officer.

He made us feel better when he told us that the fee for the paddock club was over six hundred and with our front row stand seats we were looking at a grand, minimum. And, yes, even as an important sponsor, Harry would've had to pay that. We were impressed. Who could help feeling privileged? I was determined to get the best out of the situation. As for Catha, she launched headlong into a conversation with said Press Officer about advertising opportunities and promotion deals. The only problem was that he didn't seem to take in what she was saying but kept answering her with how many revs, how many laps, how many seconds it took for a wheel change and so on. This may have been because he couldn't hear her properly for the noise – sort of high decibel heavy metal with a base throb of engines firing up. In fact, I noticed some of the more savvy guests had brought their ear baffles. Lucky sods.

Mind you, I was having enough trouble breathing, let alone talking. The air was a hot soup of oil, axle grease and petrol. I looked round for Harry. He was in a tight knot of men in spacesuits. No doubt about his priorities. Total amnesia as far as women were concerned. Catha and I included.

I said, 'Let's get out of here and find our seats.'

She nodded. Now that the Ferarri man had put his ear baffles on too, there seemed even less point in us hanging around.

Front row stand seats at ninety-five pounds a throw. Terrific. Okay, so the wind blew the drizzle in under the roof and there was an icy draught slicing across our ankles, but we'd got some hot slabs of delicious pizza before we left the paddock and were tucking in with gusto. There wasn't long before the start and, when the public address system came on to announce the grid positions, it was so loud that Catha dropped the last bite of pizza in her lap.

'Why don't they turn that thing DOWN?' she shouted.

As soon as the race started it was obvious. The roar of forty-six Formula One engines hurtling past at close quarters, all wrapped around a crescendo of exhaust fumes and scorched rubber, battered the senses into the sort of terminal confusion usually associated with Alzheimer's. To communicate with the patient one had to shout.

Catha shouted. I read her lips. They said, something, something, 'Serious brain damage.'

I shouted back, making sure to exaggerate my lip movements. 'Making me feel dizzy.'

She shrugged helplessly as six tail enders hurtled past full throttle, one with brakes screaming as it hit a wall and exploded. The public address system thundered into action to detail the horror of the scene above the approaching roar of the race leaders already nudging the bend to start on a second lap.

I put my mouth against Catha's ear. 'Let's just go with it. Concentrate on the race,' I shouted.

153

She nodded mutely. She was using some of the paper napkin from her pizza to stuff in her ears at the time.

Trouble was that the cars went by with such speed that however quickly you swivelled your head all you could see was a blur. Okay, so the loudspeakers tried to tell you what you'd seen but the only certainty was that if you turned your neck right to left fast enough you'd end up suffering whiplash.

After ten minutes of this Catha turned to the man behind and shouted at him, 'How long does this race last?'

'Great, isn't it?' he shouted back.

'I said . . .'

He mimed something and held up three fingers as another clutch of belching monsters roared past. Then he punched the air. Pointing at her watch, Catha mimed did he mean three minutes or three hours?

'Or three days?' I shouted.

Whichever way we looked at it, it was too much. Catha and I left our seats to shelter at the back of the stand where the noise was marginally less and tried to work out how to improve our lot.

'We haven't even got a car to go and sit in.'

'We could go back to the paddock. I spotted a nice bar and a restaurant.'

'I want to get some distance on this thing,' she said. 'I'm afraid my eardrums are pierced. They hurt. Do yours?'

'It's my brain,' I said. 'Turned to jelly.'

'I'm so cold too.'

'And wet.'

We wandered off with no particular plan. Catha said we ought to look for the press enclosure because journalists were a resourceful bunch. I favoured following the course of the motorway until we found a service station. Then we ran up against a long stretch of chicken wire. This appeared to serve as a stockade, protecting a whole caravan park of big trailers. They looked inviting, warm and dry and far enough away from the action to be reasonably quiet. There were groups of other people with their noses pressed to the wire looking longingly in too – much like displaced refugees gazing across a border fence. Later we learned that they were simply the fans of the drivers. Anyway we were about to go through a gap in the fence when a security guard stepped across our path.

154

'No admittance,' he said.

'Just try and stop us,' Catha retorted, and to my alarm she made two fists and held them up towards his face. That's how desperate she was.

Quick as a flash, he noticed her security cuff. 'Whose guest are you?' he asked.

'Harry de Burgh Walton,' I said importantly.

'The Walton's team trailer is third on the right,' he advised and with that he let us pass.

I'll never be sure whether or not we finished up in the right trailer. We were too excited to be in the warm and dry and quiet to care.

'Well, this'll do nicely,' Catha said shrugging off her dripping fur.

'Great. And there's even a telly. We can watch the race and chat about it afterwards with the best of them.' I clicked it on.

'You sure that's necessary?' Catha asked. 'I mean a car is a car is a car.'

I clicked it off happily enough. 'Oh, and a mini bar, look!'

'Oh, and . . . Ali! What wouldn't you give for a nice hot shower?' And she drew the curtain back on a neat cubicle with a shower basket stuffed full of gels and shampoos.

No need for further comment. We both undressed, stepped out of our mud-caked boots, drew the curtain after us, switched the tap to hot, and selected high power. Bliss. We went to town with the Crabtree and Evelyn, used all but a dribble, but Catha and I always get such pleasure out of soaping and re-soaping each other that I don't think any but the most mean-spirited would begrudge us.

'Ah! I feel better for that.' Catha sighed luxuriously as she switched the shower off. 'Quite human again. Oh, but we should've located the towels before we . . .'

I pulled the curtain aside and spied a big fluffy bath sheet. I was just about to step out and reach it down off its hook when the door of the trailer suddenly flew open. I stepped back into the shower and closed the curtain double quick. We heard what sounded like three or four men shuffling in, all talking at once. A general melee.

'Mind, mind, this way . . . on the bunk . . . gently now . . . lay him down . . . clipped the kerb . . . turned over three times but he's alright. The doc's had a good look and he's . . . just help me get the rest of his clothes off.'

And then another softer voice said weakly, 'How's the car?'

'D'you want the bad news or the bad?'

'Written off?'

'The good news, Barry, is you're alright. The injection the doc gave you'll help you sleep and then we'll send the physio in.'

'The blonde one?'

A general guffaw. The group started back towards the door and someone remarked on Barry's powers of recovery before the door slammed shut. The draught from outside made us both shiver.

Catha mimed 'Where did we leave our clothes?' but I couldn't remember. I shrugged. I mimed that we'd give it a couple of minutes. By then he'd be asleep. We heard him sigh. Sure enough it wasn't long before the sound of deep rhythmical breathing reached us.

We stepped out from behind the curtain cautiously. Our clothes were pretty widely scattered. The only real problem was that Catha's fur had been on the end of the bunk and the sleeve was firmly wedged under Barry's legs. Catha motioned me to help her tackle this first.

We had to lift the duvet they'd covered him with to get a better view of the way the sleeve was caught under his thigh. This slight motion seemed to unsettle him and he turned on his side. Unfortunately, in doing so, the sleeve got clamped between his knees with the cuff caught in the fold of his groin.

'Oh, damn!' Catha breathed.

I motioned that I would put my head under the duvet and gently disengage the sleeve if she would watch his face and forewarn me in the event that he started to wake up. She gave me a thumbs up.

It was lovely and warm under the cover. There was a wholesome odour of soap and sweat, and just enough light leaking under the duvet's edge for me to discern the well-defined musculature of his legs, the dark triangle of public hair and shadow above his carelessly draped testicles and penis.

I went for the cuff of Catha's coat first, easing it back towards me inch by inch until a little fur brushed his balls – no more than an eyelash's blink – but his penis twitched immediately. I stopped, waiting for Catha's warning that he might be going to wake.

Nothing. My bottom was getting cold. I gave the cuff a harder pull. Unfortunately Barry clamped his thighs tight together in a sort of involuntary reaction and I lost my advantage. His penis twitched more markedly too. I withdrew my head from under the duvet.

'Hurry up,' Catha whispered. 'What's keeping you?'

'It's his penis,' I said.

'Let's see,' she said and knelt down beside me.

We both put our heads under the duvet. I gave the cuff of her coat another little tug and sure enough the penis jerked. It was more or less like a puppet on a string. Catha had a go. The same thing happened. Then I had a turn.

Then she nudged me. 'Oh, this is silly,' she said. 'He's fast asleep. We needn't worry.' So saying, she pulled hard at the cuff and successfully dislodged it. The only trouble was his penis reacted by becoming fully erect. What's more he turned onto his back again so that it pointed straight up and, worse, the cuff of the sleeve that Catha had freed was now trapped under his left buttock.

'Oh, too bad!' Catha moaned. And she quickly ducked her head out from under the duvet to get a look at his face again. 'Ali?'

I ducked out. 'What?'

She gestured to him. 'Dead to the world.'

'Wet dreams,' I said.

'Sleeping like a baby. What d'you reckon we just lift the duvet off him and . . . ?'

'Go for it,' I agreed.

We uncovered him. Both of us stood for a moment admiring the lean fitness of his body in repose, the plump thickness of his engorged member at full stretch.

'If you lift him up slightly I'll . . .' Catha indicated that I should slide my hands under his left buttock whilst she leant over him with her face perilously close to his member, ready to disengage the sleeve the minute I'd lifted him off it.

I dug my hands down under him. His eyelids flickered open for an instant. We both froze.

Maybe he'd caught a glimpse of blonde hair. I'll never know, but he murmured sleepily, 'You the physio?'

Catha looked at me. 'Yes,' she said, her breath caressing his penis as she spoke.

'Gimme your usual,' he said. His voice was thick and slurred but he seemed to know what he wanted.

Very obligingly, I thought, Catha started to massage his thighs.

'No,' he said. 'The hand-job.'

Catha looked at me in some alarm. I shrugged. I clasped his member firmly in my right hand and started to work the foreskin up and down whilst my left hand cupped his balls to keep them out of the way of Catha who was still busy kneading the muscles of his thighs.

A long low whimper of pleasure drifted from him. I looked at Catha. Seemed like we'd both got ourselves locked into a fairly monotonous task here. Repetitive strain injury. And the outcome wasn't going to be much to our advantage either. Or, to put it another way, his bum remained firmly planted on Catha's coat sleeve.

What I had to do was to get him to arch his back. I think Catha read my mind because she nodded encouragement. I tried slowing the rhythm of my hand on his penis and shifting my grasp on its shaft so that it was nearer to the tip than the root. My intention was to get him to thrust hard upwards because in so doing he would lift his pelvis and the fur cuff would slip from under him. No luck. Even though I spied a droplet of semen forming on his knob as evidence of his excitement, he was still making no effort. Somehow I had to get him to play his part. Catha and I were in concert here.

'You'll have to give him more encouragement than that,' she said.

What could I do? I stood up and, being careful not to obstruct the passage of Catha's hands as they worked their expert way up and down his thighs, I placed a knee on each side of his hips, squatting over him as he lay prostrate on the bunk. My hand withdrew from his member to part my labia as slowly, very slowly, I lowered myself until I was sitting spread wide on him. His breath escaped him in a long low sigh. He'd had a hard day. So had I but I didn't let that deter me. I leant forward putting my weight on my arms. My hair, the blonde he had wanted, dusted his mouth and my breasts dipped onto his chest. He half raised his head as though he was searching blindly for a kiss.

I sat back. As I did so the length of his member penetrated me and I started to contract and relax the muscles of my vagina. He moaned, his head dropping back onto the pillow again. But what I was looking for was the same reaction from his pelvis. Again Catha understood better than he did. She slipped her hands under me so that her palms cradled my buttocks. She lifted me ever so slightly as I rocked over him, forwards and back. Together we judged the angle perfectly. He simply had to thrust up or lose contact with me.

Unfortunately, by the time he realised this and thrust eagerly upwards, I'd forgotten all about Catha's coat sleeve. All I could think of was how good he felt inside me and Catha, acting like a saddle for my seat, had her hands full, so to speak. This was why neither of us took advantage when he started to raise his pelvis. In fact the sleeve of Catha's coat slipped free of his weight and dangled over the side of the bunk, but by then our concentration had shifted irrevocably.

I can honestly say that it's hard to beat the tender ministrations of a woman friend in achieving satisfaction with a man. It lends the whole process, especially when one is engaged with a stranger, a degree of intimacy that ensures that the act has an extra dimension. The resilience of her dear hands cushioning my buttocks, the way they guided and supported me as I bore down on his rigid tool, lunging upwards into me, lent the moment a special poignancy.

'Ah, Catha!' I cried as I climaxed.

Barry opened his eyes wide, glanced up at me and then past me to her. He came. As if it was too much to comprehend he lay very still for a moment. Then he opened his eyes wide and said, 'Where's your white uniform? You're usually buttoned up tight to your neck. If I'd known you were starkers I would've . . . And who's she?'

'The nurse,' I said quick as a flash.

He watched Catha shimmy into her leggings, funfur and antelope boots in some bewilderment.

'Pulse normal,' she said. 'Blood pressure A-okay.'

'You feeling better?' I asked him as I dived into my clothes.

'Well, I think . . . never better. Yeah, I feel great, really great, but . . . what happened?'

'Bit of an accident,' Catha said as she hurried to the door.

'I mean, you had a bit of an accident.'

'Just one of those things,' I said, following her out. 'Better luck next time, Barry!'

It wasn't only the thought of a six-hour traffic jam that influenced Catha in favour of another helicopter ride. She had a sort of faraway, dreamy look and kept saying what a revelation Silverstone had been and how it had inspired her to get back and see Sir Jonathan asap. She said that peeping between her hands at Barry's member plunging in and out of my vagina, the whole picture framed between the inner curve of my buttocks and upper thighs like the drapes of stage curtains, had had the same effect on her as watching a play in the theatre.

'A good play?'

'The best sort of theatrical experience is life-enhancing,' she said.

'And leaves the audience feeling deeply moved.'

'You should've had a go with him too.'

'No,' she responded. 'However involved one gets one simply doesn't get up there on the stage and mix it with the actors.'

'But it sort of whetted your appetite?'

'Yes, it's definitely put me in the right frame of mind for Sir Johnnie,' she said.

When we finally connected with Harry in the paddock he seemed pretty pleased with life too.

'So what did you think of it?' he asked.

'Terrific,' I said.

'Like you imagined?'

'Well . . . better,' Catha said. 'Specially the crash.'

'Which crash?' Harry seemed surprised.

'Barry's,' I told him and Catha nodded enthusiastically.

'Could've been fatal,' Harry admonished. 'But they got him out in one piece. Something of a miracle.'

'That's just the word I would've chosen myself,' I said.

'Anyway he's made a full recovery,' Catha told him.

'And that's the understatement of the year,' I added.

Chapter 13

After the din and grime of Silverstone, there could have been no more welcome invitation than Bruce's to join a shooting party in the Scottish Highlands. The thought of a long weekend amidst the peace of the heather-covered hills which surrounded the isolated splendour of his family's ancestral pile rather rode rough shod over any objections we might have had to the word 'shooting' in his invitation.

The fact that Bruce extended his invitation to include Sir Jonathan made the prospect even more pleasing to Catha – who was finding that her protector was backward at coming forward, so to speak. Their discussions about whether or not to have sex before marriage, whether or not sex mattered at all, indeed whether or not sex had any relevance beyond that of procreation, and if it did whether or not it could be seen as the by-product of a patriarchal society's need to control women, etcetera, was putting a brake on Catha's future plans. Not to put too fine a point on it, all her yaketty yakking was about to bring this relationship to a screeching halt.

Transposing their philosophising to another setting might just do the trick. The last untamed piece of wilderness in the British Isles must be conducive, Catha said, to Sir Johnnie letting it all hang out. No comment.

In fairness I should add that her concerns regarding Bruce's invite were also environmental. On the one hand, she was critical of the Forestry Commission's activities in the Highlands, and this visit would afford her a practical over-view. On the other, she wanted to suss out the prospective value of the legacy Bruce had promised her charity once he had inherited the estate from his mother. The job came first, right?

I was getting dressed to go and meet Max when Serena rang and blew me away. That is to say that the minuscule doubts I was beginning to entertain about the peace of the Scottish moors started to inflate. Bouncy-castle time. But I didn't tell Catha what Serena said.

'Ali? S'me and I want your advice.'

'Speak up, can you? Who is that?' I said. I'd recognised the conspiratorial whisper but this was the first time she'd ever rung me and I was shocked.

'S'me, Serena. Oh, Ali!'

'What?'

'To cut a long story short—'

'Yes, could you,' I said. 'Because I've got to be in Balham for a business meeting in half an hour.'

'Stefan's booked a weekend in the Highlands like he did last year and this year our host turns out to be none other than, guess who . . . Bruce.'

'What?'

'You remember. He and I had it off at the charity thingie and he was so . . . oh, so heavenly. Oh, Ali, what am I going to do?'

'Cancel,' I said simply.

'But it cost a fortune.'

'You mean Stefan has to pay for the privilege?'

'Yes, well, it's the only way they can keep these estates going. A thousand pounds a day Stefan's paying actually. But he doesn't begrudge it. He's quite keen to be supportive of these heritage type places with their quaint sporting rituals,' Serena explained defensively.

'Well, Catha and I are not having to pay a penny,' I said and knew I sounded smug.

'You? Well, they have private guests in the main house but in the Hunting Lodge they have paying guests. They have to fund things by— You? You and Catha?'

'Must be a different weekend.'

'Next weekend?'

'No.' I breathed a huge sigh of relief.

'Stefan's into some business thing up there too. With Don.'

'Who?'

'You remember at the charity hop I was meant to be with him but he went off with someone else and I described him to Stef and it turned out that they'd played golf in Florida last year and—'

'Okay, hold it there,' I said.

'Yes, but Ali.'

'I just have to think this one through.' I paused a moment and Serena observed a respectful silence. 'What does someone like you do in the Highlands?'

'Not much,' she admitted. 'There are no shops. Not even pavements. I listen to my Walkman mainly.'

'So why does Stefan take you?'

'I'm even learning golf. He's bought me a lovely outfit. Lots of socialising, you see. But with Bruce there . . . oh, Ali, I'm creaming myself at the thought of him. What'm I going to do? Why does Stef take me to these places? Well, to show me off, why else? Because he's proud of me.'

My antagonism flooded back. I remembered hating her. I said, 'Want my advice, Serena? Just get ill, grumbling appendix or something painfully incapacitating, pronto.'

How come no sooner had I solved one problem than another raised its head (or cock)? Max, he of the 'I-only-love-you-for-your-mind' was next to make his presence felt. And some conundrum that turned out to be.

By the time I got to the photographic studios in Balham he was stripped off and laid out on a battered chaise longue reading some hard-porn mag from the US. Bad news. He was intent on getting a hard-on. So when he glanced up as I made my entrance, I was already on my guard as he said, 'Hey, Alison, am I glad to see you!'

'Hi, Max,' I said and glanced at Jasper crouched in the shadows. He made a gesture to me which clearly indicated that Max was having a tough time getting it up.

'Hi, Jasper,' I said. 'How's it going?'

'Now you're here,' he said. 'Everything'll slot into place.' And he added an aside to the recumbent figure on the couch. 'No need to beat your brains out any more, Maxie. Once she's got her clothes off . . .'

'Thanks,' I said. 'But no thanks, I'm not taking them off.'

'No need.' The photographer stepped out from behind the camera to reassure me. 'But if you'd go into the cubicle, undress and put the towelling robe on . . . ?'

This didn't seem to be an unreasonable request and, besides, he was handsome in a ragged sort of way. When he

163

explained, 'Just want to shoot off a few rolls, see what we come up with, artistically speaking,' I saw no reason to stand in his way, or Jasper's or Max's, come to that.

I hadn't had a decent photo of myself taken for ages and with Jasper praising the photographer's creative talents, I started to feel reasonably enthusiastic. In fact, once I'd got my things off and was modestly draped in the long voluminous robe, I began to relax and feel quite inspired myself, artistically speaking, of course.

'This for the book cover?' I asked.

'No need to be pedantic about things,' Bill stated. All the while, the *click-click* of his camera punctuated what he said and the insistent *pop-pop* of the flash illuminated his balletic movements as he crouched, climbed a ladder and swayed around us.

'Oh, great!' he said as I turned. 'Now if you just . . . fantastic! You really are . . . lovely, and look up and . . . a natural. And now just tilt the head a little more . . . wonderful half smile and again! Oh, yes, oh, yes, and that lovely strand of hair like silk a little more . . . and now if you untie the belt of the robe and . . . oh, well done!'

Natural break whilst he ripped open the pack of new film with his teeth and jettisoned the one he'd already used. He was acting like he couldn't wait. You can always tell a good photographer by the way he treats his sitter. There's got to be mutual respect. And I was feeling flattered. I was feeling like the cat's whisker. He had a job to do and I was going to give it to him. I was going to give him all I'd got. Professionally speaking.

'Just sit down here,' Max said, patting the dusty velvet of the chaise longue beside him.

And Jasper said, 'Why not? See what develops.'

'If you just drop one shoulder of the robe,' Bill suggested as I sat beside Max. 'And . . . oh, brilliant! That's it! Chin up and a half turn of the head to the right . . . look past my shoulder, angel. And let the robe slip a little more . . . You've done this before,' he exclaimed.

'No, never,' I said. 'Honestly.'

'I don't believe you. Waddya think Jasper?'

'One thing's for certain,' Jasper enthused. 'She's got what it takes.'

'What about me?' Max interjected, rather petulantly I thought, as Bill started clicking feverishly again.

'Yes, what about Maxie?' Jasper asked Bill.

'Relax. I got his left hand in the last shot.'

'But I'm the author of the book,' Max explained. 'And I don't think Alison'd dispute—'

'And his father's putting up half the money,' Jasper told Bill. 'So the boy's got a right to be in the picture.'

This was news to me but explained why the project had taken off in such a big way. Not much of a surprise though, since I already knew that his father had oiled the wheels of academe to get him his research post in the first place. Poor Max. And now Bill was directing him to play a more cental role he looked as though he'd got stage fright. He'd gone white, his eyes had glazed over in a fixed stare at nothing in particular in the middle distance. Somehow I had to help him connect.

'I said,' Bill insisted, 'put your hand on her right breast. What's stopping you?'

I looked down, taken-aback to realise just how far the towelling robe had slipped open. It was cold in the studio and my nipples were erect. But my main concern was that Max's hand was trembling a few inches in front of my breast, apparently unable to make contact. I already knew he had a block when it came to penetrating a woman. He was a knickers-on-man when it came to sex, I was already aware of that. But it was only now that I grasped just how deep his inhibition went. It was crippling. He was like the rabbit caught in the glare of a headlamp, unable to move. Poor Max.

Just grab her tit,' Jasper said, his exasperation getting the better of him.

'Don't,' I told Max quietly. 'Don't worry. Just give me your hand and . . .'. Very gently I took his hand and guided it onto my breast so that his fingers barely dusted my nipple.

'Ah!' Max cried and flung his head back as though he had suffered an electric shock from a live socket.

'Fantastic!' Bill cried, clicking away furiously. 'No, don't shut your mouth, Max, but open your eyes and . . . oh, brilliant! Give it to me! Go with it!'

Meanwhile I'd caught hold of Max's other hand, cupped it in my own and had pressed it hard down onto the warm flesh of my other breast.

'Ah!' Max cried out and this time his head fell forward onto my shoulder.

'Great!' Bill shouted and started to shin up the ladder so he was shooting down at us. 'Now press and lift both her tits together to that her flesh spills out over the top of your fingers.'

I increased my pressure on Max's hands, forcing them to lift and squeeze my breasts together. He tried to lie back on the chaise longue away from me, so I laid back with him and prised apart the centre and index finger of each of his hands to allow my hardened nipples to peep out.

'Oh, please, no!' Max whimpered.

'Brilliant!' Bill exclaimed.

'Nice one,' said Jasper.

I couldn't see Max's expression any longer since now we were both lying prone on the chaise longue with me on top, both of us looking up into the lens of the camera. My head rested back on Max's right shoulder and he was looking up to the left over mine.

However, I was aware of something hidden from the camera, something that neither of the others could see. Max was getting hard. The shock of succumbing to the sensuous pleasure of flesh on flesh might have hit him like a knock-out punch but his penis was going to beat the count. It was springing to life in spite of him. In the hollow of my back, immediately above the cleft of my buttocks, I sensed movement, his member twitched and began to enlarge.

'Help me,' he gasped.

I was struggling to dislodge his hold on my breasts so that I could turn and face him to offer reassurance, but his hands were stuck fast like limpets. To get him to release his grasp I wiggled my bottom. He'd just about unclenched his fingers when Jasper said, 'Give it to her, Maxie.'

'Oh, do shut up,' I said.

'Yes,' Bill told Jasper. 'When you've got two natural performers like this you give them their head. You do not make crass remarks. You show a little sensitivity, okay?'

'All I said was . . .'

'We know what you said,' Bill snapped. 'But if you are set on interrupting the inspirational flow . . .'

'On the contrary. I want them to get on with it.'

'I shall have to ask you to leave the studio, I'm taking the photos.'

'I hired you,' said Jasper.

'I'm not just one of your commercial hacks, Jasper. My work has integrity.'

'So get on with it.'

'And if you want to jerk off on that . . . ?'

'Who says I'm jerking off? I just got a twist in my underpants,' Jasper snarled. 'What's it to you if I put a hand in my trousers? You want to make something of it?'

As luck would have it Max was so diverted by this argument that for a moment he had straightened his fingers to turn towards Jasper and Bill and get a look at them.

I took advantage of his loss of concentration to turn over and face him. I spread my thighs quickly so that his penis briefly slapped my pussy. And, before he had time to cry out his surprise, I'd stoppered his mouth with my own, darting my tongue briefly in between his lips. He turned his head sharply to the right so that my mouth was on his ear.

'I don't want you to come inside me,' I whispered. 'That understood?'

'But . . .' he stammered. 'I wanted to, I mean, I want . . . I mean . . . if you'd . . .'

I was getting a handle on this man's psychology alright. The more I denied him the more demanding he'd become. 'Nonsense,' I said.

'But, Alison . . .'

'We can't get intimate with people here.'

'No? But . . .'

Even as I said it I knew that I was close to forgetting that we were being watched. Jasper had been effectively silenced. The *click-click* of the camera was growing ever more distant.

'You get on top of me now,' I said. 'Then you'll be fully in control. I won't have the advantage. I don't want it. Nor do I want you to slip into me accidentally.'

Max said, 'You're right, and dislodged himself from under me and climbed on top.

I looked up at him and said, 'Just keep your penis well away from my vagina, you got that?'

'I got it,' he said and swallowed hard. Then he added, 'You mean you don't want me in there?'

'Did I say that?'

Max blinked as though trying to clear his head. He pushed himself up on his hands to look down at me without his penis losing contact with the cushion of my pubis. 'But suppose I want to?' he asked.

I didn't answer him straight off. I ran my fingers up through my hair so that it fanned out on the faded crimson velvet. I heard another film on auto-rewind before it was ejected, the sound of foil on a fresh reel being snapped open between Bill's teeth, before I said, 'With people watching, Max?'

'Yes, but that makes it—'

I put a finger on his lips. I understood. The presence of a third party gave him a licence that in normal circumstances he lacked. The idea of the photographs put the whole thing at the once removed. With a couple of voyeurs on tap Max felt much safer than he would've done if we'd been alone.

As though in a move to get away from him, I shifted my position slightly so that his member slotted neatly into position between my thighs. And then, on the pretext of trying to protect myself from the dangerous intimacy of this new position, I slid my hand down and grasped his tool, making sure that my supposed attempt to block its path into my vagina slid back his foreskin.

A moan was wrenched from deep inside him. The shock to his system was such that he was no longer able to support his weight on his arms. He fell forward onto me. However, I could not fail to notice that as his chest subsided onto my bosom his buttocks lifted so that his rigid member was now angled straight at my entrance. Poised to penetrate the barrier of his own inhibitions, he hesitated. My hands slid around his hips to gently massage his bottom – so gently that he could not be sure whether I was inviting or resisting.

What is it about a woman like me who always responds to a man by trying to be helpful? Nature and nurture, and all that stuff about propping up the male ego? The missionary position? Well, that's okay by me as long as I get juiced up in the crush. And, quite frankly, I defy any sex therapist to do a better job than I did that day. I mean, Max took the plunge. Big time. Years of abstinence, the iron shackles of his restraint, suddenly fell away from him and he emerged a free man. Or, to be more precise a raging bull.

With a great shout of triumph, he descended into me. I was vaguely aware of Jasper cheering and the clicking of the camera increasing to a frenzy. I think the ladder crashed over too because Bill had to leap back as Max wrestled me to the floor, his hands diving and delving over my body, his mouth frantically searching for mine, for my eyes, my ears, my nipples. All the time he was thrusting deeper and deeper with his plump penis gyrating and thumping closer and closer to my womb. If I put up a struggle, tried to fend him off, it was only in an attempt to slow him down so that he wouldn't climax too quickly. No chance.

'I'm coming!' he shouted, as though it was the most amazing thing in the world, as though it was a moment of truth that he simply had to share with all and sundry, a magical experience that came out of nowhere.

But I knew better. It came out of me. For that reason it was my victory. But then he started to sob.

'Max?' I enquired tenderly. I combed my fingers through his hair and tried to lift his head to get him to look at me as one might a recalcitrant child.

'Can never thank you enough, Alison,' he gasped. 'Want you to know . . . you sprung a trap that I . . . I didn't hurt you or . . . did I? Oh, Alison, will you marry me?'

What could I say? This was not the moment. 'Cool it, Max,' I said. 'How was that for you, Bill? You got some good shots?'

Bill didn't answer. But Jasper said, and I noticed he was zipping up his flies at the time, 'You've given us plenty to play around with. Don't worry. Bill was right in there with you. So was I. Great stuff.'

After Jasper had dumped a handful of tissues in the wastebin, he added, 'You're right, Max. I can see all sorts of spin-offs. Merchandise. A blue movie. Maybe even an audio book for the visually disadvantaged.'

But Max wasn't listening. He just stared at me as though I was some sort of saintly apparition or something. It quite spooked me. Finally he asked, 'You want to think about it?'

I pretended to misunderstand his question. All I said was, 'Ugh, ugh,' and shook my head. 'No way am I starring in a blue movie. In fact . . . Jasper, I shall want to vet any photos that you might select for the book.'

'Sure,' Jasper agreed. 'We'll have a session in my office.'

'No,' Max interjected. 'I mean, will you marry me?'

I could see he was still up there, head in the clouds, and I didn't want him to come down to earth with too much of a bump, so I said I'd think about it.

I thought about it for quite a while and then said I'd give him a definite answer after Scotland. I'd have time to sort out my head while I was there. Little did I realise . . . However, I was pleased to tell Catha that she wasn't the only one to have had a proposal and we set off on the train for Inverness with plenty to discuss.

Vis-à-vis marriage, the Inter City hadn't even pulled out of Kings Cross before we'd drawn a line under that one. Catha said that marriage had been invented by men to keep tabs on paternity. It had to do with inheritance and property rights and no one had any rights over us. I agreed. What's more I said love and marriage did not necessarily have any connection. She said that was patently obvious. End of story.

We settled back into our seats and spread out magazines and coats with careless abandon. By the time the train hit Hertfordshire it was obvious that the driver had lost contact with the brakes. As we hurtled through the outer reaches of North London I said that the Japanese could keep their Bullet Trains. Catha was making a call to her office at the time and arguing the toss about expenses for the journey, but she snapped the mouthpiece shut on her mobile to remark, 'Which reminds me, Ali, I want to make it plain here and now that I despise blood sports.'

'Meaning?'

'Meaning bullets.'

'Oh, shooting, right, Me too. Goes without saying.'

So far we were agreed on all points. We went on to discuss our wardrobes. Catha had bought a simply lovely negligee for the occasion, a floaty chiffon thing trimmed with swan's down. I'd packed my silk kimono. I wondered if she was imagining us holding a sort of levee in our bedroom. She said, no, but that we might 'descend', as she put it, and partake of a cold collation or salmon kedgeree or something in the breakfast room in stylish deshabille. She was wrong.

The fact of the matter is that Catha and I have a sort of

five-star, Michelin Rosette mind-set that had not prepared us for the rigours of a Scottish castle. The truth dawned only slowly. We had to change trains at Edinburgh where it was already getting dark. Not only were the days already shorter but the temperature had taken a nose-dive towards Antarctica. However, we were soon ensconced in another train with hot air throbbing round our ankles, picturing supper in the baronial hall in front of a vast log fire whilst a piper played a bit of a skirl.

At Inverness we were met by someone called Buchanan in a mud-splattered Land Rover. He tucked a big plaid rug over our knees which we thought rather a quaint custom – until, after several minutes struggling to get the back window to roll up to no avail, we had quite a spat over which one of us had got more than her fair share of the blanket.

After some thirty miles, which took ages because of the way the road twisted and turned, and a further mind-numbing stretch of rutted mud track with our teeth chattering, we arrived at the castle. By this time it was well after midnight and we'd been on the move for fourteen hours. Catha said she was going to forgo supper and simply snuggle up in bed. We couldn't see much of the outside of the place because all the lights were off but, against the pale moonlit sky, various turrets and mock fortifications stood out above what appeared to be a vast Victorian mausoleum.

As Buchanan was unloading our suitcases, one half of the double entrance doors opened to spill a little light onto the imposing sweep of the front steps. And there, to our delight, stood Bruce in a woollen dressing gown and sheepskin slippers with a big rug flung about his shoulders.

'Welcome,' he said. 'To two intrepid travellers!'

'Quite a trek,' I said.

'But great to be here,' Catha told him.

He stepped back into the great marble hallway with its twin staircases swooping up into the dark to get a better look at us as Buchanan dumped our suitcases, said goodnight and slammed the door.

The sound echoed for several seconds before Bruce, with a wink at Catha, said, 'Quite a contrast in settings.'

'I beg your pardon?' Catha asked.

'To the last time I saw you.'

As I observed (post Henley) Catha regarded the whole incident of having been a castaway on a desert island as something of an aberration – a mere blip on the heart monitor of life – and she wasn't going to give it undue emphasis now.

'Oh, that,' she said airily and then got more serious. 'Has Sir Jonathan arrived yet?'

'Gone to bed,' Bruce told us. 'Like everyone else. Because we want an early start in the morning.'

Catha glanced anxiously at me but, before either of us had a chance to say anything, Bruce had continued, 'Kirsty is going to show you to your room. I've put you in the Nursery Wing. Warmer. One of the boilers blew up yesterday.'

'How awful,' I said.

'No, indeed it happens all the time but . . . Kirsty?'

Several dogs preceded Kirsty – an Irish wolfhound, a dalmatian and two black labradors. They circled us without much interest and one of the labradors raised his leg on Catha's suitcase. Thank heavens she'd walked away to study a lifesize portrait of a woman in a pink sashed ball gown.

Kirsty gave the dog a kick, Bruce didn't take any notice. He was watching Catha looking at the oil painting. 'My mother. In her heyday.'

'Looking forward to meeting her,' Catha purred.

Tired she might be but Catha never quite lost sight of her modus operandi. Her charity was ever present in her mind. The proposed legacy was dependent on the demise of Bruce's mother. And she wanted to judge for herself the dear woman's life expectancy.

'Indeed,' Bruce said. 'But she doesn't stay here.'

'I thought she owned the castle?'

'So she does,' Bruce explained. 'But she lives in a caravan by the loch.'

'In a caravan?'

'Went down there one night to take some pot shots at salmon poachers. Liked it so much she never came back.'

'How wonderfully eccentric!' Catha enthused.

'She says its much warmer. And there's no mile walk to the bathroom either, just a little Elsan outside the door.' Bruce turned to Kirsty whilst Catha and I exchanged worried looks. 'Kirsty, you put the radiator on in the Schoolroom for them?'

'Aye.' And that was all Kirsty said. Like Bruce she was

dressed for bed but, judging from the way her hairnet was askew on her frizzled hair, she'd already been there and couldn't wait to get back. She picked up our bags and made for the stairs with the dogs in close attendance.

'Night!' Bruce called from the echoing depths below as we hurried after Kirsty up the stairs.

Alarmingly, no sooner had we made it to the first landing than Kirsty dropped both our bags and clutched at the bannister, panting wheezily.

'So selfish of us,' I said. 'We'll carry our own bags.'

'You alright?'

'If you could just lead the way?'

It was a long slow journey with the dogs continually brushing against our legs and criss-crossing our path, but at least Kirsty knew where the light switches were as we crossed landings, plunged down cavernous corridors and finally ascended a narrow wooden staircase hidden behind an oak door.

'Actually the room isn't bad,' I said after Kirsty had left with the dogs.

There was a silence. Catha and I listened to the click and scuffle of the dogs claws on the bare boards as they retreated into the night.

'Quite pretty chintz,' I said, closing the curtains. 'Someone made a big effort with this room in the nineteen fifties.'

'Oh, fancy, and I thought horsehair mattresses went out long before that,' Catha said.

'And look over here – a table all set for breakfast, little gilt teacups and lace napkins and things. Maybe we'll be served up here.'

'Sweet,' Catha said. 'Except I can't really see anything. Isn't there another light?'

Investigation proved that there wasn't.

'I thought Kirsty was meant to have put the heating on.' I felt the radiator. It was stone cold except for a scorching hot patch near the valve. 'Ouch!' I said.

'You could've fooled me,' Catha said. 'I can see my breath.'

'Lucky we brought some cold weather gear. Apart from your flimsy negligee and my . . .'

'I stopped to watch Catha dive into her suitcase for a cashmere sweater and a pair of wool tights, socks, gloves and a scarf. She put them all on and got into one of the high narrow iron beds. It let out some horrid squeaks.

'What'll you wear tomorrow though?' I asked her.

'In the old days,' she said philosophically, 'people used to be sewn into their winter clothes and not take them off till the summer.'

'Yes.' I took a selection of clothes from my own bag. 'Just have to enter into the spirit of things.'

'Tell you what, Ali, might be best to go out with the rest of them tomorrow.'

I agreed. 'A good tramp over the moors will warm us up no end.'

'Bed's damp.'

'Oh, no!'

'Get in this one with me. Switch the light off. Get a bit of a fug up under the blanket.'

'I wonder how Sir Jonathan is coping,' I whispered.

'Probably want to move to a hotel tomorrow. We didn't pass one though did we?'

'No, don't leave me here, Catha!' I was so tired I felt quite tearful as we clung together under the bedclothes.

'Feel better in the morning.' Catha rubbed my back a little.

'Yes. I curled one of my legs between hers and slowly, slowly we warmed up and slept.

Or did we? Because I don't think much time had passed before we were both sitting bolt upright, ears straining. The sound of a terrible disembodied wailing emanated from some distant reach of the darkened building. Coming closer one minute, and the next receding in wave upon wave of inhuman cries.

Catha's fingernails dug into my arm. 'The place is haunted!' she whispered into my ear.

'Oh, Catha, please!' I hissed. 'I didn't know you believed in ghosts.'

'I don't, she said but she didn't sound at all certain. 'There must be a rational explanation. We'll ask Bruce in the morning.'

Chapter 14

The following morning, and the first of our Scottish sojourn, brought several surprises. Firstly, daylight revealed that the breakfast table in our room – so daintily set with bone china and lace napkins – was in fact overlaid with a fine net of cobwebs. On closer inspection we found a dead moth in the teapot and assorted petrified gnats and fossilised flies in the teacups. Under the table itself, and obscured by the drape of the drawn threadwork cloth, was a dusty collection of sweet papers, condoms and miniatures of crème de menthe – all empty. Speculation as to the age of this treasure trove led Catha to observe that the British Museum might be interested. However, as I was quick to point out, condoms were made of pigs' bladders in the Middle Ages and these had the unmistakable stamp of a twentieth-century french tickler about them.

We finally arrived at breakfast, led by our noses – the smell of fried kippers being particularly pungent. A big pot of porridge was bubbling on a hot plate and some twenty people were buzzing with anticipation of the day ahead. It was then that we were in for our second surprise. Catha made straight for Bruce and questioned him about the ghostly keening we'd heard in the night. There was a rational explanation but not one much to Catha's liking.

'Oh, that!' Bruce said cheerfully. 'Just the dogs hunting. They chase the rats through the house at night.'

Catha took some time to recover from this piece of information and was, in fact, halfway through her first bowl of porridge before she spotted the love of her life seated some way distant along the refectory table. He was halfway through recounting how he'd tracked a wounded deer during last week's hind cull, shooting it as it lay panting in a pool of its own blood.

'Johnnie!' Catha interjected sharply. If I detected the note of warning in her voice I don't think anyone else did.

Sir Jonathan leant forward and inclined his head to acknowledge her and called, 'Wondered how long it would take you to recognise me.'

But Catha wasn't to be blamed for that. Sir Jonathan, obviously an old hand at Scottish weekends, was transformed from a sleek city gent to a country squire in layers of sweaters, tweeds, a muffler drawn up to his ears, half-finger mittens and a knitted balaclava. Catching her look of surprise, he pointed to his head gear and said, 'Apologies to the lady guns but over half of all body heat is lost through the head. Acts as a sort of chimney.'

Now Catha has enough trouble with the word 'lady' without being called a 'gun' and I have to say that neither of us had ever been referred to as 'lady guns' before.

This was going to take some digesting, along with the kipper that followed the porridge. I started frantically to think of excuses for Catha and I to be excluded from the shooting part of the party. I was sure that she must be thinking along the same lines. But then Bruce distracted me by pointing out through the great windows of the dining hall to the courtyard where Buchanan was loading wicker hampers into the Land Rover. He was deep in discussion with the Head Keeper and ten young men who, Bruce explained to me, were to act as beaters for the day. He went on to say something about hoping the birds would fly high because that made for better sport, and I was just coming down in favour of a sudden migraine and leaving Catha to make her own excuses when her voice rang out.

'I think every woman should learn to shoot,' she said. And she glanced along the table at Sir Jonathan. 'One never knows when it might come in handy.'

There was a general murmur of approval but my heart froze. Only I had understood the subtext of her remark. This was hardly the moment for her to turn hunt saboteur. And she knew the penalties for manslaughter let alone murder. I felt I ought to have a quiet word with her.

I made as if to rise to go and sit next to her but Bruce caught me by the elbow. 'There's something I must tell you,' he said. The man opposite had noticed Bruce's hand

176

restraining me and was quick to remark, 'Presumably you are taking the lady novices under your wing, Bruce, as per usual?'

Another general murmur of approval.

'Have you built them a hide?'

Approval turned to merriment. But then Sir Jonathan cut in, 'I'm taking care of Catha. I've a twelve bore Remington for her to try.'

'Oh, that'll do nicely,' Catha said, with a loaded glance to me.

'Can I come with you too?' I asked Sir Jonathan.

'I'm surprised at you!' Catha said, playing shamelessly to the gallery with an exaggerated lift of her eyebrow. 'Wanting to be gooseberry.'

Get her, I thought, giving me attitude at this stage in the proceedings. Let her swing for it. Anyway, Sir Jonathan said, 'Sorry. Shall want to get some shots in myself.'

'He's got a great eye,' Bruce said. 'He must think the world of Catha. Normally he gets the biggest bag by far but if he's going to be distracted by showing her the ropes . . .'

'What did you want to tell me, Bruce?' I interrupted him.

'Oh, yes, er, well. Indeed it is best you know although . . . Catha will obviously be fully occupied. But someone she knows called Don is here.'

'Don?'

'Apparently they first met at the charity do where I first . . . and subsequently they . . . and I had no idea that . . . except of course I knew that I'd . . .'

'But Don isn't here,' I said, looking anxiously down the length of the table.

'No, he's staying at the Hunting Lodge with her.'

'With her? With who?'

'Oh, damn,' he said. 'Not very good at it. Wheels within wheels and all that.'

Suddenly it clicked. 'You don't mean that Don is staying with Serena who you . . . met at the self-same charity dinner?'

'Yes,' he said. 'But she's here with her husband.'

'Stefan?'

'Oh, you know him too?'

'Well, yes, but . . .'. My mind was racing.

'Small world,' Bruce said. 'But I think it'll be alright because Don is sensitive to the fact that Catha has come here to be with Johnnie. And he respects . . . well, apparently they had a bit of a dust up at the opera over Catha. So Don's not going to join the shoot today. He's here on other business anyway and . . . Well, just an unfortunate piece of mistiming. In fact, it was only because poor Serena had a nasty attack of food poisoning three weeks back and I had a cancellation for the Lodge just now that . . .'

'Tricky one,' I said.

'Will you tell Catha or . . . ?'

'No,' I told him. 'Ignorance is bliss.' I looked along the table to where Catha was scowling and stabbing her kipper before adding, 'She's set on making this weekend the turning point of her romance with Johnnie. Oh, and of course, settling details of the proposed legacy with you.'

I managed not to hit anything. This wasn't difficult because Bruce's shouts of 'Keep your head up,' combined with anticipating the ghastly bang when I squeezed the trigger, made me shut my eyes a lot of the time. Perhaps even more frightening was Figgie, the dotty old bat who turned out to be Bruce's mother, the Countess of the caravan. Her enthusiasm was such that she took pot shots at anything that moved, including a squirrel, a beater, a dog, the branch of a tree and, at one point, me. In fact Bruce called up the Head Keeper on his two-way radio.

'Hamish,' he said. 'What did the Countess have on her cornflakes this morning?'

I didn't catch the reply but Bruce had a sort of knew-as-much look in his eye as he said, 'Then you come over here and help her load her second gun, you with me?'

Figgie seemed irritated to be interrupted by Hamish and called him a rascally bastard until, without a word, he drew a hip flask from his pocket. Then she followed him quietly enough and together they sat down behind some gorse bushes.

This was all very well but it did mean that Bruce could concentrate on his prey. Almost immediately he was released from his filial duties, he shot three birds as they rose in a tight group over us. When they plummeted from the sky, the two black labradors raced to retrieve two and the third fell close to us, its wings fluttering pitifully. I followed Bruce to fetch it. He picked it up and twisted its neck. As he turned to me in

178

triumph my eyes filled with tears.

'What's the matter?' he asked in some alarm.

I was too choked up to reply.

'Have you hurt yourself?'

I nodded mutely. It seemed the easiest way out.

'What happened?'

Almost without thinking I limped a few paces, using my shotgun as a sort of crutch.

'Give me that,' Bruce said quickly. 'Did you sprain your ankle?'

I nodded.

'A rabbit hole, was it?'

I nodded again. 'But where's Catha?' I asked, since whenever I lie I need the comfort of an ally.

'She and Johnnie are placed in the lea of the hill,' Bruce said, pointing to a blank bit of sky. Then he called, 'Hamish, will you come over here?'

This goes to explain why within minutes I was being driven away from the scene of carnage in one of the estate's Land Rovers. Hamish had lifted me into the passenger seat and said. 'I'll hae ye back to the castle in ten minutes and Kirsty'll slap a poultice on ye. She's a dab hang wi'th'ice.'

Ice! As if that mausoleum wasn't freezing enough. The thought was more than I could bear. As we sped along, I said with some urgency, 'I can't go back there, Hamish. Please! I've got to go somewhere warm. Isn't there a little pub with a big log fire somewhere near?'

He shook his head. 'Ten miles hence,' he said. He glanced sideways at me as he changed gear to negotiate an outcrop of rock. 'I've a big fire at my croft. Keeps in all day with a few turves on.'

'Oh, Hamish, is it far?'

'Nearer than the castle. You wantae gang there?'

In answer I kissed him. I just couldn't stop myself I was so grateful. He laughed with surprise and I looked at him for the first time. He was about thirty. The wind and his laughter had already etched a delicate fan of lines at the corner of his eyes. The weather had tanned his skin and reddened his lips. Some long untidy strands of coppery hair stuck out from under his tweed cap. His hands on the steering wheel were . . . I closed my right hand over his left one . . . were large and capable, their skin rough and calloused.

I said, 'So sorry to give you all this trouble.'

He didn't answer. He changed gear again and looked down to the floor. 'Is the ankle swelled yet?'

'Oh, dear, um . . .' I made a show of feeling down my leg and reminded myself that I had to limp when I got out of the Land Rover.

I limped so convincingly, and with so many pained 'oohs and ahs', that Hamish picked me up and carried me the length of the path to his front door, which he flicked open with one finger on the latch. A nudge of his shoulder, and we were in. The walls were thick, the window small and a smoky warmth pervaded the room.

I locked my arms around his neck and whispered in his ear, 'Oh, heavenly!'

He set me down on an old rag rug in front of the hearth. He unlocked my arms with some difficulty, the lines at the corner of his eyes crinkling up as he smiled. Then he kissed me.

'Now,' he said. 'I'll riddle yon grate and liven the fire for ye.' He took off his cap as he knelt beside me on the rug. His hair was surprisingly long and glinted a reddish gold as he knocked the turves off the logs and a few small flames flickered to life. He used the poker to prise the logs apart and then leant his head down close to the floor near my feet and started to blow into the grate. I watched, mesmerised, as he sucked in air and puffed it out, his cheeks acting like bellows, the tumble of hair over his eyes glowing ever brighter as the flames rose and the logs started to whisper and then shout with a crackle of sparks.

My exclamation of 'heavenly' as we'd come in through the door seemed almost prophetic. The way he looked now put me in mind of those angels with their pink cheeks puffed up, the sort you see at the corners of antique maps to illustrate the direction of prevailing winds. My hand went out to stroke his hair but at that moment he knelt up and sat back on his heels. He saw my outstretched hand. He grabbed it roughly.

'Now listen to me,' he said. 'I've to hasten to the shoot. They can't do without me.'

'Nor can I,' I said.

He let my hand drop. 'And the Countess needs me.'

'So do I.'

'She's less time than you.'

'Meaning . . . ?'

'Meaning there's all the time in the world for you and me. And you'll still be here when I get back this evening.' With that he stood up and started to make for the door.

'Well, I wouldn't count on that,' I said.

He turned and looked down at me, 'If your ankle's that bad,' he said, 'you'll no' be straying far. And if you're laid up like a wounded hind I'll track you down soon enough.'

I looked back to the glow of the fire. 'You're right,' I said. 'I'd forgotten about being lame for a moment. I'll still be here.'

I heard the click of the latch on the door. 'But Hamish . . . ? He didn't wait for the end of my question. The door slammed shut behind him. I sighed, stretched and lay out full length on the rug before the fire. Bliss. The first time I'd been warm since Inverness. But it wasn't only the fire that warmed me, it was the anticipation of pleasures to come.

The wind sighed outside, making me feel even cosier. I turned slightly, wriggled my skirt up around my hips and bent my knees allowing them to fall apart so that the hot breath from the fire circulated around my thighs and caressed my fanny. I thought about Hamish and my hand travelled down, snuck inside my panties and started to stroke my clitoris. He would come back smelling of the scent of heather, with the sure step of the native hunter. He would uncover his head and let his angel curls fall. A strange mythical creature, like a unicorn almost, he would sprout a golden horn. On the other hand, he would take me like a peasant with his rough hands, he would be impatient, kind of bestial, and thrust his penis straight into me without . . . Suddenly I heard the click of the latch behind me. The door opened and, punctuated by a quick draught closed again. He couldn't wait!

'Hamish!' I exclaimed without turning.

'You whore!' said a familiar voice. Quick as a flash Stefan had traversed the room and was standing with his back to the fire looking down on me. I didn't move. I hadn't even had time to detach my hand from inside my panties. I'd have to brazen it out.

I said, 'Oh, hi, Stefan.'

'Surprised?' he asked.

I said, 'The only surprising thing about your visit here is

181

that you're having to pay a thousand pounds a day.'

'Worth every penny,' he replied. 'To keep warm.'

He really made me mad – the way I could never get one up on him. I went to sit up but he pushed me back down with a foot on my shoulder, pinning me to the floor.

'Carry on with what you were doing,' he suggested. 'Don't let me disturb you, darling.'

'God, I hate you,' I said.

'No, I mean it,' he protested. 'I like to watch. I love to see your face when you come, the way your eyelids flutter and your lips part. But pull your sweater up first because I like to see your breasts tremble and heave too.'

I leapt to my feet then and demanded, 'How the hell did you know where to find me?'

'That's easy,' he said. 'Binoculars.'

'You weren't on the shoot.'

'I was joining at lunchtime and getting the lay of the land. But that reminds me . . .'. Suddenly he took my arm and walked me to the door and back to the fire again. 'I thought so,' he said.

'What? Thought what?'

'That the limp was a no-no. Even from five hundred yards, Alison, I, me, Stefan can tell when you're play-acting. And how! What a drama queen!'

I sat down with a jolt on a battered sofa to one side of the fire. I felt pretty defeated. I put my head in my hands.

'I'll kiss it better if you like,' he relented.

I shook my head.

'I've got some magic ointment. The sort you like.'

What was it about this man that transfixed me, made me tremble in his presence? I had to save myself from him. I have to save Catha from Don too, because there was another example of a woman drawn by a man to her downfall like a moth to a flame. Suddenly I remembered a hundred questions I had to ask Stefan. I started with a minor one.

'And what about Serena?' I asked.

'What about her?'

Because I had a conscience I always imagined other people must have one, even Stefan. I said, 'Well, don't you feel guilty about leaving her unguarded with someone . . . like Bruce about?'

'Bruce! The Scottish laird!' He laughed uproariously at that. So he still doesn't know, I thought.

'If I was worried about her being seduced, Don is a much more likely candidate.'

'Don?'

'In fact, he'd be doing me a favour. It's one of the reasons I've left them alone together.'

'You've got to be joking,' I exclaimed.

'I tell you, Ali, she is relentless in her adoration of me. She thinks I can do no wrong, well, okay I can't but even so . . . it's not healthy and it's driving me up the wall.'

My turn to laugh. But I wasn't going to spoil her secret. I wasn't ready to. Maybe I never would be.

I said simply, 'Well, I have it on good authority that Don is a reformed character. So I wouldn't hope too much for your wife's seduction. He may have been a bit of a goer in the past but now all he wants is to settle down.'

'A leopard doesn't change his spots,' Stefan said with feeling. 'Believe you me.'

'And I have that on the best authority?' I asked.

'It takes one to recognise one.'

'Well, can't argue with that.' On this point I had to take him seriously.

'Look at me,' he said in his uncompromising way.

I looked, I wanted him. But I was going to save myself for Hamish. Stefan put a hand up under my hair so that it rested on the nape of my neck and then he pulled me slightly towards him. He only had to touch me and I felt naked. I struggled. I pulled away from him.

He said, 'Okay. There's something important I have to discuss with you.'

But I wanted to find out more about something else before he changed the subject. 'How well d'you know Don?'

Stefan shrugged. 'It's just a business connection. I designed a software package to keep track of the money he rakes in at his casinos. So happened he was coming up here anyway to fix a deal for some timber off the estate. Log cabins for some pleasure park in Albania. Got to plug the gap now Sir Jonathan's cut him out of a contract for timber from the rainforests.'

'Rainforests? You don't mean from Brazil?'

Stefan shrugged again. 'Guatemala or Nicaragua or . . . why?'

If it wasn't one thing it was another. I shivered. I could see a moral crisis gathering like a great thundercloud over Catha's head. How come she'd got herself involved with, not one, but two treacherous men? First Don. Now Johnnie. I almost hoped she'd shot the latter, because when she found out he was destroying the rainforest she'd—

'But you won't deflect me that easily.' Stefan cut across my thoughts.

'What?'

'Why are you hacking into my Web Site?'

'Why am I . . . what?'

'Don't act dumb with me,' he said angrily.

'Why am I . . . ?'

'It must've been you who pasted a notice asking to buy my personal address.'

'Has the world gone crazy or what?'

'I told you the address: 'ali.sons.xxx.pussy.com'. And when I refuse to sell it, my personal site is flooded with porno pix of you.'

'But I don't know what you are talking about,' I cried. 'I'm barely computer literate.'

'Barely, my arse, or rather, your arse!'

I slapped Stefan. He slapped me back.

I started to cry – mainly because I couldn't make any sense of anything. I couldn't think of anything to say either so he went on, 'And this avalanche of images of your pretty bottom, your pert breasts, all those parts of you I photographed and photos that you threw away because you were afraid I'd show them to friends or . . . how dare you, Ali! And all this on some pretext of being a visual taster for a forthcoming book entitled *Modern Mating Rituals*!'

'Ah, no! Ah, no!' I gasped.

'Ah, no, indeed.'

'Tell me it isn't true,' I cried. 'How could he do this to me?' I leapt up, tearing my hair. My distress was obviously so genuine that Stefan changed tack.

'Who?' he demanded coldly.

'It must be Max. Or Jasper.'

On Stefan's insistence I explained how this had all stemmed

from my new job as a research assistant on a serious academic project for a visiting American professor at Cambridge called Maximillian Chopin Smith.

'It could only happen to you,' he said.

'No, because, in a manner of speaking, something similar has happened to Catha too.'

And I went onto explain how her new appointment as Chief Fundraiser for a highly regarded charity had pitched her headlong into ever-more compromising sexual liaisons with unsuitable men. While I was at it I also touched on our resolution to replace lust with love. One thing I can say for Stefan – he's a great listener. And he always tries to be constructive.

'And I just don't know what we can do about it, Stefan.'

'Stay home and lock yourselves in a cupboard.'

'No, but seriously.'

'Declare yourselves a disaster zone.'

'How can we stop being exploited?'

'Business is about exploitation, sweetheart. And I'll bet my bottom dollar you both do your share with the men. But, since you ask, there's only one solution for you two and that's to work for yourselves.'

'But that takes money. Unless . . . you fancied . . . giving us a start up?'

Stefan shook his head. 'If I want to take a gamble, I've plenty of off-the-wall projects of my own, thanks. Anyway, you know Catha wouldn't accept money from me.'

I couldn't argue with that. I couldn't argue with the idea that to be truly independent a woman had to work for herself, either. But what could we do? We'd often discussed setting up in business but so far all our ideas had come to nothing.

'Maximillian what?' Stefan asked.

'It doesn't matter.'

'I rather think it does.'

'Chopin Smith, but I'm not going to marry him,' I said. And this makes it easy for me to refuse Max, I thought.

Stefan stood up suddenly and crossed to the door. 'Perhaps you should marry him,' he said.

'Stefan, please!'

'Could be a solution.' He opened the door.

'But, Stefan!' I sounded a bit urgent because I just hated

the idea of him giving me away so lightly. Yet I knew it was silly of me to feel like that because it was something he had, in a manner of speaking, done before. More importantly – I never liked him to leave without making love to me.

'Goodbye, Mrs Chopin Smith,' he said and shut the door.

I was alone. I just couldn't believe he could be so unfeeling. I felt really abandoned and miserable. Even the warmth of the fire seemed to be on the wane. I gave the logs a vicious poke. And I thought about what I was going to say to Max.

However, it wasn't long before my anxieties about Catha got the upper hand. If she had made it up with Sir Johnnie, found some way to rationalise his love of blood sports, it was going to be up to me to tell her that he was engaged in the worst form of environmental vandalism. A man who could kill rainforest, could kill deer and birds, could kill dolphins even. I shuddered at the thought. And then remembered that if, one the other hand, Catha had had a decent quarrel with him she would have gone back to the castle on her own. She'd be there now – cold and lonely without me.

As soon as Hamish returned I would ask him to drive me there. Meanwhile I decided to make good use of my time by the fire. I found a tin bath in the kitchen, dragged it in front of the hearth, filled the kettle, took my still damp clothes off and hung them on a string over the mantle to dry. This would save me braving the icy wastes of the bathroom at the castle with its claw-footed tub that served as a tomb for an impressive assortment of spiders.

I was glowing from my bath and wrapped in an old blanket when Hamish walked in. He smelt of the open air and the gorse. The rough tweed of his jacket sleeve rubbed my bare shoulder as he put an arm around me and drew a clutch of feathers from his breast pocket. He'd collected them for me, along with a sprig of heather for luck.

It seemed a bit ungracious to ask to be taken back to the castle immediately. Anyway he said he was cold and tired after a long day and he lay down on the rug by the fire and lit a cigarette. I made as if to step over him and get my clothes but he caught my ankle. I explained I was a bit concerned about Catha not taking to blood sports. He told me not to worry because Bruce had actually barred her from the shoot after a complaint from Sir Jonathan that she was a danger to others in the party.

This news came as a relief and I asked Hamish what had happened. He wasn't sure exactly but Sir Jonathan had stormed off back to the castle to pack up and leave. Better and better. One down, one to go. I asked what had happened to Catha but he just said, 'Ne'er the twain shall meet again.'

'Well, in that case, Hamish,' I said, as I lay down on the rug beside him. 'I'm not in quite so much of a rush as I thought.'

I suddenly felt very languid. As if the fire knew its master was there, it flared up, bathing us in its warmth until we both seemed to be melting.

Lazily I stuck some of the feathers in my hair. Between slow puffs on his cigarette, Hamish stuck some more in the bush of my pubic hair. I eased his jacket off. Whilst I was doing so he decorated me some more with a whole necklace of smoky kisses, plus one on the lobe of each ear.

As I slowly undressed him, I covered him with my own kisses. He threw away his cigarette and his caresses grew ever more lingering. The remains of daylight faded from the little window until the whole room was licked by the stuttering flames of the fire. Together we sank into a lazy dream of arms and legs, of curves and hollows that seemed to interlock and unlock, fold and unfold, plug and unplug until the boundaries of our bodies merged beyond the point where we knew what belonged to who or who was what.

He slipped inside me with such ease and so unhurriedly that I felt I'd sucked him in there as naturally as drawing breath. He moved about inside me and I moved under him and over him and to the right and left. But neither of us accelerated our movements in an effort to reach a climax. It just happened along with the hiss of the fire and the sigh of the wind outside. I came and he came and we slept.

Oh, I felt so guilty in the morning. Poor darling Catha, all alone and freezing in that monstrous barn of a place with me all cuddled up in the firelight.

Hamish drove me at top speed – which was to say at about twenty miles an hour – along the rutted track with its lethal outcrops of rock. Bruce was in the echoing hall looking strained.

'Well, done Hamish!' he said. 'Where did you find her?'

Hamish looked a bit embarrassed so I explained to Bruce that I'd fallen asleep by Hamish's log fire and he hadn't had the heart to wake me.

'Indeed,' said Bruce. 'Have to rustle up a search party though,' and he turned to me. 'Catha hasn't been sighted since yesterday afternoon. Stormed off across the moors on her own. Fear the worst, I'm afraid, since she doesn't know the terrain.'

'Oh, no!' I cried.

'I'll gather ye dogs,' Hamish said and turned on his heel and left.

'Oh, no!' I cried. This was not a situation I'd foreseen and was worse than my worst nightmare.

Bruce was ignoring me to dial the phone. He said, 'Ringing the Lodge. Need every man we can muster.'

'Oh, Catha!' I gasped. 'She could've died of exposure.'

'Shut up,' Bruce said, and then to the phone, 'Who's that?'

I sank down on the bottom stair, cradling my head in my hands as Bruce continued, 'Well, Stefan, one of our lady guns has gone missing and we have to—' After a brief pause, Bruce said, 'No, not Alison but her friend Catha has not been sighted since—' Another pause.

I could hardly breath the tension was so great.

Then Bruce went on, 'What d'you mean – she's there? With Don? You mean she's . . . in bed with Don at the Lodge. I see. Well, there's a thing. My father always said ladies were more trouble than they're worth on a shoot but . . . and you agree, but . . . Well, indeed, yes, all's well that ends well. Thanks.'

Chapter 15

The trouble for someone with high ideals like Catha is that they've got such a long way to fall. The speed and depth of her descent became clear on the journey home. It was as though all her inhibitions had been blown away and she was in free fall. Even her usual reticence had gone out the window and she raised her voice over the rattle of the train to tell me, to tell the whole carriage, what had happened.

'Our bodies are fine-tuned as one instrument,' she shouted, 'the concord of our physicality being expressed by the miraculous way that we both climaxed together. Emotionally and intellectually too, we—'

'Sssh!' I said because I'd noticed the man in the seat across the gangway was beginning to look distinctly uneasy.

'Oh, I don't care who hears, darling,' Catha declared, following my gaze with a disdainful look towards him. 'I want to shout it from the rooftops.'

It was going to be a difficult journey. I said, 'Hey, did you know Sir Jonathan is into buying up rainforests?'

'Yes, I'm well shot of him.'

'And he was supplying Don from the same source?'

'Don pledged his support for the environment in the early hours of this morning,' Catha responded with a faraway look in her eyes. 'He even promised to rethink his Albanian strategy. He's incredibly sensitive to the emission of gases affecting the stratosphere too and the discharge of chemical effluent and . . . But where was I? Oh, yes, I was about to begin at the beginning.'

What could I do except allow her to work off her head of steam? I settled back in my seat and, before I closed my eyes, I noticed that the man across the gangway had closed his too, and had discarded his newspaper the better to concentrate on Catha's story:

'Of course I had no idea where I was going but, looking back now, I think some ulterior force directed my steps to the Hunting Lodge. Extrasensory perception, call it what you will. All I know is that suddenly I was looking in through a lighted kitchen window. And there, like a vision, he stood four square gazing out like the captain of a ship scanning the sea.'

'He saw you?'

'No. It was already dark. It was his own reflection he saw. I stood transfixed. It seemed too incredible that he should be there in that wild inhospitable place just at a point in time when I had lost my way and feared I might die of exposure. In such a situation a person can hallucinate and see a mirage. Which was why, when I went to knock on the door, I did so tentatively.

There was a pause and I knocked again. He flung the door open. He seemed as shocked as me, as disbelieving, if you like. I stood transfixed. He stepped outside. He touched my cheek with the back of his hand as though to reassure himself that I was real. I caught hold of his hand for the same reason. He pulled me to him and our mouths collided in a bruising kiss.

It was like we were one immediately. As though every chink of light, every pocket of darkness that described the separate silhouettes of our two bodies had to be erased. His right leg forced a way between mine as he stepped towards me again and, with his arms around me and mine around him, our bodies closed in on each other. He sighed a long deep sigh of recognition and, as he did so, I breathed in the breath he had exhaled. As if intoxicated and unsure of keeping my balance I clung to him even harder. Sensing my anxiety, he walked forward, forcing me back into the darkness beyond the sharp oblong of light cast outwards from the kitchen door across the rough earth.

I'm unclear about what happened. And isn't that always true of real happiness? In particular, the essence of happiness is in a forgetfulness of time. It could have taken two minutes or fifty, it could have been on a feather mattress or a bed of nails, neither of us would've known the difference. From the abrasions on my back and his legs and arms, we guessed afterwards that we must have landed up in a clump of gorse bushes but, by the time we discovered our injuries, we were delighting in them. Whether we shouted or whispered our avalanche of endearments, we couldn't recall. And the stars that I saw could've been in my head or they could've been the Milky Way. But, as Don said later, we made our own Big Bang, so what the hell.

It was only later that I had my wits about me – enough to be able to report to you now what happened in some detail . . . oh, okay then, I won't . . . oh, okay then, I will. It was after we'd bathed each other's wounds and I had kissed and licked each of the scratches on his arms and . . . oh, look, just say if you don't want me to go on but . . .

Okay than. We got into bed and, to begin with, we were laid out like two corpses, immobilised side by side, eyes open, staring unseeing at the ceiling. Slowly a strange rasping sound impinged on my consciousness which Don said was noise pollution spilling out from Serena's Walkman in the room next door. This was the first time I had been aware of anyone else's presence at the Lodge. And, as Don said, Serena wasn't really there but lost in a world of tit-and-bum-club music. This meant that she had the volume set high enough to make her prematurely deaf and meanwhile ensured that she would remain oblivious to any noise from us.

Warm and safe at last, and in the company of my one true love, I relaxed completely. Remember that so far our only meetings had been brutalised by circumstance and cruelly limited with regard to time – in the Ladies' at the conference centre, in the Organ Room at Glyndebourne and in the gorse bushes of a Scottish moor. Now we had the luxury of a double bed for a whole night and at last there was no need to hurry.

Paradise. Don started to explore my body in the most non-intrusive way and I reciprocated. Whilst our hands worked gently but ceaselessly to grasp and pull each other ever closer, our tongues travelled like blind caterpillars into every nook and cranny: mine tracing the whorls of his ear, the sinews of his neck, the arch of his armpit, the soft drape of his balls, the hard ridges of his stomach, while he tasted each of my fingers and toes and wriggled into the deepest recess between the lips of my labia to flicker against the engorged knot of my clitoris. In fact he brought me expertly to climax with his tongue before he even presumed to enter me. Bliss. Oh, and when he did enter me he was not only big, bigger, biggest but he rolled me up on the feather pillows with my knees behind my ears so that his penetration of my vagina was deep, deeper and deepest. He reached so deep inside me, Ali, that he touched my soul. No really, he went so deep into my psyche that it was as if his semen ejected into my bloodstream and his aura erupted in my brain. The ultimate fix. I didn't resist, for the first time in my life no part of me held back, oh, how can I explain . . . except to say that, well, just talking about it now brings me to the point of climax again. Every muscle and nerve in me cries out for him now. Oh and, Ali, he's a stockings and suspenders man. From here on in I can't wear tights, even crotchless ones.'

Catha lent back exhausted and closed her eyes briefly as I glanced at the man across the gangway. Wide awake now, he was having a desperate stab at his newspaper but, between the jolting of the train and the trembling of his hand, he was rereading the headline he'd first read in Inverness. What was more, and I couldn't help noticing, the jiggling of his newspaper bore no relation to the rhythm of the train. Catha opened her eyes and looked at me in an enquiring sort of way. Obviously I'd have to say something. I said, 'Great stuff.'

'What's the matter with you?'

'Nothing.'

'Anyway . . .'

'What?'

'After we'd finished, well, that's when it began.'

'What?'

'Our realisation that we shared an emotional compatibility and an intellectual closeness. We talked. About everything. Endlessly. We talked till dawn. A true meeting of minds as well as bodies, Ali.'

She droned on about how they were going to share the rest of their lives together, how they had to have their own space and he was going to set her up in a flat in Dolphin Square and wasn't this true love? Ad nauseam. Dolphin Square – I ask you. I grew more and more alarmed. It wasn't just that this picture of Catha as a kept mistress was totally out of kilter with everything that'd gone before and a negation of all her principles, it was the image of Don as a dependable and faithful suitor which somehow did not ring true.

Catha talked, Stefan's warning echoed louder and louder in my head. When it came to the psychology of sex, his judgement was second to none. He wouldn't have questioned the idea that Don was no longer the promiscuous rake he'd once been without evidence to the contrary. Stefan knew. I knew. But how could I tell her? Only one thing was certain – because of her mistrust of my ex I couldn't say that it was him who had told me.

I said, 'I know you're on a high, Catha, and I'd be the last person in the world to . . . But how can you be so sure?'

'Sure of what?'

'Well, that he . . . well, that his intentions are really as honourable as—'

'You're jealous.'

'I mean, suppose,' I persisted, because I desperately didn't want her to get hurt, 'just suppose, that he was one of those chameleon characters who agree with everything . . . well, a bit of an opportunist in fact – brilliant at striking deals and getting his way with women.'

'He said you'd put up a fight to keep me,' she sneered.

'It's not that. It's just that I care. Just that I don't want you to be taken advantage of . . .'

'Bitch!' she said.

'More likely he wants to keep me out of the picture because I can be objective about him whereas you . . .'

'End of conversation!' she said with an awful finality.

The man across the gangway folded up his newspaper and slumped against the window with his eyes closed.

'I shall never speak to you about Don again,' she added. 'Never.' Of course I felt wretched. But at the same time I knew that there is one thing that no woman, not even Catha, can resist and that's discussing her lover in endless detail with a close woman friend. And I was the closest. I had history on my side. I had sown the first seeds of doubt. All I had to do was wait.

My own priority was to make it plain to Max that he had blown it. Not only had he lost the chance of me accepting his offer of marriage, but he had lost my services as a researcher on the book. I had to tread carefully though. I wanted his undertaking to remove the porno pictures of me flooding the

Internet via ali.sons.pussy.xxx.com.

Less than a week after returning from Scotland I had a meeting set up. I'd been willing to go up to Cambridge but he said he was down in London and so, for convenience sake, we could meet up at the photographic studios in Balham.

I'd rehearsed my speech. It went: 'Now look here, Max, you've betrayed my trust. Not only on a personal level but on a professional one. You've single-handedly corrupted this project and twisted it out of all recognition. You've changed the goal posts. And never mind that – you have exploited me, my person, by using my body in a tawdry advertising stunt for financial gain. I shall never forgive you. It goes without saying that my marriage to you is out of the question. Furthermore, unless you oversee the removal of the intimate pictures of me on the Internet, I shall take legal action.' Uncompromising stuff.

I rang the doorbell and announced myself via the entryphone. Max was waiting for me on the landing outside the studio. As I came on a level with him I began, 'Now look here, Max—'

'Ssssh!' he said and caught hold of my hand, pulling me into a little kitchen almost exclusively furnished with dregs of coffee in polystyrene cups.

'Now look here, Max—'

'Hey, hey, am I glad to see you!'

Frankly I was alarmed by his appearance. Beads of sweat stood out on his forehead and his mane of hair was standing up on end. However I was determined. 'You have betrayed my trust,' I went on.

'Say that again!' he breathed. 'Why should you ever forgive me? You hate and despise me. Don't tell me. I know. I even exploited your body for . . . well, what can I say? But have pity on me. Now in the hour of my distress who can I turn to but the one person who understands?'

'Whatever's the matter?' I said. 'Tell me, Max.'

'See, it's like this.' He took a deep breath to calm himself as I smoothed the hair back from his furrowed bow. 'See, I met someone.'

'Who?'

'I met the person I'm going to spend the rest of my life with. Okay, so berate me. Okay, so I thought it was you. But you'll understand, Ali, that my psychological turmoil when you showed me how to fuck . . . when you got me to come inside you, well, it kinda clouded my judgement somewhat, which isn't to say that I don't like you or—'

'Don't worry Max,' I implored. 'Oh, please, I do understand. And congratulations. Who is she?'

'Well, that's not something I'm at liberty to tell you.'

'Why not?'

'Because my understanding is that you know her.'

'I . . . ?'

I hadn't even got to grips with this turn of events before a hard cockney voice called from the studio, 'Max, I got my knickers off, what you waiting for?'

'I don't think I know her,' I said.

'No, no, she's not the one that I . . . She's the one I told you answered my ad remember?'

'No.'

'I had the one reply.'

'You mean the only woman who'd answered your personal ad? When we first met?'

'You got it!' Max said. 'And she's agreed to let me practise on her now. I mean the full bit. Penetration. Because so far I only done that with you and I got to get into the habit.'

'The habit?' I tried to be calm to quieten him. 'You mean so you can be sure you can satisfy the lady you're going to spend the rest of your life with?'

Clasping both my hands, he nodded, mute with gratitude. And after a pause he said, 'As things are I don't think it's a problem I can surmount without a camera.'

'You mean you reckon that in order to perform you've got to have a third person present taking pictures?'

He nodded mutely again before exclaiming, 'Ah, Ali, I knew I could rely on you.'

'It's not a very practical proposition,' I told him. 'Long-term.'

'But it's a start.'

I had an idea. 'Okay, give me the camera and I'll do my best.'

The owner of the cockney voice turned out to be thick set with generous white cushions of breasts and thighs. Before we walked into the studio she had arranged herself provocatively on the chaise longue. With one leg over the curved back and one dangling to the floor, her fanny was spread wide and glistening to our view. On seeing me, she sat up and slapped her plump legs shut.

'What the bloody hell . . . ?' she said.

Max did his best to counter her accusations that he was a pimp, that I was a madam, etc, and that she had been duped. It was only when I told her that Max was a pimp and that I was in his employ too that she began to relax. Not the most auspicious start to a photo shoot, particularly as I'm one of those people who are continually surprised by the way her photos turn out. If I aim at a person's face I tend to get a foot, if I point the lens at a landscape it's inevitably obscured by a finger or a brick wall. However, as things got under way, I was emboldened by the knowledge that in this case it was the process that counted rather than the end result. Recalling Bill's athletic performance of some month's before, I darted this way and that, climbed the ladder, crouched low on the floor and clicked away madly, all the while exclaiming, 'Oh, well done! Lovely! This way a little and . . . oh, brilliant! Now look at me and . . . oh, fantastic!'

It worked. The woman began to show off. She thrust her breasts out, scooped them up, squeezed them together, tweaked her big brown nipples to make them hard, wiggled her bum, laid back and, with her hands between her legs, spread her pussy and stuck her tongue out.

Her performance, combined with the click of the camera, worked its magic on Max. With eyes tight shut, he ploughed into her and she, with her ankles crossed behind his back, had him trapped. For a moment it looked as though he might panic and he tried to stand up, but she was still there with him, her legs resting across the top of his hips encircling his waist, her hands clasping his neck, still riding him with her bottom slapping his thighs. She was a real pro. Come hell or high water she was into her routine and she wasn't going to let go. He went with it, braced his legs, met her thrusts with his own, then laid her back onto the chaise before they rolled off onto the floor.

I was still clicking. I was clicking so fast that the only image recorded would have been a streak of lightning or else the film should've snapped. It didn't. Okay so the lens was pointing at anything by this time, floor, ceiling, my face, my lap, but it didn't matter. In particular it didn't matter because there was no film in the camera.

When Max had shot his load and she was looking for her knickers, I told him – no film in the camera. He was shocked. I said, 'It's like swimming. Once you've done it you never forget. And you, Max, just did several lengths without your water wings.'

'You gave me the confidence,' he said with tears in his eyes.

'You'll never look back.'

'How shall I ever thank you, Alison?'

'Just tell me who she is. The one you said you're going to spend the rest of your life with.'

'I promised not to because . . . it was part of the deal.'

'Forget it,' I said. 'I'm just happy to have been able to help. And now, if you wouldn't mind, as I'm feeling a bit drained, could you call me a cab?'

I didn't dwell on the identity of the mystery woman in Max's life because of other developments. Firstly, I was horrified to discover that Catha had resigned from her charity. She said that this was because she had finally accepted the fact that she was abusing their trust by allowing herself to be abused in their service. A crisis of conscience, in other words, about raising funds in exchange for sexual favours. But I wasn't convinced by this argument. It seemed to me that her resignation more likely stemmed from her wish to devote herself one hundred per cent to Don, and this made me frightened for her. But when I broached the subject Catha denied it. She went further by saying that the seeds of doubt I had planted about her lover had begun to prey on her mind. In fact, over the course of the next few days, her anxiety got the upper hand. However, we'd just begun to discuss ways of putting Don to the test when we were overtaken by an event of such magnitude that it made us forget about everything else.

We received through the post a cheque for thirty thousand pounds from an anonymous benefactor who apparently wished us to have the opportunity of setting up our own business. Nothing could have been more unexpected or better timed. The brief note that came with the post-dated banker's draft said that a more detailed letter would be following. We were excited and bewildered in equal measure.

Of course I thought of Stefan and his comments that we would never be truly free until we were self-reliant in business, but then I remembered his 'I've plenty of off-the-wall projects of my own, thanks' dismissal too. And, as Catha pointed out, we'd had dealings with so many rich men over the past few months, all of whom had thought we were the cat's whisker, that it was impossible to guess which one of them had made this munificent gesture.

It wasn't a huge amount, of course, but more than enough to get us started. Catha favoured a book shop with a coffee and juice bar so that people could browse whilst taking refreshment. I was afraid they'd spill juice on the books. Catha said she wouldn't want them to buy the books anyway because she'd only stock books that she wanted for herself. She saw the virtue of my idea that we should make use of all our newly acquired connections by setting up an agency dealing in stately home swaps but she said that the market would be a bit limited and I had to agree. She said we had to think of something more ethically sound. I said we wanted a money-spinner. She pointed out that there need not be a contradiction – one only had to look at the way ethical shares had taken off on the stock market. And so on.

Once the initial novelty of our situation had worn off though, Catha's fears about Don resurfaced with a vengeance, and I felt responsible. This was why, in spite of Catha's misgivings about the underhand nature of such a move, we fetched up in the offices of an investigative agent specialising in due diligence (the latter being the trade term for poking your nose into other people's private affairs to ascertain their true characters).

Catha's ambivalence about whether or not she should go ahead with such an enquiry into Don's life was resolved only when I managed to find an agency run by a woman. Catha had said she wasn't going to show her vulnerability to any old gumshoe in a dirty mac, and I respected her for that. I accompanied her to the agency office to give moral support. Nothing, though, could have prepared me for the interview that followed.

We were shown into the rather tatty office of the head of the agency and there, seated behind the desk, was none other than DS Wordsworth. She greeted Catha wordlessly by shaking her hand, all the while staring at me. When she made to shake my hand I stepped back sharply. The ghost of a smile made the scar near her top lip blossom into a little white star. As her eyes bore into me, I knew she was remembering me bent over my bed with my bare bottom exposed to her gaze. The scar on her lip stretched as her smile broadened and I knew that she knew that I knew what she was thinking.

'You two know each other?' Catha queried.

'Only briefly acquainted. Do please be seated.' DS Wordsworth indicated a small sofa before she continued. 'Some months ago in the course of routine duties.'

Catha shot me a puzzled glance as she sat and I realised that the jumbled confession I'd made to her after the day of the 'bomb' – remember, we hadn't been on speaking terms after she'd walked in on me and that young journo – had contained only the briefest details.

I faced the figure behind the desk and said, 'I thought you were in the police.'

'Forced to resign on account of over zealous exercise of investigative procedures,' DS Wordsworth said in a tone that suggested there was more to this statement than met the eye. *I'll bet,* I thought, *for 'investigative procedures' read 'strip searches'. They copped the fact you weren't only stripping way beyond the call of duty, but touching and kissing and . . .*

'How very interesting,' Catha said, her interpretation of DS Wordsworth's innuendo being quite different. 'Fascinating to meet a woman with first-hand knowledge of the sexism that, as one always suspected, is rampant in the police force.'

I sat down beside Catha and placed a protective hand over hers. DS or now plain Ms Wordsworth saw my move and stood up. No stranger to interview techniques, she stepped from behind her desk to sit opposite us across a low coffee table. Her suit was crisply tailored and her legs, encased in high gloss tights, made a rasping noise as they slipped and slithered against each other whilst she settled herself comfortably into a leather armchair.

Finally she answered Catha with, 'The more testosterone, the more elevated the libido.' And of course no observation could've been better designed to engage Catha's interest.

They launched forthwith into a far-reaching discussion of

male power structures, glass ceilings and even the fact that men's intellectual objectivity was based on the visibility of their genitals. What a bummer. Before I knew it she had Catha eating out of the palm of her hand and yet . . .

'What does your friend think?' Ms Wordsworth was saying, and both of them turned to look at me.

'What?'

'We thought you were listening.'

'About men's genitals?'

'No, darling.' Catha gave an indulgent little sigh as though I was prone to this sort of mistake. 'About whether or not a trap should be set for Don or whether—'

'Sophisticated surveillance techniques can be very long winded,' MS Wordsworth interrupted. 'Covert work is always time consuming and, therefore, more expensive.'

'What sort of a trap?' I asked.

'Well, like . . .'. And Catha did look shame-faced. 'Getting someone to try and seduce him.'

'Who?' I asked.

Quick as a flash Ms Wordsworth came in with, 'I have a couple of very attractive young women on tap for that sort of thing.'

I'll bet, I thought. I'll bet her job interview with them had been pretty much to the point too.

Catha seemed a bit dubious. 'Perhaps if I could be present?' she asked, lamely adding, 'I mean hidden in a cupboard or . . .'

'I run a professional outfit here,' Ms Wordsworth responded sharply. 'Amateurish tactics are out as far as I'm concerned. You are employing me to be dispassionate and objective. There's no doubt whatever that any meddling by those emotionally involved can prejudice the proceedings.'

'No chance you could do it?' Catha asked trustingly. 'I mean, rather than one of your . . . girls?'

'Well . . .'. Ms Wordsworth's gaze caressed my legs and her tongue briefly licked the scar on her top lip. 'At a price, I mean if the price was right and we came to some . . . arrangement, I might consider—'

I stood up. I'd had enough. 'Catha, I don't think you should make a snap decision on this one. The consequences could be far-reaching.'

Catha stood up too. 'Ali's right,' she said. 'We'll sleep on it.'

Chapter 16

Solving a problem by sleeping on it isn't helped by having a sleepless night.

I made no bones about my mistrust of Ms Wordsworth and I told Catha that, in my opinion, it was possible that she disliked men so much that she might rig the evidence. She was the sort of ball-slicer who had little time for subtleties. Even if she hadn't before, now that she'd been sacked by the police, she had a chip on her shoulder bigger than any of the bull dykes Catha had had to deal with on her Women's Studies course. She might well make Don out to be a male chauvinist pig even if he wasn't.

I hit home. Catha paced the floor. 'So what am I meant to do?' she cried.

'Drop the whole thing.'

'I can't. Not now. It's as though I've set something in motion that . . . it's like I'm on a high-speed train that won't stop till it reaches its destination.'

'You've got to find out about Don?'

'I've got to. And I can't rest until I do.'

'Okay, okay, so . . . well, perhaps one of the young girls she mentioned might be more—'

'No, it's too obscene. Total strangers. It has to be someone I know and trust. Someone with a degree of integrity, someone I know I can . . .'. Suddenly she stopped dead and stared at me as though she had seen a ghost.

I gasped. We'd both had the same idea at the same time. 'No, no, Catha!' I begged. 'Please don't lay this one on me.'

She resumed pacing my bedroom. 'But I trust you more than anyone,' she said. 'Besides which, in a way you bear a responsibility because it was you who raised doubts about Don's fidelity in the first place.'

Her turn to hit home. What could I say? 'Darling, I don't want to have to seduce him.'

'And I don't want you to but . . .'

'But supposing I did?'

'The point is you wouldn't have to try too hard.'

'But . . .'

'On the other hand you'd have to try hard enough to give him the opportunity.'

Talk about a can of worms. Panic stations. I said, 'Oh, Catha, please! If I do seduce him you won't believe me and if I don't you won't either.'

'I will.'

'You won't.'

'But with you . . . I could be there to see for myself, I mean, to witness the outcome, couldn't I?'

'Well, that's true.'

'And, I mean, you wouldn't be accusing me of amateurish tactics if I hid in a cupboard or . . .'

'Oh darling, of course not. In fact I'd like you to.'

This seemed a good way of allaying her suspicions both before and after the event. And we might have got some sleep then except there were so many details to settle, so many pros and cons to weigh up regarding the venue, what I would say to Don and what I wouldn't and what I'd wear for the meeting too.

Don had just got back from Albania, where ostensibly he'd gone to convert his plan for a pleasure park into one for a bird and small mammal sanctuary. So in the morning I psyched myself up to phone him. I had to ask Catha to leave the room because it was going to be a tricky one and she agreed that I must concentrate because the whole thing'd never get off the ground if I didn't sound convincing.

He seemed surprised to hear from me and was immediately worried that something was wrong with Catha. Once I'd reassured him and explained that, as her closest friend, I simply wanted the chance to chat with him about a couple of things, his voice relaxed and he became very friendly.

'Don't worry,' he said. 'I know you two are very close. And there's no way I'd want you to feel excluded, Alison.'

'Well, thanks,' I replied.

'In fact I'd want you to feel very much included,' he positively purred. 'Where shall we meet? Want to come here?'

'I'd prefer more neutral ground actually.'

'I understand.'

I put it to him that the Holiday Inn was a kind of public and private type of place and that I'd leave a message at reception for him. I was just about to explain that occasionally I even had access to a private room there through a business connection when there was an enraged shriek from the hall and I put the phone down quickly.

Had Catha flipped already, just because I was having a confidential word with her lover? *This bodes ill*, I thought, and hurried into the hallway. She was standing there, reading a letter she'd just opened. She thrust it towards me as though the paper was scorching her fingers. I took it quickly.

It was from a solicitor in the City. It set out the terms and conditions imposed by the anonymous donor of our thirty thousand pounds. The main thrust being that the money was intended for the launch of a mail-order business in upmarket sex toys to be called, 'Dildos R Us'.

Needless to say, I shared Catha's dismay but not the depth of her fury. What put a brake on my anger was an uneasy feeling that I'd heard something like this somewhere before.

'Of all the low-down dirty tricks!' Catha raged. 'You wait, just wait. We'll nail this con merchant, this piss artist, if it takes us the rest of our lives! Who does he think he is? Some little tin pot god playing cat and mouse with our destiny!'

It was then that I recalled Stefan's remark about there being a gap in the market for quality sex toys – when I'd taken my dildo to him for repair. And yet, at the same time, he'd expressed total disinterest in such a project. Well, one thing was certain, I couldn't give any hint of my suspicion to Catha. After all, it *was* only a suspicion, and I often seemed to credit him with being a malign influence on my life only to discover later that he was innocent of any involvement. And this, I suppose, simply demonstrated that I still hadn't got him out of my system.

After I'd agreed with Catha that we'd get our own back it was easy enough to distract her attention from the letter. I told her that the meeting with Don was arranged.

'As easily as that?' she said.

'Because he's concerned about you. Afraid I might have some sort of bad news or something.'

She smiled dreamily. 'The poor darling,' she said. 'Did he say anything about wildlife in Albania?'

And with that she calmed down completely.

It was cosy to be back at the Holiday Inn again, the setting for the start of our adventures. My interviews with the respondents to my personal ads seemed eons away, as did their eventual climax with my High Court judge in Room 203. To think it was only ten months. Yet we'd come a long way. Or at least Catha had. She was on the verge of achieving her goal – to replace lust with love.

We'd booked an Executive Suite so it didn't look too bedroomy, and we checked in at least an hour before Don was due to arrive. We had to familiarise ourselves with the geography of the room. Not difficult this – it was the usual L-shape with vestibule and bathroom as one entered, trouser press and double wardrobe leading into a large overheated space of thick carpet. The standard paraphernalia of kingsize bed with padded headboard was, as we had hoped, neutralised somewhat by a wing chair, desk, coffee table and lots of nondescript prints in elaborate frames on the walls. For Catha, though, the most important feature was the wardrobe.

'Oh, no!' she said.

'What?'

'Why did they have to put in a shoe rack?'

'Put some pillows down so it won't be too uncomfy.'

'Oh, no!' she said.

'What?'

'The hot pipes run through the back of it.'

'Well, you're going to have the door open a smidgen so you can see out.'

'I shall fry. And there's a whole raft of those captive hangers on the rail too.'

'Be careful not to jangle them.'

'I won't because I won't stand up.'

'And that reminds me – your bracelet.'

'What?'

'That could jangle too. I meant to tell you to take it off before we left home.'

'I'll push it up under my sleeve.'

'Listen, darling,' I said, unzipping my overnight bag, 'more importantly, am I to wear the dress with tights or the suit with stockings and suspenders?'

'You decide.' Catha's voice was muffled because she was testing her hidey-hole inside the wardrobe and making sure that she could see out. 'But whichever you choose wear your overcoat on top so you don't look as though you're intending to stay the night.'

'Get real,' I said. 'It's eighty degrees in here.'

'Well, if it's eighty out there, it's at least a hundred in here.'

'I'm going to wear the suit then because it's the best compromise.'

At that Catha stepped out of the wardrobe and said, 'But not with the stockings and suspenders.'

'Oh, look,' I told her. 'We've been through all this – I've got to feel sexy in myself or I won't put out the right vibes.'

'But I told you, he's a stockings and suspenders man. So it's too much of a come-on.'

'And I told you that if you're right about him there's no way he's going to discover what I've got on in the way of underclothes.'

'The trouble with you is,' she complained, 'that if you wore a potato sack you'd still look so bloody available.'

I faced up to her. 'So what d'you want? You want me to wear a veil to cover my face like a muslim woman?'

She had no answer to that. I think we both recognised that our nerves were stretched to breaking point. She watched silently as I stripped off, pulled on my tiny cache sex with lace heart covering my pubes, my garter belt, my seamed sheer stockings and half cup bra.

'Couldn't you wear something a bit more . . . modest?' she said as I shimmied into the tight skirt of the suit.

'What? Like a chastity belt?'

'Only in the way of panties, Ali,' she apologised.

I responded by ripping a pair of french knickers out of my overnight bag and pulling them on over my cache sex. 'Satisfied?' She swallowed hard and I felt sorry for her. 'Look, Catha,' I said, buttoning the suit jacket up to my neck. 'This outfit is about as demure as I can get.' And with that I sat down on the edge of the bed with my legs tightly crossed.

'But you're not going to sit there?'

'If I sit on the bed he has to sit in the wing chair.'

'Just don't flirt with your eyes,' she said.

'I don't.'

'You do it all the time. In shops, in buses, everywhere.'

'Well, as I'm not aware of it . . .' I shrugged. 'But I'll be careful what I say.'

'You won't be too obvious?'

'No, I've already agreed I'm not going to say that I fancy him rotten.'

'Because you don't.'

'The closest I'm going to come to broaching the subject of sex is to say, "Gosh, Catha is so lucky! Pulling an attractive man like you!"'

'Yes, I think that's about right. I mean, it gives him a cue that he can pick up or ignore and . . .'

'And it keeps your name in the frame too.'

'Yes.'

'Time's getting on, Catha.'

'Yes, so just show me how you're going to arrange yourself on the bed.'

Fat chance. She arranged me. And a very awkward position too, propped up against the headboard but with my legs sort of tucked under the bed to one side.

'I feel like a sacrificial victim,' I told her as I watched her climb into the wardrobe.

'Well, what d'you think I feel like?' she asked as she pulled the door to behind her and her voice became muffled.

'Like a cannibal's dinner climbing into the pot?'

'I don't think I can take this for long.' Her voice increased in volume slightly as she propped the door open a chink and sat down.

'Well, I can't either,' I said. 'I'm getting cramp with my legs like this.'

'So make it quick.'

'Sssh!'

Sure enough there was a short pause and then a gentle knocking on the door. I simply had to change position and swung my feet up onto the bed as I called,' Come! Door's open!'

In a flash he was inside with the door closed behind him.

He leant back against it looking through into the room at me. He made no move towards me. He said nothing.

With Catha's exhortation to be quick uppermost in my mind, I said, 'Gosh, Catha is lucky! Pulling an attractive man like—'

I didn't have time to finish because he made it to the end of the bed in a couple of bounds, grabbed my ankles and yanked me sharply towards him so that, before I knew it, my bottom was perched precariously on the end of the bed, my hair and my hands trailing behind me above my head.

'Hey, Don,' I gasped. 'All I said was—'

By which time he'd clamped my knees under his armpits and was biting my inner thigh where it curved out above my stocking tops.

'Catha!" I yelled.

'Don't worry about her,' he said, snapping open the buckle of the snakeskin belt to his trousers, whilst keeping my legs securely trapped under his arms.

'Catha?' I implored, but more feebly this time because, as Don released his trousers, his member bulged into view.

'I won't tell her if you won't,' he told me.

Where the hell was she? What'd got into her? The silly, silly cow. No sign of her. Not a sound. What was she up to?

Oh, okay, okay, I thought, *so if this is the way the cookie crumbles* . . . and as Don's hands slid up the insides of my stockinged legs to pull aside the leg of my panties, all sorts of thoughts flashed across my mind: I remembered Catha's original description of Don as a sexual juggernaut with no brakes careering down a hill, I recalled her saying what a turn-on it'd been for her to watch me having sex at Silverstone, I remembered . . . okay, so I'd show her.

His hand was into the french knickers and had encountered my cache sex and was now pulling that aside too. I'd let her have it. If she didn't want to rescue me . . . if she . . . wanted to see how far . . . he'd go . . . He'd decided to get my panties off and I lifted my right hip and then my left to make it easy for him . . . I wouldn't hold back, I'd go with it. Front-row seats for the greatest show on earth? *Well, are you going to see a performance, baby,* I thought. *Here goes! And here's one time I'm not to blame either. Here's one time I'm being a true friend to you and all you can do is . . . land me right in it!*

207

He was stepping out of his trousers. I bent my knees up and finished wriggling out of my panties. He snatched them from me and buried his face in them, sniffing like a wild animal. Then he leant towards me and stuffed them in my mouth. I spat them out, grabbed at his shirt and ripped it open. I tried to sit up further, wanting my tongue as well as my eyes to feast on the sinewy muscles that latticed his broad chest. He pushed me back and turned me over face down. I only just saved myself from falling off the end of the bed by kneeling up and trying to crawl to the headboard. His hand shot down between my legs and grabbed at my bush to hold me back whilst his other hand twisted into the hair on my head. I kicked backwards. He caught hold of my foot and ran his fingernail along the length of its sole. I fell forward with the shock, my face in the bedclothes, my hands grabbing at the pillows.

He used the moment to his advantage. He placed a hand on each of my buttocks and, with his palms pressing down, he eased them apart and spat into the crevice of my bottom. Then he used a finger to spread his spittle around my anus. With a tremendous effort, I dragged myself panting up the bed until I managed to anchor myself by clinging onto the padded headboard. I closed my eyes, waiting for the next onslaught. Nothing happened. I opened my eyes.

He had sat down in the wing chair, holding his hands up against the chair back as if to say 'Peace, peace!' as though to say that he had no intention of forcing me.

My eyes travelled down to his spread thighs and the solidity of his rigid member. I slid off the bed, letting my jacket slip off my shoulders at the same time. I stepped out of my skirt, which had ridden up in a tight band around my waist. Then I undid the front fastening of my bra and stroked my nipples which were already hard. I licked my fingers and spread them across my breasts to make them glisten. He hadn't moved, his hands still resting on the chair back above the level of his shoulders. Only his eyes were busy exploring me inch by inch as I stood naked before him.

I went to sit on his lap. Facing him, I spread my legs and then placed a knee on each side of his thighs on the corners of the chair seat so that I was in a position to lower myself onto his cock.

His member was so elongated now that it was curving away

from me towards him so, with one hand holding the arm of the chair, I used the other to guide his penis backwards to my opening, the taut skin of his knob stoking the pouting lips of my labia as I did so.

His eyes closed. Gradually, I introduced him inch by inch into the innermost folds of my flesh. And, because I was very wet, he slid gently and soundlessly like an oyster from its shell into an open throat.

He sighed and it was then that I bore down on him with all the force I could muster, contracting the muscles inside my vagina so that they closed around him like a vice. The surprise, the agony and the ecstasy, were so great that he arched his back with such violence that the chair tipped over and we crashed to the floor.

Winded for a moment, but still coupled together, we lay still. I was the first to recover. I started a slow rhythmical pumping, my pelvic bone nudging against his as he lay under me. But then he suddenly wrenched himself free and stood up, lifting me with him, his hands under my armpits. He rushed me backwards against the far wall, pinning me there and re-entering me by thrusting upwards. My hands were flung above my head, I dislodged a couple of prints which crashed to the floor, whilst a third dangled dangerously in its heavy frame above my head. He saw the danger, pulled me from the wall and back down onto the floor again. Together we thrust furiously, rolling this way and that, first him on top and then me, until our roller-coaster progress was impeded by the coffee table.

I pulled off him and sat myself on the glass. My legs were wide apart as though astride a saddle and my pussy was leaking moisture. His head was under the table and he looked up through the glass. I imagined what he saw: my sex like a mineral sample, a slice of amethyst put on display to exhibit the fine tracery of rings rippling outwards, compressed by the forces of nature into a semi-precious stone and displayed behind glass.

When I judged he had looked enough, I slid backwards so that I knelt on the other side of the table, licked the place where I had been sitting, and pressed the lips of my mouth to the glass. Now I could see him watching mesmerised, his face slightly distorted through the glass as though he was

209

underwater, his eyes unblinking as though he had drowned. Slowly I disengaged my mouth, leaving a little pool of saliva to mingle with the moisture that had oozed from between my other lips.

Then I leant across the table, my hands clutching the outer edges of the glass, and pressed down so that my breasts were squashed against the cool hard surface and spread out above him like two white clouds.

After a moment his hands grasped my thighs and he pulled himself slowly out along the carpet until his face was directly under me, between my legs. I squatted back and he started to tongue me. I forgot to let go of the table, though, and the glass top started to slide off onto the floor. He sensed me tense up and pushed me back out of the way just in time.

I saw him look at the now-empty frame of the table. He picked me up and sat me inside it so, whilst my bottom rested on the floor, my legs were raised and dangled with my knees supported by the struts that had held the glass. My sex was open to him and it was like he had me in a cage without bars. He straddled the frame of the table with me inside it and pushed his penis into my mouth. I sucked hard. He was close to coming. My hands started to fondle my own sex so that I could come too. He caught hold of my arms, stretched them above my head, forcing me to stand up. Then he lifted me clear of the table and kissed me as he held me in his arms before he threw me onto the bed.

He re-entered me with a great explosion of energy and I came in a long-drawn-out orgasm with a shuddering cry. He came soon after and the length of his body convulsed against mine, his head thrown back before he subsided slowly onto the pillows beside me.

My God, I was thinking, *Catha's right, he's brilliant at it.*

He said, 'My God, it's hot in here.' After a few deep breaths he sat up and added, 'Don't go away. I'm just going to take a cold shower.' He loped off into the bathroom, calling back, 'If you have the lips of your labia pierced for me, darling, I'll buy you some diamond studs to wear there.'

I heard the shower start up before I shouted back, 'D'you say that sort of thing to Catha?'

'Catha?' he shouted above the noise of the shower. 'Have to be careful what I say to her. All that crap about greenhouse gases? No. I just keep my head down and let her rabbit on.'

Maybe it was the mention of rabbits that made me think of it but I shouted, 'How'd it go in Albania, Don? The wildlife park and so on?'

He laughed and called back, 'Successful trip. Met the president's nephew. Got the nod to add onto my original plans. A luxury hotel and two ten-storey blocks of holiday apartments as well as an extra—'

I don't know what he said next. There was a sudden clattering of hangers on the rail inside the wardrobe. Catha fell out of the door, spun full circle and, like a whirling dervish brandishing a hanger above her head, she gave a bloodcurdling yell and launched herself into the bathroom.

All hell broke loose. I heard what sounded like the shower curtain rip, followed by a deafening crash, the sound of a violent struggle was punctuated by crashing glass. I tried to get up, found my legs were too weak and my hand automatically reached for the bedside phone. I asked reception for help, they called the police.

To cut a long story short, a captive hanger, once its metal spoke has been unhitched, makes a pretty lethal blunt instrument. But after the doctor on call to the hotel had bandaged him up, Don was pretty sportsmanlike and refused to press charges. As for myself, I dismissed the offer of a rape counsellor as wholly inappropriate. In fact, at the time it was only the hotel manager who seemed disinclined to listen to reason. And I couldn't really blame him. The room did look a bit of a tip.

It wasn't until the squad car had given us a lift home and we were indoors that Catha spoke.

'What happened?' she said.

'What d'ya mean what happened?' I snapped.

'Did he seduce you?'

'What's got into you?' I shouted. 'You were there, weren't you?'

'Well, I was and I wasn't,' she said.

It turned out that she'd caught a flash of Don streaking past the wardrobe to grab my ankles and the shock of that, combined with the stifling heat, had made her pass out. She'd missed the action and had only come to afterwards, when he'd flashed past on his way to the bathroom. She'd reached up to grab at the dress rail to pull herself upright and one of the links of her bracelet had got caught on a hanger. So there she was chained and helpless in the dark or, as she put it, held captive within the torture chamber of her own mind. It was only when she heard Don's disparaging remarks about the environment and his treachery regarding Albania that she found the strength to wrench herself free.

'Well, did he or didn't he?' she persisted.

'In a manner of speaking,' I said.

'How far did he go? The whole hog or . . . just tell me,' she demanded.

'Sorry, Catha,' I said.

She went into a steep decline after that. She turned her face to the wall and wouldn't get out of bed. I tried everything to rouse her but all she'd say was that she'd given up on the human race. I got into bed with her and gave her cuddles, rubbed her breasts, kissed her and gently worked on her clitoris. Nothing seemed to have any effect. She remained determinedly rag-dollish. I pretended Ms Wordsworth was coming to tea. I made out there was a letter for her from the Gun Lobby demanding that she delete the phrase 'shooting from the hip' from her paper on 'The Deconstruction of Male Language'. Oh, and another from the solicitor of Bruce's mother's estate leaving her half a million. I even set up a game of strip poker and ended up playing with myself. It got lonely.

After a couple of days I knew I couldn't cope. I was getting depressed myself. I had to talk to someone. I rang Stefan.

He said, 'Hi, sweetheart, how you doing?'

I told him.

He said, 'I'll be round in five minutes.'

'No,' I said. 'You mustn't.'

'Why not?'

Since he knew of Catha's reservations about him already, I said rather feebly, 'Well, because of Serena.'

'Oh, she's gone,' he said.

'I beg your pardon?'

'Yes, I sold her.'

'You what?'

'To someone you know.'

'What?'

'Well, that is oversimplifying the matter,' he said. 'But I'll explain when I see you. In five minutes.'

'No, Stefan, you mustn't . . .'. But the phone had already gone dead. I hurried back to Catha and slid into bed beside her, feeling more protective than ever. It wasn't long before the front door bell sounded.

'Don't answer it,' she said.

'But it might be someone—'

'I've opted out of society,' she said.

'Well, I'll just tell them "Not today thank you", okay?' and with that I got out of bed.

I opened the front door a crack. Stefan kicked it wide with his foot. I raced ahead of him down the hall to bar his way to Catha's bedroom. I stood with my arms outstretched, my back to her door.

To my horror he shouted down the length of the hall, 'Oh, so that's where she's hiding, is it? The silly bitch! Just wait till I give her a piece of my mind.'

He slammed the front door shut behind him and strode towards me. He thrust me aside and threw the bedroom door open. Catha was sitting bolt upright in bed, her knees drawn up under her chin. Within seconds she'd been transformed. She looked just like her old self, like a magnificent she-dragon breathing fire. At last! It'd worked!

Unimpressed, Stefan plonked himself down on the end of the bed with his back to her and kicked off his shoes. Catha's eyes narrowed and she fixed me with an accusatory stare.

To redirect her attention back to Stefan I asked him, 'So what's the explanation? I mean, you can't have got rid of Serena by selling her? Selling your wife? No one'd believe that.'

'Ha!' Catha hissed. 'I would!'

Stefan shrugged his jacket off and slung it past me onto a chair. 'Oh, listen, sweetheart,' he said, as though Catha wasn't there. 'Serena had to go. And you know the one thing she really understood was shopping. I had to get a price for her or she would've felt undervalued and I didn't want that. She had to leave me with a sense of her own worth. If it was the last thing I did for her . . . I couldn't just give her away for nothing, now could I?'

My head was full of conflicting emotions but Catha came

to the point. Interested in spite of herself, she asked, 'And might one enquire what the bride-price was? What did you ask? Two cows and a pig, or what?'

'Thirty thousand pounds,' Stefan said, stepping out of his trousers.

Catha and I were being overtaken by events, I could see that.

'Thirty thousand . . . ?' I gasped.

'Did you say thirty . . . ? Catha glanced anxiously past Stefan to me.

'But as I told you, Ali . . .'. Stefan was pulling his shirt over his head without unbuttoning it.

'That was the upshot of what had been a much more complicated deal. In fact it was the way I explained it to Serena. Max paid me that sum in an out-of-court settlement for something else.'

'Did you say Max?' I gasped. 'You can't mean . . . ?'

'Maximillian Chopin Smith,' Stefan said and lay back casually on the bed with his hands folded behind his head. 'Once heard – not a name that's forgotten.

'Not . . .' Catha asked me bewildered '. . . your Max?'

'He'd hacked into my Web site.' Stefan addressed Catha for the first time but still didn't look at her. 'I don't know if Ali told you.'

I nodded my head wordlessly. I was too winded by this turn of events to speak before he continued. 'Traced Max easily enough. You'd told me where he was based and the publisher's name featured on the junk flooding my site. I told him I didn't take kindly to having my info corrupted. Or my name. I was no cheap porn merchant. I had a reputation to protect worldwide.'

'You had a reputation? What about mine?' I cried.

'You never had one to start with.' He dismissed the suggestion with a wave of his hand – which he let fall so that it brushed Catha's thigh.

Catha pulled her nightdress down smartly which meant that the shape of her breasts and even her pubic mound became much more pronounced under the thin material.

But Stefan appeared to be too intent on telling us what'd happened with Max to notice. 'I got in touch and told him straight off that I was going for litigation. And, as it concerned the Internet, it was a cross-border case, so I was going to sue in France. That's what convinced him I wasn't messing. French law is much more punitive when it comes to privacy and defamation. He begged for a meeting. He came down to London. Had dinner at our place and he and Serena fell in love.'

'Thirty thousand,' was all I could think of saying.

'Yes, well, I wouldn't have got that much in damages but, taking into consideration the expense of defending himself in France . . .' Stefan's interest tailed off. He changed tack. 'So now I've got time to devote to helping you two get back on track. Sort your lives out.'

'And you started by sending us thirty thousand to set up "Dildos R Us"?' Catha's voice was gently beguiling.

I held my breath.

Stefan rolled over on his side to look at Catha. 'I told Max I wasn't in it for personal gain. I said I'd donate the money to a deserving cause.'

To my amazement Catha started to laugh. 'And so you have!' Stefan placed his hand on her pubic mound and she stopped laughing, but she didn't push him away.

'I've news for you,' Catha continued. 'And I'm sorry, Ali, I should've told you, but we agreed that there was no way we could be compromised by accepting it for ourselves. I sent the money to my charity.'

'Oh, but, Catha!' I was taken aback, but I could see that Stefan was really angry.

His eyes narrowed. Then suddenly he smiled, his gaze travelled the length of Catha's body to where his hand rested just above her sex. 'Then you could say,' he pondered, 'that I am a defender of the environment. A benefactor of all that you want to preserve, of all you hold dear.'

'Only by default!' Catha laughed.

'Even so . . .'. He coaxed and wriggled his hand a little further down so that the tips of his fingers came to rest out of sight between her legs.

I felt a twinge of jealousy. I laid down on Stefan's other side whilst Catha made an effort to be stern. She said, 'Your trouble, Stefan, is that you equate power with sex and vice versa.'

He rolled onto his back and placed his other hand on my

pudendum so that he lay with a hand on each of us. He said, almost like he was swearing on the Bible (only in this case it was two bibles), 'And your trouble is that you try to remove power from the equation. And that, my darlings, is against nature.'

Catha felt obliged to answer him. 'Ah, well, now this is something we must discuss.'

'Words don't always help,' Stefan told her.

Catha had another stab. 'As someone who has been deeply involved in the deconstruction of male language, I—'

'And revolutions in Women's Studies cut no ice down at the local pub.'

I don't know if it was because the fingers of his left hand were beginning to explore her sex in the same lazy way that those of his right were easing their way into mine, but I could tell from the tone of her voice that Catha was having difficulty concentrating. She was in danger of losing her thread. However, she'd had a lot of practice, so I wasn't surprised to hear her try again. 'Or to put it another way, men's invention of a self-serving vocabulary—'

But Stefan cut across her with, 'More news! Or have you heard? About Bruce?'

'What news?'

'His Mum kicked the bucket and disinherited him.'

'No!'

'The game warden, Hamish something – Ali'd know – copped the lot.'

'But Bruce must've had an inkling!' Catha protested.

'No one did.'

'*Well, I did*, I thought. I'd guessed there'd been a special relationship between them. But all I said was, 'I've got news too.'

'Tell us.' Stefan demanded.

'Yes, do!' Catha said.

'I've been declared *persona non grata* by a certain hotel chain. Afraid I've been officially barred for ten years.'

Stefan turned his head to smile at Catha before slipping a finger deep into my vagina as he said, 'Well, in that case, we'll just have to stay here.'

'Could be a blessing in disguise,' Catha sighed.

A Message from the Publisher

Headline Liaison is a new concept in erotic fiction: a list of books designed for the reading pleasure of both men and women, to be read alone – or together with your lover. As such, we would be most interested to hear from our readers.

Did you read the book with your partner? Did it fire your imagination? Did it turn you on – or off? Did you like the story, the characters, the setting? What did you think of the cover presentation? In short, what's your opinion? If you care to offer it, please write to:

> The Editor
> Headline Liaison
> 338 Euston Road
> London NW1 3BH

Or maybe you think you could do better if you wrote an erotic novel yourself. We are always on the look-out for new authors. If you'd like to try your hand at writing a book for possible inclusion in the Liaison list, here are our basic guidelines: We are looking for novels of approximately 80,000 words in which the erotic content should aim to please both men and women and should not describe illegal sexual activity (pedophilia, for example). The novel should contain sympathetic and interesting characters, pace, atmosphere and an intriguing plotline.

If you'd like to have a go, please submit to the Editor a sample of at least 10,000 words, clearly typed on one side of the paper only, together with a short resume of the storyline. Should you wish your material returned to you please include a stamped addressed envelope. If we like it sufficiently, we will offer you a contract for publication.